DEAD CENTER

A TRUTH SEEKERS NOVEL - BOOK FIVE

SUSAN SLEEMAN

Published by Edge of Your Seat Books, Inc.

Contact the publisher at contact@edgeofyourseatbooks.com

Copyright © 2020 by Susan Sleeman

Cover design by Kelly A. Martin of KAM Design

1

The guns came out of nowhere. Big men. Tall men. Assault rifles. Bursting through the front door, their bodies cloaked by darkness. The gun barrels creeping out of the shadows like fingers. All pointing at her. Ainslie. Just a woman at home minding her own business.

She shrank to the floor in the shadow between her sofa and the wall. Hidden for now. Terrified to move even an inch. A fraction of an inch.

Was she going to die right there? In her place of refuge? As a forensic photographer, she'd shot the aftermath of home invasions, and they'd never ended well. Never!

The men stormed closer, the lights on their guns sweeping the room as if they were hunting prey, a cold wind rushing in behind them.

The light landed on her face, blinding her.

"Hands," the gunmen yelled. "Show me your hands."

"Please," she cried out as she raised her trembling arms. "I don't want to die."

"US Marshals," he said. "We're not going to shoot you if you keep your hands where we can see them."

"Marshals? Thank you, God!" She heaved out a breath

and nearly forgot to keep her arms raised. "I'm a forensic photographer. Used to work for PPB." These men weren't with the Portland Police Bureau, but she wanted them to know she was one of the good guys. "My name's Ainslie. Ainslie Duncan."

"Ainslie." A familiar voice came out of the dark like a warm blanket on a frosty night, even if she couldn't place it.

"Drake Byrd," he said.

"Drake! Oh, good." Sierra's brother. Her boss's brother. *Perfect.* Ainslie had met him once at a crime scene. "Tell your buddies to put their guns down. It's just me here, and I'm certainly not armed."

"Sorry, no can do," Drake said, his voice sharper. "We had a call that Vito Bittner was holed up here."

"The escaped convict? Here?" She shook her head in bewilderment. What did the brutal murderer who escaped from the Multnomah County Courthouse at his pretrial motion have to do with her? She pondered the question, forgetting about her raised arms.

"Hands," the first guy snapped.

She quickly lifted them up. "Sorry. Why would Bittner be here? I don't know him."

The first deputy stepped out of the shadows, his eyebrows raised. "You said your name was Duncan. You any relation to Ethan Duncan?"

"Ethan? My brother?" A queasiness that she'd gotten on a regular basis since Ethan developed a drug habit when they were teenagers started in the pit of her stomach. He'd been clean for a year—well, if you didn't count the last month of some heavy drinking—but he was locked up in the Multnomah County Detention Center awaiting trial for a crime he didn't commit. She'd tried to get him released, but the judge had set Ethan's bail too high, and she and Ethan couldn't possibly pay it. He'd been arrested on Friday night and arraigned at the courthouse the same day Bittner escaped.

"Is he an inmate at MCD?" the deputy asked.

She didn't like his tone and lifted her chin. "Yes."

"Your brother was in the holding cell with Bittner when he escaped," he stated flatly.

"So." Her shoulders rose in solidarity with her chin, even though her heart dropped. Ethan hadn't mentioned being in the same group as Bittner, but it didn't matter. "Just because Ethan might have been in a cell with the guy doesn't mean he—or I—know him."

The deputy pinned his dark eyes on her. "Pardon my skepticism, Ms. Duncan, but this can't be a coincidence."

She had to agree, but had no explanation for the phone call.

He looked at Drake. "Stay with her. We'll finish clearing the place."

"No one else is here," she said.

He ignored her and marched off with the other men. The wood floor vibrated under their boots as they invaded her rental house.

"Can I put my hands down?" she asked Drake.

"Sorry, no."

"Seriously, Drake. It's me, Ainslie. You've met me before. I work for your sister at Veritas Center for crying out loud." The world-renowned forensic lab processed DNA for private individuals and handled crime scene forensics for law enforcement agencies. The center was owned by experts in DNA, toxicology, osteology, computers, and trace evidence. Sierra headed up the trace evidence division.

"Sierra never told me that." His accusatory tone bit into Ainslie.

She didn't like his response. Unfortunately, once people learned of Ethan's incarceration, they formed an instant

3

distrust of her, as if she were guilty by association. "Does she tell you everything about her work?"

"Not much about work lately. Our conversations are all about her upcoming wedding." The corner of his mouth quirked up, but he quickly flattened it out. "When did you start there?"

"A few months ago."

"Ainslie!" Another familiar voice sounded from the front door, but the stress in this guy's tone was unusual for the calm, unflappable man. "Ainslie! Where are you? Are you okay?"

She looked beyond Drake to see Grady Houston, the weapons expert at Veritas Center and the man she'd had a huge crush on since the moment they'd laid eyes on each other. His tall linebacker-shouldered body filled the door-way, taking over the room like he always did when he entered. At least taking it over in her mind.

Large and in charge. And in her heart.

Of all the people to show up when she needed her wits about her, not a distraction.

He stepped into the foyer's dark shadows, but she could still make out his khaki tactical pants, black T-shirt, and leather jacket. He didn't wear a jacket just because of the cool April weather, but also to hide the Sig Sauer he kept holstered at his hip.

His sharp gaze searched the room like a heat-seeking missile.

She knew the moment his eyes—so brown that she couldn't even describe the depth of the color—connected with hers, a zing of awareness would shoot through her. He was the last person she wanted to deal with tonight. The very last. And she prepared herself for another assault on her senses. This one feeling just as deadly.

Grady marched across the room, hating that sweet, adorable Ainslie was cowering in a corner. Big tough Drake being a bully. Holding a gun on her.

Grady didn't like it. Not one tiny bit. He curled his fingers into fists to keep himself from crossing over there and decking Drake. He might respect Sierra's brother, but Grady was going to put an end to this. Right after he got a good look at Ainslie to make sure she wasn't hurt.

Wishing someone had turned on the lamp so he could get a clear look at her face, he locked gazes with her. He'd always admired her eyes, a russet brown color very much like those of a dog he'd owned growing up. Right now they were wide and terrified, and her pain sliced through him like a hook tearing into a fish's mouth.

Grady swallowed and concentrated on erasing his anger so he didn't sound harsh. "Are you okay? I heard about this on my scanner."

"I'm fine," she said, her soft Texas accent quavering. "Would be better if Drake let me put my arms down."

Grady eyed Sierra's second-to-youngest brother, who had a reputation in the family as the bad boy with often contentious opinions. "Come on, man. Give Ainslie a break. She works for us at Veritas, so I can vouch for her. Totally not a criminal and surely not someone who would harbor a fugitive."

Drake narrowed his gaze, clearly not trusting her. "I guess that means you know about her brother, then?"

Grady didn't even know she *had* a brother. She kept to herself, and he knew very little about her personal life. Or at least she avoided Grady. "What about him?"

Drake's eyebrow went up toward inky black hair that ran

in the family of five brothers. "He was in the same holding cell as Bittner the day he made his escape."

Shocked, Grady shot a look at Ainslie. "Is that true?"

She pressed her lips together, seeming disappointed in him for some reason. "That's what they tell me. But Ethan wouldn't have anything to do with a guy like Bittner. Not even back in the day when Ethan was struggling with a drug addiction and needed cash. Bittner probably scared my brother half to death."

Seriously? She didn't know if her brother knew this major criminal? Grady might not still live in Nebraska with his family, but he was close to his siblings and they shared nearly everything about their lives. If they were in a holding cell with a killer, he would have heard about it.

"You don't know?" When her disappointment grew into a full-fledged scowl, he regretted the question.

"I know he's locked up at MCD for a crime he didn't commit." She gave him a glassy stare. "I have no idea who he talks with because he doesn't tell me about his life there. Says he wants to spare me from the horror of it. So, whoever made this call tonight must know something I don't. Either that or it's a weird coincidence."

Grady was normally a trusting guy, but something seemed fishy here for sure.

"Mind if I turn on a light?" Grady asked, trying to buy time until he could figure out what to do.

"Go ahead," Drake said. "But don't touch anything else."

Grady switched on the nearest lamp, the light flooding the room. It highlighted several framed photographs that he was sure Ainslie had taken. The landscapes were vibrant and dramatic, showing him a side of her that he never knew existed. She had a very scientific, linear mind on the job, but obviously she had a creative side, too. A softer side. And, for some reason, that made him even madder about the way

6

she was being treated tonight. About the way he'd reacted, too.

He needed to give her brother the benefit of the doubt. Maybe offer another explanation. But what? Who would report Bittner being in the house if they had no knowledge of Ainslie or Ethan?

An idea popped into Grady's head, and he looked at Drake. "What if this is a swatting call? Been a rash of them in the city lately, and they haven't found the perpetrators."

He didn't bother to explain the swatting to Ainslie. As part of the law enforcement world, she would know it referred to falsely reporting an emergency to a police department to cause a Special Weapons and Tactics— SWAT—team response to a physical address.

Drake shook his head. "Call came from Ainslie's cell."

"No way!" She glared at Drake. "My phone's on the table. Take a look at it. You'll see I didn't make the call."

Drake eyed her. "I don't think you did. Caller was male, but he could've used your phone, and you could've deleted the call. Phone company records will be more accurate, and we'll request those."

Grady looked at Ainslie. "Swatters often spoof their calls to make them look like they came from the location they're reporting."

Her gaze softened a fraction. "Since no one used my phone, that has to be the explanation. I rent this house. The caller might not know who lives here. Maybe he selected the address at random."

"Did Ethan ever live here with you?" Grady searched her freckled face for answers.

She nodded, setting her reddish-brown hair swinging over her shoulders. She usually wore her hair in a ponytail at work, and he loved seeing how silky soft the thick waves looked.

"He lived here for about six months," she said, thankfully oblivious to Grady's wayward thoughts. "You think that's why I was targeted?"

"Could be." Grady heard footsteps pounding down the hall. He reached for his sidearm and spun.

"Whoa." Drake swung his rifle at Grady. "Never draw down on a fugitive apprehension team. Unless you have a death wish."

Grady held up his hands and gaped at Drake. Grady knew this guy. Had been to parties with him. Socialized. And here he was aiming an assault rifle at him. Unbelievable. "No need for you to point that rifle at me either."

Drake scowled. "You inserted yourself in our op, and I'll do whatever it takes to have my guys' backs."

"Don't worry. I understand." Grady slowly lowered his hands. "Trust me."

Three tough looking guys with submachine guns matching Drake's rifle marched into the room. Grady recognized the HK MP-5, the weapon of choice for many law enforcement agencies. He'd analyzed countless 9mms discharged from these weapons and fired his share of this model as well. A sweet gun for sure.

"We're clear. No sign of Bittner." The first deputy shifted to glare at Grady from intense gray eyes. "Who're you?"

Grady didn't like the guy's tone, but he would answer. "Grady Houston. Weapons expert at the Veritas Center. Ainslie works for us."

The deputy lowered his gun. "And you were just in the neighborhood or what?"

"I live nearby and heard on the scanner that something was going down at Ainslie's place, Deputy...?"

"Zander. Carl Zander." He raised a brow. "And you just happen to know her address?"

"Gave her a ride home one night when her car wouldn't

start." Grady widened his stance. He didn't like being on the defensive when he wasn't doing anything wrong, and Ainslie wasn't either. "Look. Ainslie's mighty uncomfortable over there. At least let her put her arms down and get up."

"Go ahead." Zander waved a hand. "But keep your hands where I can see them."

She glared up at the deputy and got to her feet.

Grady wanted to help her up. Maybe hold her close until she got over the shock of four armed men bursting into her house. No way he would, though. They'd been dancing around an intense attraction to each other for months. The very last thing she needed tonight was for him to make a move. Supporting her and getting these deputies to take a hike would be far more beneficial.

"As you said, Deputy Zander, the place is clear," Grady said. "I'm sure you didn't see any sign of Bittner. Why not apologize to the lady and take off so we can get her door fixed and move on?"

"Apologize for doing my job?" Zander said. "Hardly."

Grady didn't like this guy's attitude. "Then just take off."

Zander slung his rifle strap over his shoulder. "I have some questions for Ms. Duncan before I go. Maybe you should be the one who takes off."

Grady firmed his shoulders and eyed the guy.

"Hey, hey." Drake stepped between them. "Why don't we take it down a notch here? Grady just wants to help."

Grady couldn't believe the usual instigator in the Byrd family was making peace, but Grady was thankful for his intervention before things escalated with this He-Man.

Zander focused on Ainslie. "I'll need to search you."

"That's not necessary," Grady snapped and started toward them before the guy touched Ainslie.

Drake held out a hand and gave Grady a warning look. Grady wanted to ignore him. How he wanted to. Problem was, they were doing their jobs. If he interfered, he would be arrested. No point in fighting it. In the end, Zander would still search her.

Zander stopped in front of Ainslie and kept his focus on her. "Hands on the wall."

She glared at him but complied.

Zander started the search, running the back of his hand over Ainslie's T-shirt then yoga pants. Grady gritted his teeth. The clothing was form fitting enough to prove she wasn't carrying. Zander had to know that. He could've forgone the detailed examination if he'd wanted to.

As the search played out, Grady's anger vibrated like a jackhammer attacking concrete. He wanted to deck the guy so badly he could taste the need for it.

Zander stepped back. "Go ahead and have a seat, Ms. Duncan."

"I'll just join her," Grady said.

"No!" Ainslie settled on the sofa covered in a soft blue fabric and straightened her shirt as if she was trying to erase Zander's touch. "I appreciate your support, but I can handle this on my own."

He had to work hard to keep his mouth from falling open. Sure, he got that they'd been avoiding being alone with each other for months in that unspoken dance, but tonight she needed someone on her side. Was she so troubled by the idea of him being with her that she'd rather face these deputies alone? It was looking that way.

"You heard her," Zander said, seeming to enjoy Grady's discomfort. "Take a hike."

Grady ignored Zander and locked gazes with Ainslie. "You sure you want me to go?"

"Positive," she said with an unwavering voice.

"Okay, then," he stated, more for himself than for her, but he still couldn't make his feet move.

Zander cocked an eyebrow. "Need me to walk you out?"

Grady ground his teeth and spun toward the door. He got his feet moving, one foot in front of the other. One step. Two. Each one feeling like he was betraying Ainslie. How pathetic was that? She wanted him to leave—fairly ordered him to go—and he still couldn't shake the feeling that he was letting her down.

Outside, he shook his head in the nippy air. Clearly, he had more than a physical thing for her. Sure, he'd avoided being alone with her. She did the same thing. But it didn't matter. Not one bit. Over the past few months he'd somehow come to care for her.

Question now was—what was he going to do about it?

2

Ainslie couldn't believe Grady showed up tonight of all nights. She watched him walk away. Watched his powerful but hesitant stride, his hand sliding through his warm red hair, a sure sign he was angry, maybe frustrated. At the door, he glanced back and scratched his close-cut beard. He made eye contact. Held it for a long moment before disappearing into the dark of night.

She wanted to call out to him. To beg him to come back and help her through this interview with Zander, who was watching her carefully, but she clamped down on her lips. Encouraging Grady to return would give him the wrong impression. Maybe encourage his interest in her.

With her brother's issues, she was in no position to start a relationship. And even if she was, Grady was all kinds of wrong for her. She'd grown up in Texas, where football ruled. With a brother, her life had been all about football, something she had zero interest in, and Grady was a huge watch-sports-every-chance-he-got kind of guy. Not something she would want in her life. Ever.

"Ms. Duncan," Zander's insistent tone broke through her thoughts.

He stood, feet planted wide and towering over her. She didn't like the way he was pinning her with a skeptical look. She shifted her focus to Drake. He didn't look anything like Sierra, but then she'd recently learned they didn't share the same birth father. His gaze held the same intensity as Zander's, but there was a kindness mixed in. Maybe, even if he'd held her at gunpoint for some time, he could be an ally.

"When you're ready, tell us about your brother," he said.

She didn't want to talk about Ethan with anyone, but they weren't exactly asking. She kept her focus on Drake because Zander scared her. She took a long breath. "One of Ethan's middle school friends—Wade Eggen—was shot outside Ethan's house. Ethan came home and found Wade clinging to life. He'd been beaten up and shot in the head. The neighbor saw my brother standing over the body and called 911 before Ethan had a chance to make the call. He was detained by the police. Forensics revealed his blood on Wade's body. Plus Ethan owns a gun of the same caliber as the one used to shoot Wade. As a result, Ethan was charged with the crime."

"And your brother's explanation for his blood on the body?" Zander demanded.

"He's been going through a rough time lately. I don't know what, but something's bugging him, and he's been getting drunk and picking fights in bars. He was at a going-away party for a co-worker on Friday night and had an altercation, so he was bloody and bruised when he got home. The fight took place in the parking lot with no witnesses. Forensics proved Ethan had blood from an unknown person, but he doesn't know the name of the guy he fought with, so he can't prove anything."

"All sounds suspicious to me," Zander said.

"I'm confused," Drake said. "Why didn't they do a ballistics test on Ethan's gun to compare to the recovered slug?"

"The bullet is lodged behind Wade's right eye and extremely close to the brain—so close that removing it could endanger his life. The doctors left it in, and experts reviewed a CT scan of the bullet. They concluded it's a 9mm. Ethan's gun is a 9mm Beretta." She shrugged and let them draw their own conclusions.

"Sounds like they got their guy then," Zander said.

Drake shot a tight look at his fellow marshal. "I don't know about that. It's not proof positive."

"My point exactly," Ainslie said.

Drake shifted to face her. "You work at Veritas, and Grady seems like a friend. Can't you get him involved in reviewing the documentation?"

"No," she said and left it at that. She'd considered asking Grady to give it a look, but as one of the top ballistic experts in the country, his services would come with a steep price tag, and she couldn't afford his fee.

"You should get him on it," Drake said. "No one more knowledgeable about weapons and ammo than Grady."

Zander shifted his stance. "We'll be getting a warrant to review your recent phone calls. Tell us now if there's anything that might be a surprise, or it will go badly for you."

"What? Like I talked to Bittner?" She rolled her eyes. "Go ahead and look at my records. I have nothing to hide. And also, I have a security camera, so you can look at that, too, and see that Bittner didn't show up here at any point."

Zander shook his head. "You could've deleted the video. He could have come to the back door. You have a camera there, too?"

"No." She raised her chin. "But the camera would still have caught the motion of anyone walking to the backyard. And the videos are uploaded to my provider's server first, so

14

even if I deleted one, you should be able to get a warrant for the file on their server."

Drake met her gaze, his expression tighter now. "Do you have any reason to think your brother might've been in on Bittner's escape plan?"

She shook her head. "He's innocent, and he's convinced we're going to prove it, so why would he do anything to stop that from happening?"

Drake pinned her with his gaze for a long, uncomfortable moment, and she almost squirmed under his intensity but somehow managed to resist.

"Let's pray it all works out for him," he finally said.

Zander snorted. "You're both forgetting something. Bittner could've threatened your brother or your family if Ethan didn't help."

Ainslie met his gaze. "Until this call, did you have any reason to suspect Ethan's involvement with Bittner?"

"No," Zander said. "But you can be sure we'll go back and review everything the minute we leave here."

"There must be something more you can tell me about the call that brought you here," she said.

Zander folded his arms over his chest. "Call came into the 800 number we set up to report any sightings of Bittner."

"Did the caller give his name?"

"No," he said. "Our detectives are working on tracking the call back to its source."

"Then it seems to me you don't have any facts at this point to think it's legitimate." She returned his stare with a tense one of her own. "I would think you would've tracked down the source before breaking down my door."

Zander grimaced and, for the first time, she managed to put a chink in his tough exterior. "Was a judgment call, and we had to act fast."

She wanted to snap at him for not being more thorough,

but it would only serve to make him angry, and what good would that do? She had to move forward not look backward. "And what about me? Am I now under suspicion for being an accomplice, too?"

Zander took a long breath and let it out slowly, his gaze fixed on hers.

"I think the best thing we can do is put a deputy on protection detail for you," Drake said.

Zander shot a look at Drake. "Protection detail? I was thinking more like putting a tail on her."

Drake faced Zander. "I'm inclined to think Ms. Duncan is a victim here and could be in danger. But in either event, a deputy with her at all times solves both issues."

Zander rolled his eyes. "And who's going to babysit? You?"

"Glad to take the first shift." Drake changed his focus to Ainslie. "If there's something else we need to know about Bittner, now's the time to tell us. He's a killer without remorse, and he'll gladly eliminate anyone who gets in his way."

Grady watched the last deputy's car pull away from Ainslie's house. Zander still believed Bittner had been there, so he'd called in a forensic team to lift prints. It had taken them hours to complete the job. Grady believed Ainslie, but if Bittner threatened her brother, he could see someone lying in that situation. He didn't think Ainslie would lie, but he knew from past experience a person didn't know what they were capable of concealing until they were put in a difficult situation.

Right. Like *that* was something he needed to be thinking about tonight.

He shoved the memory back into the folder he'd worked hard to keep closed for years and stared across the street to where Drake sat in his SUV. He appeared to be settled in for the night. Why, Grady had no idea, but he was going to find out what was going on.

He crossed the road in the spitting drizzle so common in Portland in March, and by the time he reached Drake's SUV, he'd lowered his window.

"You staying?" Grady asked, bending his head against the soft rain.

Drake gave a clipped nod. "Protective detail."

Interesting. "So, what? You all believe Ainslie now?"

Drake rested his hands on the wheel and took a long breath. "I'm inclined to believe her. Zander, not so much. We'll have someone on her until we bring Bittner in."

Grady wasn't sure if he should be glad about this or question it. "I don't want anyone harassing her."

Drake shifted on the seat and eyed Grady. "Just what is your relationship with her?"

Grady wished he knew the answer to that, but even if he had, he wouldn't share it with Drake. "We work together. That's all."

"Right." Drake rolled his eyes.

Time to move on.

"I'll be putting our team on tracing the call."

"I expected as much. With all the contacts you guys have in law enforcement, you'll have no trouble getting the information you need. Let me know if I can help."

Glad for the cooperation, Grady nodded and started to walk away, but then an idea popped into his head, and he turned back. "About the protection detail. Ainslie will be staying at the Veritas Center until Bittner is captured."

A cocky smile crossed Drake's face. "I knew there was

something going on with you two, and her staying at your condo proves me right."

"She won't be staying with me. I'm sure Sierra will agree to let her bunk with her." Each of the Veritas Center partners had a condo in the west tower of the building.

"Good luck with that." He smirked. "If you can get her head out of the clouds."

"Clouds?"

Drake grunted. "Oh, c'mon, you have to have noticed that she's obsessed with the upcoming wedding."

"Oh, that." Grady thought about Sierra's actions since she'd gotten engaged to FBI agent Reed Rice. "She seems able to focus just fine at work, but otherwise, yeah, you're right. She does have her head in the clouds."

Drake scratched his jaw with a hint of five o'clock shadow. "I've always thought about her as one of the guys. She had to be with five brothers, you know? So I never expected her to go all girly on us. Not in a million years."

Grady had to agree, but then, he didn't know a thing about what planning to get married might feel like because it wasn't in the cards for him. To make a lifetime commitment, he'd have to tell his potential spouse about his past, and he wouldn't reveal the secret he'd carried since he was nine to anyone for any reason. Even for the life he'd often thought he wanted. One he was watching his fellow partners at Veritas, one by one, claim for themselves. Claim a happiness he didn't have in his own life.

"Hey, you guys aren't looking for another investigator on your staff, are you?" Drake asked.

Grady was thankful for the question to get him out of his own head. "You want to leave the marshals?"

Drake gave a sure shake of his head. "I'm asking for Aiden. Since he donated his kidney to Dad, we're all worried he'll get hurt on the job and figure he should start looking into something a bit tamer than his ATF gig."

Aiden loved his job, and Grady couldn't believe he'd be thinking about leaving it. "He know you're asking around for him?"

"Nah. Just thought I'd check."

"We don't have plans to hire anyone else right now, but you should talk to Sierra about it. I'm sure she wants to see Aiden in a less risky job, too."

"Yeah. Once she comes down from the wedding high."

"But then there'll be the honeymoon high and wedded bliss high. Then kids."

Drake laughed and held up his hands. "Okay, got it. I won't wait."

"I'll just go tell Ainslie that she's staying with us."

Drake's mouth dropped open. "Um, dude, I'm no expert on the ladies, but maybe asking would be better."

He was right. Grady wanted to blast through the damaged door, grab Ainslie up, and haul her to his truck for safekeeping. That wouldn't go over well with any woman, and he'd never do it, especially not with someone who didn't want to have anything to do with him. But the thought proved how much he actually cared about her, and he needed to be mindful of that so he didn't fall even more for her. Not unless he wanted to be in a world of hurt. Which he didn't.

"Catch you later." Grady tapped the truck then dug out his phone. He stopped on the sidewalk leading up to the small bungalow hunkered down in the dark shadows of tall pines and waited for Sierra to answer.

"Grady?" One word, but he heard the fatigue in it.

He brought her up to speed on Ainslie's situation, including sharing Drake's role in the raid. "I'd like it if you'd call Ainslie and invite her to stay with you."

"Poor thing," Sierra said. "Of course I will. As soon as we hang up."

"I'll give her a ride or follow her over to the center. And you should know, Drake will be tailing her, too." He explained about the protection detail.

Sierra sighed. "I hope he didn't give Ainslie too much trouble."

"He was tough but fair," Grady was happy to report. "Now, Zander was another matter."

"She must be a mess. I'll call her and get the spare bedroom ready."

"Thanks again."

"No worries. I think I'm turning into Bridezilla, and I need a distraction from wedding planning." She laughed, and the call ended before he could agree with her.

Feeling more optimistic for Ainslie, Grady headed up the walkway. His first job was to find a way to secure the front door. He could do that while Ainslie packed. Near the open door, he heard her phone ring, so he assessed the damage while she held a conversation with Sierra.

Ainslie protested several times, but then Sierra must have found the right enticement, as Ainslie sighed out a long breath and agreed to stay with her.

As soon as Ainslie ended the call, Grady knocked on the doorjamb. "Ainslie?" he called to keep her from worrying about who'd come to her door now. "Can I talk to you for a minute?"

She pivoted in a graceful turn. She was five-six and moved with the elegance of a dancer. He'd always liked watching her, especially the curve of her neck when she had her hair up. Long, slender, delicate. He was almost afraid she might break if he ever held her in his arms the way he wanted to.

"Why are you still here?" she asked tersely.

Okay, fine. Burst that holding-her bubble. "I thought you might need help securing the door."

She turned her attention to the doorframe and tsked. "I've been so focused on trying to figure out who might've made this swat call, I forgot about the door."

"Would you like me to take care of it for you?"

She looked at him then. Really looked at him, her gaze connecting and holding. What she was looking for, he had no idea, but he remained still under her study.

She let out a slow breath between pursed lips. "That would be nice."

He'd expected to have to argue with her, but this ready acceptance worried him even more. He'd have to keep an eye out to see if she was feeling defeated and if he could help with that. But for now...the door. "I don't suppose you have any wood in the garage."

"I don't use the garage, so I don't know what's in there, but feel free to look."

He nodded. "If there's nothing there, I'll run to the Depot for some plywood. They should still be open."

"That would be nice," she said again. It was as if, in agreeing to the help, she was trying it on for size. "You should know I'm going to be staying with Sierra until Bittner is caught. Drake must've called her, and she insisted."

He didn't know if he should play dumb or say something. If he admitted he was the one who suggested she stay at the condos, she might change her mind. Better to keep the information to himself. "I'll just check the garage while you pack, and I can follow you over to the lab."

"Sounds good." She looked over his shoulder. "I'm assuming my tail will come along, too."

"He's got your back and your best interest at heart."

"Yeah, I picked up on that." A tight smile lifted the

21

corners of her mouth. "Seems like a great guy who'd be fun to know, assuming I can get past him holding a gun on me."

"There is that." Grady tried to ignore her comment about Drake. He might not be free to pursue her, but he didn't like hearing she wanted to get to know Drake.

Grady took off for the garage, her comment lingering. What did she need to get past with him so she could get to know him? Tonight told him that he badly wanted that, and it also reminded him he would never have it. He was no more ready to reveal his secret now than he had been on that life-changing day.

3

Ainslie turned onto the Veritas Center's driveway and took a moment to enjoy the unusual architecture highlighted with soft moonlight before pulling into the parking structure. Two six-story towers were connected with a skybridge at the top and a single-story building on the first floor that served as the main entrance. She still couldn't believe she'd gotten the job here. The place was world-renowned for cutting edge forensics and DNA. Her dream job for sure.

Grady beeped his horn behind her, and she jumped.

Right. He'd tailed her.

She pressed her fingers on the reader to open the gate and pull into the garage, winding up to the top floor where the partners parked, Grady and Drake right behind her.

On the one hand, he was being pushy. Typical Grady. On the other hand, he was being considerate in making sure she got to Sierra's condo safely. And yet, he was also trying to control her. She didn't think he was intentionally doing it. He'd served on Delta Force for many years and had a fierce protector personality. He just wanted her to be safe. She'd seen him do the same thing for others in her time working here. Men and women. If he thought his help was needed, he jumped in, and only then did he look.

She found his compassion and desire to do the right thing appealing and irritating at the same time. Appealing usually won out. Not tonight though. Maybe it was because of all the testosterone that had been flowing through her house with the deputies there. Maybe she was lumping Grady in with them.

She parked near the door and got out to open the trunk of her Honda Civic. By the time she'd removed the first bag, Grady was by her side, taking the handle from her hand. She thought to argue, but what would have been the point? He was a gentleman—opening doors and helping people at work. Even fixing her door. Besides, he wouldn't give the bag back no matter what she said, and she was too tired to argue.

She picked up her camera cases and started for the door. She glanced back at Drake, who'd turned off his ignition to spend the night in his vehicle.

Grady rushed ahead to the door and pressed his fingers on the print reader then pulled open the steel door. "Have you ever been to the condo tower?"

She shook her head.

"The first three floors are empty." He held the door open for her. "Nick and I are on four. Kelsey and Devon got married last month so they're on five with Sierra. Emory and Blake, and Maya on six. We'll cross over on the skybridge here."

He stepped down a hallway, and she followed.

As it opened to the glass-enclosed bridge, she took in the view of the city, the lights twinkling in the distance and the puffy clouds sliding by in the moonlight overhead. "I always wanted to see the view from up here."

He stopped mid-bridge and glanced back at her. "You

should have said something to one of us. We'd have been glad to show you."

She wasn't sure what to say to that, but he seemed to be waiting for a response.

"I...um...I don't know." She shifted her camera bags. "All the partners are really nice and everything, but you are still my bosses."

He arched an eyebrow. "Sierra is your boss. The rest of us don't get involved in who she hires in her department."

"Fair enough, but...I mean...if I did something really off the wall, you could have me fired."

His eyebrows hitched higher. "I could *recommend* it, but Sierra holds all the power in hiring decisions for her department. Trust me, she would feel free to ignore anything I said. She runs her department, and it's ultimately her decision. Same is true of all the partners."

Ainslie hadn't known that and wasn't sure she was glad to know it now. That information removed an obstacle that she'd lodged firmly in place as a reason not to fall for this guy.

He tipped his head at the wall of windows. "So, what do you think of the view?"

She looked out over the city and itched to get out her camera, but the glass reflection would ruin any pictures. "I wish I could capture it."

"I saw the landscape photos at your place and assumed you took them."

She nodded. "Landscapes help me put the horrors I see on the job into the perspective of God's universe."

He tilted his head and moved close enough that she could catch the damp scent of his leather jacket. "I don't know how you and Sierra handle working murder scenes."

She looked up at him, wishing he weren't near enough

that her awareness of him felt like a physical pull. "You work crime scenes too."

"Only occasionally when Sierra calls me out for a ballistics consult. And honestly, they're usually less gruesome than what I saw in the service."

She couldn't even imagine what he'd witnessed or how he'd dealt with it. "That must have been tough."

"Tough?" He shrugged. "Yeah, I guess, but God doesn't give us more than we can handle with His help."

She wasn't so sure about that. He'd been piling things on her shoulders since her mother died, and Ainslie was cracking under the weight. Not something she wanted to talk about when she was already tired and dragging from the adrenaline draining from her body.

"We should go." She skirted around him and rushed across the bridge to the stairwell, jogging down the steps before he caught up to her.

Yeah, she was running from him, and she didn't care if he knew it. She wasn't sharing personal things and getting involved with this guy. She shot into the hallway on the fifth floor.

"Last door on the left," he said, closer behind than she'd thought.

Ainslie pounded on the door, catching her breath from her mad dash. Maybe from the rush of emotions Grady's nearness raised. She'd dated in the past. Had her share of long-term relationships even. But this thing with Grady was different. Way different, and she didn't understand it. Sure, he was good looking. Handsome. Buff. But it wasn't just a physical attraction. That she knew for sure.

The door opened, and Sierra marched out. Even in bare feet, she was four inches taller than Ainslie's five-six and towered over her. She wore gray yoga pants and a turquoise

T-shirt that formed to her fit body. She ran her gaze over Ainslie and frowned.

"You poor thing. What a perfectly horrible thing to have happen." She gathered Ainslie into a hug.

Shocked at the personal response from her boss, Ainslie didn't know how to respond. She let Sierra hug her. Surprisingly, tears pressed at the back of her eyes, but she wasn't a crier. Before the tears started to fall, she backed away and took a long breath. "Thank you for letting me stay with you."

"Of course. Think nothing of it." Sierra pushed the door open. "Now come in and have a cup of tea, and we'll get you settled."

Ainslie glanced back at Grady and swallowed hard. She wasn't used to accepting help. In fact, before tonight when she'd let Grady barricade her door, she never did it. *Never.* It always felt too much like the charity of her childhood that had been forced on her and her family by people with questionable motives. But in her weakness tonight, she'd not only agreed to stay with Sierra but had let Grady board up her house, too.

One offer of help would lead to another and another, and then other people would soon control her life again. She'd worked hard to learn to stand on her own two feet— and to make the money she needed to do so. And tomorrow, when she was rested and this aberration of growing dependence on the partners left her, she would take time to rethink the night. Maybe she'd go back home. But right now, she needed to send Grady packing before she let her attraction to him sway her into letting him help even more.

She faced him and took a firm stance. "Thank you for securing the house tonight and following me over here."

He gave a single nod as if it was a given that he would put himself out to help her. "We'll meet with the partners in

27

the morning to see what we can do to help you free your brother."

She shook her head and held his gaze. "I appreciate the offer, but I've got this and will be handling things on my own from here."

He looked confused, and, if she was reading him right, hurt by her response. "Why, when we have the resources you need?"

She curled her fingers tight to stay strong and not admit to her lack of finances. Another touchy subject for her. "Ethan and I live paycheck to paycheck, and we don't have the funds to pay you."

"No need," Grady stated firmly. "We'll cover the cost. Right, Sierra?"

"Right," she said. "We provide services pro bono all the time."

Pro bono. Just a fancy term for charity. Ainslie's childhood of poverty, of others offering charity, raised the same ugly feelings she'd suppressed for years, leaving her feeling queasy. And conflicted. She wanted to help Ethan. She *would* help Ethan, but not as a charity case. The Veritas partners might have the best of the best when it came to resources, but she would have to find another way. "I can't accept such a generous offer."

"You will!" Grady eyed her, then shook his head and ran a hand over his face. "Look. I'm sorry. I didn't mean to snap at you like that, but refusing our help makes no sense at all. We do this all the time for complete strangers. It's a no brainer to do it for one of our own."

"He's right." Sierra's gentle smile eased away some of Ainslie's anxiety. "Please let us help your brother."

Ainslie didn't want to give in, but something in the way Sierra offered her assistance didn't feel like charity. It was more like a friend being there when you needed her. Not that Ainslie had much experience in that, but she knew the offer wasn't said in the same vein as the charity of Ainslie's youth.

Sierra wrapped a protective arm around Ainslie's shoulders. "You're family, and this is what we do for family. Please don't say no."

Grady looked at Sierra with a quizzical expression. Maybe he didn't agree with the family statement, but maybe, just maybe, if he thought of her as family, this interest between them wouldn't become a problem.

"You've done so much to make my job easier these past few months," Sierra continued. "And I really want to do this for you. Please let me."

"Okay." Ainslie caved under her boss's sincerity but immediately made a mental note to find a way to track the partners' work hours so she could pay it all back. "Thank you. I know Ethan will really appreciate having you on his side."

Sierra released Ainslie and leaned against the open door. "If I could, I'd put you on paid leave, too. Give you more time to investigate the swat and this Wade guy's shooting. But we have too much on our plate at work right now. Still, feel free to use any downtime during the day for the investigation."

Tears formed in Ainslie's eyes at the sincere kindness that didn't carry the pity she'd seen so often growing up, and she looked up at the ceiling to keep them from spilling down her cheeks. "I'm so blessed by your generosity. I knew God was smiling on me the day I got the job here."

"Smiling on us, too," Sierra said. "You're a godsend for sure."

Grady widened his stance, looking tough and in charge. "Ethan's innocent, and we'll make sure he's freed."

His absolute belief in her brother brought doubt chewing

at her stomach. "There's something you should both know about Ethan that might change your mind about helping him."

Grady's eyebrows rose. "What's that?"

She didn't want to say this aloud. Doing that would make it more real, but they had a right to know. "Wade—the guy who Ethan supposedly shot—claims that Ethan's the one who shot him."

She expected an uncertain look from the pair of them, but Sierra's expression didn't change at all.

Grady simply tipped his head. "Why would Wade say that when Ethan didn't shoot him?"

Not the response she expected. Especially since Grady had seemed skeptical about Ethan at her house. "You still believe Ethan after this?"

He gave a sharp nod. "If you believe him, then I believe him."

"Ditto for me," Sierra said.

Ainslie had never experienced such unquestioning support, and she didn't know how to respond.

"Did you talk to this Wade guy?" Grady asked.

She nodded. "I went to see him in the hospital, but he would hardly look at me. I'm sorry he was hurt so badly, but he kept insisting Ethan shot him. Made me mad. So before I left, I told him I knew he was lying and that I wouldn't stop digging until I proved it."

"Good for you." Sierra stuck out her chin. "What did he say to that?"

"Nothing. Just glared at me." Ainslie shook her head. "I asked Ethan about it, of course. He says he doesn't know what Wade is up to and refuses to say anything more."

"Have they been friends long?" Grady asked.

Memories of her youth came rushing back. She had plenty of memories of Wade, but none of them could be described as fond. "Since middle school. I always thought it was an odd friendship, but they've kept in touch over the years. Wade turning on him like this is weird. I'm not letting Ethan get away without explaining. I ask every time I see him and will keep asking."

"Sometimes, telling family what's going on in a difficult situation is the hardest of all." Grady shoved his hands in his pockets and looked down at his feet. Seemed like he personally knew about keeping secrets from his family. Piqued her interest, but she wouldn't question him and take them into the personal realm. All business, all the time. That was what she needed to be if she was going to be seeing more of him while they worked to free Ethan.

"Speaking of family," Grady said. "Did you know Drake is sitting in his car watching the place?"

Sierra's mouth formed an O of surprise, and she shifted to look at Ainslie. "Grady said he wasn't a brute at your house. Please tell me that's true."

"Brute, no. He followed procedure to the letter and kept me at gunpoint far longer than I would have liked." Despite the residual anxiety from the home invasion, Ainslie forced out a smile. "I totally get it, though."

Sierra squeezed Ainslie's arm. "Thank you for being so understanding. I know Drake can be kind of intimidating." She paused, and her soft expression vanished. "Would you mind if I asked him to come up and spend the night on the couch?"

"Of course not."

She gave a firm nod. "Then let's head inside, and I'll give him a call."

Sierra stood back. "After you."

Ainslie went into the condo and headed toward a large open area where the kitchen with white cabinets abutted

31

the living room. Grady followed and set her suitcase on the light wood floor by the island.

Sierra stepped past him into the modern kitchen. "Would you like to stay for a cup of tea with us, Grady?"

He mocked gagging. "You know how I feel about tea."

"You like it as much as you like soccer." Sierra chuckled.

"Exactly. That game is so not football."

Ainslie hadn't known there was a sport Grady didn't like, but maybe she'd overestimated how much he watched sports.

"And," he said, glancing back at Ainslie, "as much as I like your company, I think Ainslie should get some rest."

"Agreed," she quickly said so he would leave. "Thanks again."

He met her gaze and held it for a long moment, transmitting a true desire to stay. Surprising. But she couldn't let him do that. For any reason. She had to get away from his influence on her so she could think about who might be behind the swat.

He snapped free and asked her to call him if she needed anything before he strode out of the condo.

Ainslie turned her attention to the space and took in the large sectional covered in a gray print that took up most of a large living room nicely decorated in muted colors. A glass coffee table was littered with scientific journals and wedding magazines. "You have a nice place."

Sierra groaned. "Ignore the mess. Wedding planning has taken up all my free time, so I've done very little cleaning."

Ainslie had seen firsthand how the stress of planning was consuming her boss, yet Sierra didn't let it interfere with her work. "Are you ready for the big day?"

"I don't think any bride ever has everything prepared." She plugged in an electric tea kettle. "But if you're asking if

I'm ready to marry Reed, then absolutely." She smiled, and her whole face radiated with utter and complete joy.

Like most women, Ainslie wanted a husband and family. She wanted to have the same kind of love that Sierra had clearly found. But that kind of commitment just wasn't meant to be right now. Not while Ethan was suffering behind bars.

Keep that in mind. She could end up working closely with Grady and could easily see forgetting that he was off limits. She wasn't going to set herself up for disappointment and heartbreak. Those were the last things she needed in her life.

4

Grady headed down to his lab. No way he could sleep now, not with everything that had transpired tonight. He'd need to spend time engrossed in his work to clear his head of Ainslie before he'd be able to get any shuteye. He had plenty of items on his to-do list to keep busy, that was for sure.

He went straight to the evidence lockers and pulled out slugs and a weapon from a brutal homicide where a husband caught his wife cheating on him and allegedly killed her and the man. All the forensics pointed to his guilt, but proving the gun that held only the husband's fingerprints fired these slugs would give the prosecutors exactly what they needed to put this man behind bars. Assuming, of course, that the slugs matched the ones he was about to fire.

He took the gun to the bullet recovery containment system—a big stainless steel tub filled with water on the back wall of his lab. The process of machining guns made each barrel unique, and as a bullet was squeezed through the barrel, the metal left distinct marks on the bullets and could be matched to a particular weapon.

Grady loaded the gun with the same make of bullets recovered on the scene and pumped off three shots into the water tank. The recoil felt good in his hands, releasing a bit of his tension. He'd love to go out back to their small firing range and take out his aggression at the swatter on his targets, but gunshots at this time of night might bother his team. Or Ainslie. She sure the heck wouldn't want to hear gunfire after having weapons pointed at her.

He moved to the end of the tank. He located the three 9mm slugs, and his thoughts went to Ainslie and the terror in her eyes when he'd arrived at her house. She'd had no idea the men busting down her door were law enforcement officers. She'd probably thought it was a home invasion. Her heart had to have been racing. Her stomach clenched. Her body filled with anxiety.

Grady slammed the slugs on the counter. He needed to do something to move forward in helping her. He got out his phone to dial Nick Thorn, the Veritas Center's cyber expert and good friend.

"Yo," Nick answered.

"I have a favor to ask."

"I'm listening."

Grady recounted the night's events, doing his best to keep all emotion out of his tone so Nick didn't ask awkward questions about Ainslie. Grady might've managed to avoid her most of the time, but it was no secret that he was attracted to her, and the others had picked up on it. Sierra even encouraged Grady to ask Ainslie out, but he'd shut down that conversation before it really got started. "Drake said the swat call came from Ainslie's phone number, but she says she didn't make the call."

"If she's telling the truth, the call had to have been spoofed to look like it originated on her phone."

So Grady had been right on track with his earlier thoughts. "I believe her."

"Yeah, you would."

"What's that supposed to mean?"

"You've got a thing for her, so of course you'd give her the benefit of the doubt."

"You think she's lying?"

"Nah," Nick said. "Just pointing out that you could be biased here."

"I need you to find the location where the real call originated, and then we'll know for sure that she's telling the truth."

Nick let out a slow breath. "You do know that could take time, right? There are different methods to spoof a call, and I first have to narrow down how they made the call. And even then, they might have covered their tracks."

Grady's gut clenched. "So you're saying it's a lost cause."

"Not lost, but don't get your hopes up."

Grady already had his hopes up. He wanted to find this caller and get him behind bars before he tried anything else to hurt Ainslie.

"Did she have any thoughts on who might be behind it?" Nick asked.

"Not that she said, other than maybe she was targeted at random and it really had nothing to do with her."

"Sounds like you don't think that's right."

"I don't. If this was indeed a swat call, they aren't usually random." Grady told Nick about Ethan, Wade, and Bittner. "She told Wade that she knew he was lying and she was going to prove it. So maybe he's trying to scare her into leaving it alone."

"Yeah, could be, I suppose." Nick yawned. "I'll grab some caffeine and get started on it right away."

"Get back to me the minute you know anything."

"You got it." Nick ended the call.

Grady shoved his phone into his pocket and looked at the gun he'd just fired. The swat could have gone all kinds of wrong, and Ainslie could've been shot. Maybe killed. The thought left Grady struggling for breath. She clearly didn't want his help, but he was going to give it. Every hour he could afford to be with her, he would be. No way he was going to let anyone try something else like the swat and take her life.

Ainslie sat next to Sierra at her kitchen island and forked up a fluffy bite of scrambled eggs sitting next to toast and several pieces of cantaloupe on her plate. Next to it was a big mug of strong black coffee, the deep, nutty aroma that drifted through the condo so enticing it had pulled Ainslie out of the bedroom like a magnet. She'd expected to find Drake sipping his own coffee on the sofa, but a replacement deputy had filled in for him in the middle of the night so he could grab a few hours of sleep. He wanted to be on duty during the day so he was back again, but he chose to sit in the parking lot to keep an eye on the lot and building.

She picked up the mug and took a sip of the piping hot coffee, trying to calm the residual anxiety from the swatting incident. She'd been off-kilter since the moment she'd come awake in Sierra's guest room. Ainslie had a good working relationship with Sierra, but the woman was still Ainslie's boss, so staying at her condo, though a blessing, was also unsettling.

Sierra swallowed her bite. "What time can you go visit your brother?"

Ainslie cupped her warm stoneware mug. "Visiting hours start at nine, and I want to be there when they open. Thank you for giving me the time to go. I'll make up for it by working late tonight."

Sierra laid her silverware on the plate. "Is Grady going with you?"

At the mention of Grady, Ainslie lifted her shoulders. "I hadn't planned on asking him."

Sierra watched her. "Something's wrong. Spill."

"Nothing's wrong."

"Then why did your spine just stiffen?" Sierra peered at Ainslie with the same intensity she used to examine trace evidence under her scope.

Ainslie didn't want to admit her feelings for Grady, but she couldn't lie, so she sipped her coffee, the wonderful flavor suddenly tasting bitter.

"It's Grady, right?" Sierra asked. "The thing you two have going on but are avoiding for some reason?"

Of course Sierra wouldn't let the topic go. She was far too tenacious for that, and Ainslie needed to say something to shut her down. "I don't want to talk about it."

"I respect that." Sierra blinked a few times, and Ainslie thought that might be the end of the discussion, but Sierra took a breath and added, "But just know that Grady's an amazing guy. Strong. Dependable. Compassionate. Hard-working. A real catch."

"And a sports lover," Ainslie tossed out.

Sierra's eyes narrowed. "Oh, yeah, that, too. He lives for his football, but still..."

"Still, I don't want to talk about it, if you don't mind."

Sierra held Ainslie's gaze. "I'll let that part go, but not my thoughts for your safety. Do you think after last night that it's safe to go to the jail alone?"

No, but... "I won't be alone. Drake will be tailing me. With his fugitive apprehension experience, he's more than capable."

"Oh, I agree," Sierra said enthusiastically. "My brother is

super good at his job, but tailing you versus being in the car with you are two different things, right?"

Ainslie agreed with Sierra, but she didn't want to because she didn't want to admit that having Grady join her would be the safest course of action. At least safe for her physical well-being. Her mental well-being with Grady in the close confines of a car would be another story all together. Too bad she couldn't just ride with Drake, but that would raise all kinds of liability issues for his department.

Sierra picked up her mug and took a long sip. "You may not know this, but Grady's former Delta Force. He'd be an excellent bodyguard."

Ainslie heard more in Sierra's voice and raised an eyebrow. "Is that your reason for suggesting he accompany me, or are you trying to push us together again?"

A sheepish expression crossed Sierra's face. "Um...well... both, I guess."

"But he's as good as my boss," Ainslie protested as she still hadn't come to grips with that no matter what Grady had said.

"What?" Sierra's eyes widened. "No. No way. You report only to me, and I'm the only one who has the power to fire you. Or even to assign you tasks. There's no conflict as far as I or the other partners are concerned."

Others? "How do you know about the others?" Ainslie searched Sierra's gaze, but she whisked her hands across her face as if trying to hide her thoughts.

"Oh, no," Ainslie said. "No. You've talked about us, haven't you? The partners."

Sierra waved a hand. "Only in passing. Not like you were on one of our agendas, but yes, it came up in a meeting."

"A meeting? You talked about me in a meeting?" Heat rushed over Ainslie's face. Blinding. Red. Humiliating heat.

"When I meet with you all, I'm going to die of embarrassment."

"Hey," Sierra said. "Nothing to be embarrassed about. It's not like we can control who we're interested in. Take me and Reed. We butted heads on an investigation, and I was still attracted to him. And look at us now."

Yeah. Love. Wonderful let's-get-married-forever love. So what? "That's not going to happen with me and Grady. First, I have to focus solely on getting Ethan out of jail, and second, I hate football. Like really and truly hate it. And I'm not big on guns either. So Grady and I have nothing in common."

Sierra drew in a breath and smiled. "Love doesn't need things in common. It just needs to be."

Ainslie sighed.

"Listen," Sierra said. "I won't pressure you to talk about this more. Just don't close yourself off from the possibility. I like to think God puts people in our lives at the exact time we need to meet them. With your strong reaction to Grady, I can't help but think God's behind it."

Ainslie groaned. "If what you say is true, then I would be going against God's will to fight this attraction, and I sure don't want to do that."

"Hey, I could be wrong." Sierra picked up her plate. "Pray about it and keep an open mind. Starting with asking Grady to accompany you to the detention center."

Ainslie knew when to give in. "I'll call him now."

"And I'll prepare a couple of to-go coffees for the two of you." She took her plate to the sink.

Ainslie made the call to Grady. He agreed and said he'd be up in a few minutes. She pushed off her stool. "I need to grab my jacket and purse."

"Good." Sierra held up a travel mug in one hand and a coffee pot in the other. "Mugs will be ready when you are."

Ainslie went to the bedroom, her mind filled with questions and doubts. About Ethan. About continuing to stay with Sierra. About Grady. Very definitely about Grady. And the swat. Who was behind it? A coincidence, or had Wade done it?

Her brain threatened to explode, and she dropped onto the mattress to bow her head.

Father, thank You for providing these amazing people in my life. Please show me if I'm supposed to accept their help. And show me Your purpose in meeting Grady, if indeed there is a special reason You brought us together. And help us to work together to clear Ethan's name.

A loud knock sounded on the condo door. Grady.

Help me with him, God. Please.

She grabbed her jacket and purse, her feet dragging as she went back to the living room while her heart rate kicked up at the thought of seeing him.

Sierra was handing two travel mugs to Grady, who was dressed in his typical tactical pants, boots, T-shirt, and leather jacket.

"The purple one is for Ainslie," Sierra said. "Black and strong. Plenty of cream and sugar in yours."

"Thanks." His gaze swung to Ainslie and locked on. His sapphire eyes lit with joy before he washed the look away, and a heated interest filled them.

Her heart responded with backflips, and an awkward silence descended on them, the room seeming to fade into the background.

Sierra cleared her throat.

Ainslie jerked her gaze free and said the first thing that came to mind. "Never pegged you for a cream-and-sugar kind of guy."

"Because you think I'm sweet enough without it?" His tone was flirtatious, his eyes alight with humor.

Not the way she'd wanted him to respond. His good mood made her want to move closer. Take his hand. Tell him what she was feeling. Instead she rolled her eyes to make light of things and looked at Sierra. "Thanks again for letting me bunk here."

"Hold on. Let me get you a key so you can come and go as needed." She hurried from the room.

Ainslie stared after her. "She's very trusting."

"I don't think unreasonably so," Grady said. "She just knows how to read people and can tell you're on the up and up."

Could that really be true? "Not how most people react when they hear about Ethan. Since he's accused of attempted murder, they think by association I must be a criminal, too."

"Ah," he said. "That's why you gave me a disappointed look last night."

"I did?"

He nodded. "When I first heard about Ethan. I questioned you when I should've supported you."

She held up a hand. "Hey, I get it. Don't worry."

"I do want to support you, you know? Through all of this." The intensity in his eyes heated up again, and he handed her the purple travel mug.

She took a sip of the hot liquid, nearly scalding her mouth, which at the moment might be preferable to the scorching look Grady was fixing on her.

"Here you go," Sierra said coming back into the room and holding out a key.

Ainslie grabbed it, and, before she could turn to leave, Sierra swept Ainslie into a quick hug and released her. "We'll clear Ethan, don't you worry. The best team in the country has your back, and we never fail. Never."

5

Nearing lunchtime, Ainslie took a seat next to Sierra in the conference room while Grady stood at the end of the table. The meeting was impromptu, and yet all the partners had made the time in their schedules to help her. Perfect, but Ainslie wasn't mentally prepared for the change in schedule. She'd thought she'd have gone to the detention center by now. Had started out in Grady's truck to drive downtown. Then she got a call saying Ethan wasn't allowed visitors until the afternoon. They gave no reason, just said it wasn't possible. As she caught up on work in the lab, Grady gathered his team together, like he'd promised to do last night. A man of his word.

The partners often met in this room, and she'd walked past their meetings many times, but she'd never attended one here, and she felt out of place. Even more so when Sierra's comment about having discussed her and Grady in this very room popped into Ainslie's brain.

Seriously, could she concentrate, or would that—and all her other worries—keep niggling away at her mind?

She ran her gaze around the table to try to judge the partners' moods. A box of muffins sat open on the table, and a few of the partners had one sitting on a napkin by their mugs of steaming coffee, but they were chatting and not eating.

Maya, their toxicology and controlled substances expert and the firm's managing partner, sat across from Ainslie, her blueberry muffin unwrapped. She'd swept her shoulder-length blond hair over her shoulders, and her striking blue eyes were fixed on Grady.

Emory, the center's DNA expert, sat next to her husband, Blake, who was a former sheriff and now their investigator. Her red hair was pulled back in a ponytail, and her face had grown plump with her pregnancy. Blake was a dark-haired intense guy—except when he gazed at Emory. Then, love beamed from his face.

On his other side sat Nick, their computer expert. He had a scruffy beard and tired brown eyes this morning, and two empty muffin wrappers sat in front of him, crumbs dotting the table.

The door opened and, wearing one of her flirty print skirts and knit tops and carrying a large mug, the team anthropologist, entered the room. Kelsey set down her mug and dropped into a chair to run a hand over curly black hair. "Sorry I'm late. Lost track of time."

"No worries," Grady said. "I was about to bring everyone up to speed. We're dealing with two investigations here, though we suspect they're related."

He turned to the whiteboard and wrote Swat and Attempted Murder, then turned around and shared details for each area.

"I've already tasked Nick with tracing the swat call." Grady peered at Nick. "Any luck?"

"Not yet." Nick looked at Ainslie. "The caller made a computer VoIP call. I assume you know what that is."

44

"Sort of," she said. "I know it stands for Voice Over Internet Protocol, but not sure of the details."

"It's a technology that allows you to make voice calls using an internet connection instead of a phone line."

"Does this mean it's less likely that we'll find the caller?"

Nick scrubbed a hand over his tired face. "Highly unlikely via the VoIP phone company, but if I can get a location another way, then we can look for CCTV in the area. I'm tracking that down now."

"You look like you might've worked late on this. Thank you so much." She made sure to infuse her words with her appreciation.

"Hey, no sweat." He lifted a bottle of Dr. Pepper and grinned. "I had plenty of fuel."

She laughed with him, but Grady kept a straight face and noted the information on the board.

He turned back to the group. "Any other thoughts on how we might find this swatter?"

"We should look into Bittner," Blake said. "I can do a workup of his known associates. Maybe I'll find someone with the skills to spoof the call and pull this off."

"I can do a deep dive on the internet for information on the guy." Nick balled up the muffin papers in a napkin.

Blake gave a sharp nod. "And I'll try to get his police file. With all of that, we should be able to piece together a good picture on the guy."

"Perfect." Grady jotted the assignments on the board.

They worked so well together. Each partner volunteering their expertise without having to be asked. Ainslie had walked by this room plenty of times when they were working an investigation and had always wondered how they handled their meetings. Now she knew and was even more impressed with their cooperation. Though she suspected they also had their times of conflict.

Had their discussion about her and Grady been filled with conflict? Did the others agree that Grady had no power over her job and she was free to date him? She thought Sierra would have voiced any opposition last night, so in less than a day, any issue with that obstacle had been removed.

Maya sat forward, pinning her focus on Ainslie. "If the swat is connected to Ethan, we should also ask him if he has any idea who might have done this."

Ainslie nodded. "I plan to ask him about it this afternoon."

Blake shifted his dark gaze to her. "No offense, Ainslie, but you're too close and emotionally involved in the situation to be objective. One of us should also talk to your brother."

"Anyone else agree with that?" Grady asked.

Everyone raised their hands and sympathetic looks were trained her way.

Grady drew in a breath as if considering the vote. What was he thinking about that altered his expression so much? It seemed serious but he shook off whatever he was feeling and planted his feet in a wide stance. "So interview by one of us, it is."

Emory cast a pride-filled look at her husband. "Blake is the most logical person to conduct it."

Ainslie gave a clipped nod. His law enforcement background made him the obvious choice. Though, she had to admit she felt a bit betrayed by the fact that they had to question Ethan's truthfulness even though she knew they were doing the right thing. "I'll tell Ethan and arrange a time."

"Thanks for understanding." Blake pasted on a tight smile.

She nodded and looked at Grady, who was writing Blake's name on the board under the murder investigation column before turning to face them. "Ainslie, go ahead and share what you know about Ethan's arrest."

Ainslie shared every detail of the shooting. "The officer took one look at his bruises and bloody hands and Wade's beaten face and assumed Ethan was the shooter."

"A likely assumption to make," Blake said. "At least enough to detain Ethan until they could sort things out."

Ainslie didn't like this fact, but it was true.

"Why did Ethan get into a fight with a stranger?" Sierra asked.

Ainslie wanted to shrug and leave it at that, but these wonderful people were here to help, and she had to share everything she knew. "Something's been bothering him lately. I don't know what, and he won't tell me. His way of dealing with it is getting drunk and picking fights. He claims there's nothing going on, but I know him. He's fighting because he thinks he deserves the pain. He started doing that as a teen and never stopped, but he's never been willing to talk about it."

"I'll ask him about that, too." Blake scribbled a note on his legal pad. "Were there any witnesses to the actual shooting?"

Ainslie shook her head. "Or at least none that the police have told me about."

"Canvassing the area for witnesses should be top priority." Blake jotted another note on his legal pad.

"You think someone else saw it?" Ainslie asked.

Blake looked up. "It's possible."

"Why wouldn't they have come forward?"

"Fear of reprisal is the most common reason." Blake set his pen down.

"I can't believe anyone would stay quiet and let my brother go to prison for a crime he didn't commit."

"Don't worry," Blake said. "If witnesses exist, we'll find them."

"We should move on." Grady's voice was oddly strangled, and his face pale. She wanted to ask what was up with the change in his behavior but would never put him on the spot in front of his team.

"What about the guy Ethan beat up at the bar?" Maya asked. "Can't he give Ethan an alibi?"

Ainslie shook her head. "Ethan didn't know him, and they fought in the parking lot. No witnesses there either. So we have no idea how to contact the guy. And Ethan's co-workers had all left for the night, so none of them can vouch for him either."

"The guy could have gone into the bar after the fight." Blake picked up his pen again. "We can ask the bar staff if anyone came in bruised and bloody that night. If so, maybe they recognized him."

"Might be CCTV cameras in the area, too," Grady said. "The time stamp could clear him."

Nick stifled a yawn. "I'm on it."

If only it was that easy. "There's something else you need to know. When Wade woke up, the police questioned him and showed him a photo array that included Ethan's picture. Wade immediately said Ethan beat him up and shot him." Ainslie sighed. "Ethan says Wade's lying."

"Why would Wade lie about this?" Blake's doubt lingered in his tone.

"I asked Ethan the same thing," Ainslie said. "He claimed he didn't know."

"I hate to ask this." Blake made firm eye contact. "But do you have any reason to doubt your brother's story?"

"No." But she had to admit with the way Ethan had been acting lately she probably should suspect something was up. Like maybe he was using again, because when he was, he lied about a lot of things.

Blake kept his focus on her, the intensity uncomfortable, and she could easily imagine he'd been a tough sheriff. "What can you tell us about the evidence behind the charges?"

"Not only did Ethan have blood on his hands from the guy he beat up, but the police found Wade's blood on his hands and clothes. The bullet that injured Wade was a 9mm, and Ethan owns a gun of the same caliber. In fact, he was carrying it at the time of his arrest."

"Had it been fired recently?" Blake asked.

"Yes, but he went to the firing range the day before so that doesn't mean anything, right?"

"Right," Grady said. "What about a ballistics comparison test? Did it come back as a match to the bullet?"

Right. Grady hadn't been present last night when she'd discussed this with the deputies so he didn't know this detail. "They couldn't do one. The bullet is lodged behind Wade's eye, and they can't remove it without risking brain damage."

"I don't get it, then." Emory frowned. "How do they know it's a 9mm?"

"They did a CT scan at the hospital and state experts reviewed the film. They declared the bullet was a 9mm and added that it could be from Ethan's gun."

Grady pinned his focus on Ainslie. "Do you know if they recovered the cartridge case?"

"I don't think so. Or at least that wasn't mentioned. Is it important?"

He nodded. "Cases have distinct impressions, just like bullets. If any were recovered at the scene, I could compare them to cartridge cases for bullets fired from Ethan's gun."

He shifted his focus to Blake. "I need to get a look at that CT scan and get my hands on that gun for ballistic testing."

Blake shifted his focus to Ainslie. "Do you know who's lead detective on this investigation?"

"Reyna Flores," Ainslie answered. "At PPB."

Grady looked at Blake. "Know her?"

He nodded. "She's good. Impartial and open-minded. Let me see what I can do about getting the file from her. Or, worst case, get her to share evidentiary findings so we know if they have anything else supporting the attempted murder charge. I'll call her right after the meeting ends."

"You should know, I used to work for PPB," Ainslie said. "I know Reyna, too. She wouldn't let me have anything official to review, but she did tell me about the evidence I shared with you."

Grady nodded and looked at Blake. "With what's been discussed so far, would you have brought charges against Ethan?"

"Not sure until I see the file, but it sounds like a good collar to me." He glanced at Ainslie. "I'm sorry. Just calling it the way I see it."

"I understand." She did and yet she didn't, but what difference did her feelings make to the investigation? She had to put one foot in front of the other and do whatever she could to move the investigation along, even if it made her feel uncomfortable.

"We need to look into Wade Eggen," Nick said. "I'll run background on him."

"And I'll look to see if he has a sheet," Blake offered. "That might lead us in the right direction. And I can go interview him at the hospital."

"He's not there," Ainslie said. "He said since they weren't going to operate to remove the bullet, he wasn't paying to lay around in bed and checked himself out against doctor's orders."

Kelsey shook her head. "He doesn't sound like the brightest bulb in the bunch."

Grady noted the info in square red letters on the board. "Call me the minute you have anything on him or Bittner. Until then, Ainslie and I'll go talk to Ethan and then do a door-to-door in his neighborhood to look for another witness."

She didn't want to spend time alone with Grady, but after hearing the partners speculate on a potential witness, she was eager to try to find one. "And we can also interview the 911 caller while we're in the neighborhood, too."

Blake glanced at his watch. "I wouldn't go now. You're best off waiting until this evening when people are home from work."

"Good point." Grady looked around the group. "Any other ideas?"

Sierra nodded. "I'll run over to Ethan's rental house to look at the crime scene. It might've been unprotected for days, but you never know what I might find."

"I took pictures the minute I learned of Ethan's arrest, but two days had passed by then," Ainslie shook her head. "I really believed what I saw on TV and in movies that the police could only detain someone for twenty-four hours without charging them. And that the person arrested got a phone call. Turns out, both are false."

"You're sort of right." Blake pulled back his shoulders. "The arresting agency only has twenty-four hours without getting a judge to sign off on a longer time. And about the phone call, most agencies will let a suspect make a call unless they think a call might do something detrimental to their investigation—like ask for incriminating evidence to be destroyed. So it's a judgment call, and the officer must've thought Ethan was a risk."

A protest climbed up Ainslie's throat, but she swallowed it down. "I can't help but feel like the officer could've at least called me. Maybe he had it out for Ethan for some reason. Not every cop is a good one."

Blake cringed. "I can't speak to the situation, but it sounds like that would've been the right thing to do."

"Can you email the pictures from the crime scene to me?" Sierra asked, likely to move them on before the discussion of a police officer's actions grew more contentious.

Ainslie nodded.

A tight smile tipped Sierra's lips, but it felt forced. "Did you notice anything unusual at the scene that would pose questions the detective didn't ask?"

Ainslie shook her head. "Everything was consistent with what Reyna told me."

"Do you know if they did a GSR test?" Grady asked.

Ainslie hadn't even thought to ask about gunshot residue. "I don't know."

"That'll be in his file," Blake said. "But honestly, just picking up and putting his weapon into his holster would put GSR on his hands."

Sierra met Blake's gaze. "GSR might be controversial, but it would be good if we could perform an independent test on the evidence."

"Yeah," Emory chimed in. "I'd love to run the DNA, too."

Nick rubbed his hands together. "And I'm jonesing to get my hands on Ethan's phone and computer files, which I assume PPB has in evidence."

"Plus, we need Wade's hospital records," Kelsey said, not surprising Ainslie that an anthropologist would want medical records. "It might shed some light on injuries that Ethan couldn't have inflicted."

"Like what?" Ainslie asked.

"Is Ethan right-handed?" Kelsey lifted her mug to her mouth.

Ainslie nodded.

Kelsey took a sip. "A possibility would be broken bones in Wade's face that would only come from a left-handed person."

Ainslie was impressed with her thinking. "I hadn't thought of that. I wonder if Reyna did."

Kelsey set down her mug. "Unless a doctor suggested it, I think it would be highly unlikely."

"His attorney will need to request the information," Blake said. "Does he have a good attorney?"

"A public defender." Ainslie didn't know if the PD assigned to Ethan was good or not. "I'll call him to ask about that."

Grady noted these items on the board. "Anything else?"

The others remained silent this time.

Grady set down the marker and gave a sharp nod. "Then let's get after it. Once we see the investigation files, hopefully we can make a hole in the prosecution's case big enough for Ethan to walk through."

6

Grady had been acutely aware of Ainslie during the meeting. It had ended and others weren't watching him, so he let his focus trail her as she walked around the room and thanked each partner for agreeing to help Ethan. He didn't know if she was doing it simply because she wanted to thank them or because she wanted to avoid getting into his truck with him to go see her brother.

Honestly, he should be the one to avoid *her* because he knew she picked up on his unease when they mentioned interviewing Ethan. Grady could easily imagine having been interviewed by a police officer in the past, revealing his secret, and choking on his words. He'd thought when Ainslie caught his discomfort that she was going to question him. His past was the last thing he would talk to her about. The very last thing.

She turned from her conversation with Kelsey and caught him watching her. Rosy red color crept up her neck and over her cheeks. He needed to do a better job of controlling his interest so he didn't make her feel uncomfortable. But how, when just looking at her sent his heart racing in a way he'd never known before?

She crossed the room to join him. "Ready to go?"

"Lead the way."

She marched out the door, her shoulders back as if she thought it necessary to defend herself around him. He didn't much like that. Maybe she felt the need to protect herself because he'd been coming on too strong whenever he looked at her.

Get control. You can do it.

In the lobby, she took a moment to greet their receptionist and the security guard, who opened the door for her. She asked about his wife, and Grady was struck by how kind and caring she was. He'd never seen this side of her. Was hard to do when he ran the other way most every time he'd laid eyes on her.

Grady nodded a quick greeting at Danny, then continued on and stepped outside. Head down against the spitting rain, he opened his truck door for Ainslie then went to tell Drake their plan. Grady had to admit he was thankful for an extra set of eyes to keep Ainslie safe.

In his truck, he did his best to keep his eyes on the road and off Ainslie, but her fruity scent that he thought included peaches and flowers, caught his attention. Or maybe he was drawn to the way her skinny jeans clung to her long legs. Or to the bright turquoise rain jacket she wore over a ribbed black sweater. Oh, man, he had to stop it. And stop it now.

"You keep looking at me," she said.

"Sorry. I'm trying not to, but..." He shook his head but kept his eyes on the heavy traffic heading toward downtown Portland. "We should really talk about what's going on with us. Maybe just acknowledging the feelings and getting them out in the open will help make it go away."

She clasped her hands together. "Do you really think that's necessary? We've done a good job of avoiding it for months. Why can't we continue to do that?"

"Because we were only successful because we managed to avoid each other, but now that's impossible." He glanced at her. "And honestly, I don't think avoidance is a good solution."

"It's worked for me. I'm not interested in a relationship right now. Getting my brother out of jail is the only thing I should be thinking about."

He didn't want to get involved either, but her rejection stung. "And after he gets out of jail? You interested in getting involved then?"

She shrugged.

The sting sharpened into a bite. "Is this apathy directed at me or all men in general?"

"I'm not sure." She sat unmoving, a pensive look on her face. "But I do know you and I are wrong for each other. I can barely tolerate football, and you live for it. In fact, I'm not big on any sports."

Interesting. "And I guess you think that's important in a relationship."

"Isn't it? Not sports in particular, but sharing interests?"

He focused on the freeway traffic, the cars in front spitting up so much rainwater he had to turn up the windshield wipers.

He'd never thought about what would make a good relationship. Never had to think about it. Not when he didn't plan to get involved with anyone. His parents came to mind. They were good role models for long-term commitment and happiness. Their love was based on their strong faith and commitment to God, not shared hobbies.

"I don't know if I agree with you," he said. "My mom loves sewing, but Dad never felt the need to take it up or sit and watch her sew. And Dad's a big hunter. Mom hates guns. Never went hunting with him even once. But they're very happily married, and the interest thing hasn't hampered their relationship."

"That's different."

"How so?"

"I don't know, but it is." She turned to look out the window.

He wanted to probe more, but it was obvious that she was struggling to find a legitimate reason why she couldn't get involved with him. First, she'd mentioned her brother's investigation. Then she'd argued about Grady being her boss. Now she'd brought up football. The only legitimate reason in his mind was freeing Ethan, and that was temporary.

What might she come up with next?

He should just tell her that he wasn't interested in a serious relationship either. But she would likely want an explanation, and telling her about his past was out of the question. He didn't want to see the disappointment, maybe revulsion, in her eyes when she learned his secret. So his best bet was just to keep his big mouth shut. To keep his eyes and hands off her. And remember she was off limits. Because he wasn't about to lead her on only to hurt her, and that was kind of what he'd been doing.

He steered their conversation toward a safer subject. "How are you doing today? You know, after the swat."

"Honestly, I'm more mad than anything." She lifted her chin in the cute defiant angle that he loved. "That some person made a simple phone call and my door was broken down, and I was held at gunpoint. It's unbelievable. Totally unbelievable. And yet it happened."

At her unease, Grady clenched his hands on the wheel. "Unfortunately, it's becoming far too common. And it's dangerous. Puts both responding officers and private citizens at risk. People have even died."

"Swatting is just so bizarre to me." She swiveled to face him. "Who even thought of swatting someone in the first place?"

"Video gamers started it. They'd make the call during a live game, and then watch the SWAT response play out in real time on their screen. They get a big thrill from it."

She shook her head. "I just don't get it. Especially when the swat is directed at complete strangers."

"More often it's targeted, and we need to remember that this caller could strike again."

She shivered.

He'd scared her. Not his intention. "It's okay. You'll be fine. You have Drake or another deputy assigned to you. And I'll be with you every time you leave Veritas, too." He glanced at her then. "You know I would give my life to keep you safe, right?"

Her mouth fell open. "But I...we...I mean, sure. I'm attracted to you, but that's as far as it goes. Offering your life seems like so much more than that."

She sounded like she was trying to convince herself that she didn't have feelings for him. He understood the struggle. Appreciated it, even, but it was irrelevant to their discussion. His desire to see her safe wasn't about love or anything like that, and he had to make sure she understood so she didn't balk at his help.

"This isn't personal." He held her gaze for a second. "It's just who I am. How I was raised and what I learned in the military. I'd protect anyone in danger."

She clasped her hands in her lap and stared down at them, sitting silently for the longest time before taking a deep breath and easing it out. "You grew up in Nebraska, right?"

Hmm. A change in subject. Avoidance? Maybe. But he wouldn't push.

"I guess you've seen the bazillion Cornhusker things in my lab." He flashed her a grin.

She nodded but didn't return his smile like he'd hoped.

"You got something against Nebraska?"

"Not at all. In fact, I don't know anything about it, except that they're big into football, and I've told you how much I dislike it."

It honestly didn't bother him that she wasn't into sports, but he was curious about the reason. "But you're a Texan. How's that possible?"

"Most Texans are obsessed with the sport, but I never liked athletics in general. I was more a *sit under the big weeping willow at the library and read* kind of person. Ethan was the opposite. He loved football and played since he was a little kid. He talked about it nonstop with my parents. I was often left out of the discussion. In hindsight, I can see I got fed up and chose to exclude myself. But back then I was jealous of the time my parents devoted to the sport. The booster club. Going to games. Stuff like that."

"My family was the same way. My sisters were kind of left out during the season, so I can understand how you feel."

"It was more than that for my mom," she said. "My dad walked out on us when I was thirteen. Haven't seen or heard from him since. At the time, the football booster club was the only social thing Mom had, and she really dove in." Ainslie sighed, and her years of neglect lived in the exhaled breath. "I even joined drill team to be a part of things. I didn't like it, but I kept at it until I graduated."

She might not have enjoyed drill team, but man, he would've loved to see her kick up those long legs on the field. Still, she had a visceral dislike for his favorite sport, and there was no hope of him ever watching a game with her. Was that a deal breaker? Could he date a woman who detested his favorite sport? He knew he placed too much importance on football. Sports in general. Maybe he was compensating for not having a significant other. If he ever formed a serious relationship, he could see cutting back. But giving it up totally? Never.

She dug her phone from her purse. "I should call Ethan's attorney and get the ball rolling on the things we discussed in the meeting."

"Of course." He knew she needed to make that call, but it seemed like she was doing it now to avoid talking with him. He was probably being too sensitive. Ha! Him, sensitive. That was a good one. He'd never been accused of that.

He checked the mirror to make sure he hadn't lost Drake and listened to her side of the call. He gathered that the public defender was finding every reason possible not to do his job. When she hung up, she let out a breath that seemed to go on and on.

He glanced at her. "Problem?"

"This guy doesn't appear to have any sense of urgency." She shoved her phone into her purse. "Or maybe he's just overworked. Either way, he's not acting real concerned about Ethan remaining behind bars."

Grady gritted his teeth. She should hire an attorney for Ethan, but he knew she couldn't afford one. He'd offer to pay for it, but that wouldn't be well received. Not when she'd seemed disinclined to accept any help to begin with.

But he also couldn't abide seeing her looking so dejected. "I promise we're taking the investigation very seriously and will do our best for Ethan."

"I don't doubt that one bit." She smiled at him, but underneath the soft curve of her lips, a hesitancy lingered.

"Something else wrong?" he asked as he concentrated on exiting the freeway to enter a busy downtown Portland street.

"Wrong?" She eyed him. "No. Why?"

"You look uneasy about accepting our help, and last night it was clear that you didn't let people help you often."

She sat silently, twisting her hands in her lap. He let her be and made the turns the GPS voice directed him to make.

"I have a thing about people butting into my life," she said. "We were dirt poor growing up and had to count on charity. Some people meant well, but others were condescending. I was teased in school, and I hated every bit of it. So when I became an adult, I vowed to stand on my own two feet no matter what."

"This isn't charity. Not that that's a bad thing either. This is just the team living our faith. Helping a fellow Christian. Investigations like this are costly, and most people can't afford them. So we help out wherever we can, and there's no reason to feel bad."

She didn't look convinced. "I wish there was a way I could pay you all back."

"We don't need that. Working for Sierra is thanks enough. She keeps giving you glowing praises and saying how you've made her life so much better."

"I'm glad." Ainslie gave a firm nod as if she'd cemented something in her mind. "I like working with her and at the center. It's so cool to be part of cutting-edge forensics, and I have no plans to leave."

"Not even if you become a famous landscape photographer and your photographs make you fabulously wealthy?" He grinned in hopes of lightening the mood.

She rolled her eyes and laughed, but she sobered quickly and pointed at the entrance to the Multnomah County Detention Center. He scanned the stone columns and facade of the tall building. He always found it odd that a jail sat right in the middle of a busy city, but it was part of the Justice Center, so it made some sense.

Ainslie picked up her purse. "You can drop me off if you want and go park."

He opened his mouth to warn her to be more aware of the potential threat to her life, but he didn't want to go overboard and scare her. "I can't let you go in alone."

He could feel her watching him, her gaze intense. "You really are taking this bodyguard duty seriously."

"You better believe I am." He passed the entrance and circled the block until he found two spaces so Drake could park, too. He killed the engine and wanted to get his gun from the locked console where the law required him to keep it while driving, but he couldn't carry on county property.

He jerked out the key and looked at her, trying to convey that warning he'd just held back. "Give me a second to check things out."

"Okay." She unbuckled her seatbelt but didn't open the door.

He stepped out of the truck. He carried his gun so often that he almost felt naked without it. Drake marched down the sidewalk. Good. He could have his weapon in the waiting area. Grady searched the surrounding area. He didn't find an imminent threat and opened the door for Ainslie.

He stuck by her side as they moved up the steps. Drake scoped out the area just like Grady was doing. He escorted Ainslie safely to the lobby and blew out a relieved breath.

She marched toward the registration desk and metal detector. He stood back with Drake, still watchful until she moved through security and disappeared behind a door.

Grady's gut clenched. He didn't like the thought of her entering a place where men were incarcerated for a variety of crimes. He could only imagine how she must feel. Something Grady could do only one thing about. Pray.

Can You help us out here, God? Help us find a way to clear

Ainslie's brother while keeping her safe? Show me what to do, please. Oh, and yeah. Along the way, help me ignore these feelings for her, because I can't do it on my own.

"Gonna be awhile," Drake said, drawing him back. "Might as well sit."

Drake chose a place where he could both face the door and keep an eye on the entrance to the jail. Not surprising. It's exactly what Grady would've done if he decided to sit down. No way either of them would put their backs to the door.

"I heard Nick is tracing the swat call," Drake said.

Grady nodded. "He wasn't too optimistic that he'd find the guy, though."

"Yeah, that's what our IT guy said, but I figured Nick could do just about anything."

"Me, too. At least that's what he's been telling us for years." Grady chuckled.

Drake smiled. "He's no different than the rest of you."

"How's that?"

"You all think you're the best in your area of expertise."

"Well, aren't we?" Grady asked.

Drake rolled his eyes. "Yeah, but clearing Ainslie's brother? I reviewed the case against him last night. I have to say, it might take even more than the wonder team's abilities to get the charges dropped against him."

7

Ainslie entered the large visitor's area filled with small square tables. Armed deputies stood in various locations, their eagle eyes fixed on her every movement. She disliked every second of being in such a foreign place and pulled in a deep breath of air that smelled like pine disinfectant. She spotted Ethan in the ugly blue prison garb that looked so much like hospital scrubs. He was sitting at a table for two, and she headed his way. His stooped shoulders and sorrowful eyes made her want to give him a big hug. She couldn't. Touching wasn't allowed.

"Hi." She tried to sound cheerful even though his normally cheerful blue eyes were dark with worry, and one was ringed with a huge purple bruise from the bar fight. His hair hung limp on his head like a mop, and his beard was scruffy. He was already a slender guy. Staying here, he was bound to lose weight.

She ignored it all and put a smile on her face. "I'm so glad to see you. How are you holding up?"

"Honestly, not so good."

She sat on the stool across from him. "I've got some good news."

His expression perked up. "I'm getting out of here?"

"Not quite that good."

His smile fell.

"But it's still great news." She scooted closer and resisted the urge to cover his hand resting on the table. "You know about the center where I work, right?"

"Yeah, they do all kinds of fancy testing for cops."

That was an oversimplified version of what they did, but she left it at that. "Right, well, the partners have agreed to investigate the charges against you to help prove your innocence at no cost."

He pursed his lips and tilted his head. "And can they prove it, do you think?"

"I do," she said honestly. "I really do."

He started tapping a nervous finger against the table. "How?"

She didn't want to share potential leads and then disappoint him. Better to wait until she had results to report. "We're working out the details."

"Sounds good." His disappointed tone didn't go with his statement.

Bringing him down more was the last thing she wanted to do, but she had to talk to him about Bittner. She shared the details of the swat, sticking to facts and trying her best not to let him know how much it had terrified her.

His face paled, his finger stilling midair. "And you're okay? Not hurt?"

"I'm fine."

"But it had to scare you to death." He let out a long shuddering breath.

"I'm okay now," she said calmly to play it down, though it was going to take a long time for her to get over the terror of the night. "I want to find out who did it. Any ideas who might want to swat me?"

He sat silently, staring at his hands that were covered with cuts and scabs from the fight. "You're the most upstanding person I know. Who would target you?"

He didn't answer her question. Asked one of his own. Was he hiding something from her?

Had he shot Wade? How could she think that way? If she was going to clear his name, she couldn't question his innocence. She had to believe in him at all costs or she might inadvertently convey doubt to the Veritas partners. "The deputies who busted down my door think this is related to Vito Bittner. That you knew him. Maybe helped him escape."

"That's nuts!" His voice shot up, catching the eye of the nearby guard. He gave them a warning look. Ethan lowered his voice and slid closer. "I didn't say a word to Bittner. I'd heard all about him and was too afraid to even look at him. Didn't want him to notice me. So I stayed in the corner of the holding cell and kept my head down. Other guys talked to him, and he bragged about himself, but he left me alone."

Poor Ethan. She desperately wanted to take his hand and comfort him. If she thought she'd been afraid during the swat, she couldn't imagine coming face to face with a guy like Bittner. And having to sit in a holding cell with him. One minute her brother had been a free man, and then he'd been locked up with a brutal killer. So unfair.

How could You let that happen? Why? Can't You see he's suffering? Where are You?

"Sis," he said. "You okay?"

She nodded, but she wasn't okay. Seeing her baby brother in this situation broke her heart. She'd taken responsibility for him since their dad bailed and their mom couldn't cope. When her mother died a few years back, Ainslie took on even more responsibility for Ethan. Now, she was failing him. Big time. And here she was questioning him and God. Making things worse. To help Ethan, she had to keep him talking.

She planted her hands on her knees and sat up straighter. "You said Bittner bragged. Maybe you heard something about a person who might be working with him to make that swat call."

Ethan gave a forceful shake of his head. "No. Nothing like that."

Okay. So that was a dead end. "What about Wade? Did he hang with anyone who might do this?"

Ethan shrugged. "I don't know much about him these days."

"But you were still friends when he said you shot him, right?"

"Sorta."

This was the first time she'd heard him waffle on his friendship with Wade. "What's going on, Ethan? You've never said there was an issue with Wade before he said you shot him."

Ethan curled his fingers into fists. "It's no big deal. We hung out a few times after he showed up in Portland. That's all."

"Did he tell you why he came here? I mean it's odd, right, with us living here?"

"He said it was about his job. Maybe it's easier to sell guns here or something."

"Wait! He sells guns?"

Ethan nodded.

"Why didn't you mention that before?"

He shrugged. "Never came up, I guess."

"Well, I can't imagine that Oregon is a friendlier gun state than Texas, but I honestly don't know about that."

"Me neither."

"But Wade looked you up, right? You didn't go looking

for him?"

He nodded. "We aren't like friends or anything. I've got enough issues to be friends with someone who sells illegal guns."

"Illegal?" She had to work hard not to raise her voice. "You didn't say that."

He scooted closer. "Because I don't know for sure. He claimed everything he did was legal. But then, I wanted to see if I could find out more about him and searched the internet. I found out he had a record for dealing stolen guns. So I figured he might be lying to me."

Ainslie resisted sighing over his decision to have anything to do with Wade after learning he was into illegal gun sales. "So why keep seeing him then?"

Ethan shrugged.

"C'mon, Ethan." She eyed him with her best older sister stare that usually got him to confess when he'd been up to no good. "You're keeping something from me. If you want my help, you have to tell me everything."

He crossed his arms and leaned back, a stubborn set to his expression. When he took this stance, he'd clammed up, and it was a waste of time to continue to question him. A waste of time today. Today only. She would come back to this topic when she returned tomorrow and press him harder. And tell Blake to push, too.

She stood. "One of my co-workers named Blake Jenkins is going to come and talk to you. He's a partner at the Veritas Center and wants to follow up on some questions."

His color paled. "Like, what questions?"

"Just basics about what happened." She kept her gaze pinned to him, and he squirmed. "I want you to think about this. If you're hiding something from me, I want you to come to the right decision to tell me what it is. If you don't, I'm not sure we can clear your name."

Grady glanced at Ainslie as they drove toward her brother's rental house in the early evening. The lights from the instrument panel on his truck and street lights highlighted her profile, shadows playing on the planes of her face. Her arms were crossed, and she was staring out the front window. Even after a long afternoon of hard work, she was still likely thinking about her visit to Ethan.

At least Grady was. On the drive back to the center, she'd said the only potentially helpful info he shared was that Wade might be into illegal gun sales. Then she'd shut down and watched out the window, her arms crossed. So Grady had let her be. The minute he got back to the center, he asked Nick to keep an eye out for illegal gun sales when doing his background check on Wade. After that, Grady asked Blake to obtain Wade's prior arrest records.

Grady looked at her again. Maybe she'd moved on. Maybe she was thinking about finding a witness.

He turned onto Ethan's street and searched ahead for parking spaces in a rundown and dangerous neighborhood —the last place he'd expected her brother to live. Sure, rents were cheaper in this area of town, but crime was high, especially drug crime. He wanted to ask why Ethan wasn't still living with her, but that was too personal even for a nosey guy like Grady to ask.

Older model cars, many looking to be held together with wire and duct tape, filled the street, and there wasn't a parking space in sight. Grady circled the block, making sure Drake stayed with him. "I never asked what Ethan does for a living."

She shifted in her seat. "He's kind of been all over the board. Getting jobs, mostly in construction, but losing interest fast. That all changed a year ago. He applied to be an electrician apprentice, and he's been in the program and doing great until the last few months. He's been really struggling to get to class and work. Something changed, but he won't tell me what."

"You think it has to do with Wade?" Grady parked and grabbed his gun from the lockbox to holster it.

"I'm beginning to." She got out of the truck and slammed the door, the sound reverberating through the quiet neighborhood.

Grady joined her and scanned their surroundings. The night was crisp and clear but clouds hung in the distance. He only hoped they finished their questioning before the skies opened up in a typical spring rain.

A car door slammed, disturbing the quiet. Drake had parked a few cars behind them and marched in their direction. He dressed much like Grady in comfy tactical clothes, but he carried himself with an assurance that said people should beware. Grady had often been told he was intimidating, but he didn't have quite the striking appearance Drake presented, and that wouldn't help their cause at all.

Grady eyed Drake. "I don't think it's a good idea for you to come along with us. The whole deputy thing will put people off."

Drake rested his hands on his waist. "I'm not in uniform."

"But you still have that law enforcement vibe going on," Ainslie said, looking apprehensive. "You're very intimidating. Trust me on that."

Drake's gaze softened, and he shifted his focus to her. "I still need to keep an eye on you."

"Station yourself in a place where you can see us," Grady said. "But pick a spot where the person we're interviewing can't see you."

Drake rubbed the back of his neck and looked around.

"Not the best neighborhood, but if that's what you want me to do, I can do it."

"Then it's settled. Keep a low profile." Grady looked at Ainslie. "Mind if we start at your brother's place? I'd like to get a look at the scene where Wade was shot."

"Sure," she said, but she didn't look at all eager to go back to his house.

"You could wait here with Drake if you prefer."

"I can handle it."

They headed down the street together, the cool night air nipping at Grady. He tugged his jacket closer and noticed that Ainslie was zipping hers. She stopped in front of a tiny bungalow with clapboard siding and a wonky porch. The nearest streetlight was burned out, leaving the house in dark shadows. She took a few steps up the walkway, the shadows deepening. An ominous feeling hung in the air.

She drew in a breath. "This is where it happened."

Grady shone light from his phone over the area. Blood, now a crusty brown, stained the sidewalk panel, and spatter consistent with a gunshot wound dotted the ones nearby. Other than that, the scene was unremarkable.

She crossed her arms as if protecting herself from the crime. "Except for the blood, there's nothing out of the ordinary."

"Yeah," he replied, but wished he'd seen something that would break this investigation wide-open. "So let's go talk to the person next door. Maybe they saw something that night."

They made their way to a worn wooden porch with peeling green paint. Light spilled out from a large picture window. Grady knocked, and he soon heard footsteps heading their way. The door opened a crack. A security chain held it in place as a frail woman with frizzy gray hair peered at them.

Ainslie offered her a big smile. "Hi. I'm Ainslie Duncan. Ethan's sister."

The woman's penciled on eyebrows rose. "Ethan?"

"The guy who lives next door."

"Oh, *him*." Judgment lingered in her tone, and Grady saw Ainslie stiffen. "We never met, but I heard he killed someone."

"No," Ainslie said gently, and Grady was surprised she didn't snap at the woman. "Someone was shot on his walkway. Ethan didn't do it, and the man survived."

"That's better, but still. Someone was shot. Right there." She poked a bony finger out of the door and aimed it at Ethan's place.

Grady needed to get this conversation moving. "We were wondering if you heard anything that night."

She blinked and shook her head. "It happened way past my bedtime, and I'm a very sound sleeper."

"Did you talk to anyone in the neighborhood who did see it?" Grady asked.

Her mouth tightened into a grim line. "Just Malcolm. But he didn't really see anything. He was the one who called 911. He might be in a wheelchair, but he looks out for those of us who've been in this neighborhood forever."

"And where does Malcolm live?" Ainslie asked.

The woman waggled a finger across the street. "The neat blue bungalow. He's about the only person who still keeps up his property around here."

Her dejected tone hit Grady hard. It was sad to see an older woman like this living in a neighborhood that had deteriorated around her.

"We'll head over to talk to him, but is there anything we can do for you before we go?" Grady asked.

She narrowed her eyes. "Like what?"

"Take out the trash. Other chores."

She squinted at him. "Why would you do that?"

"Just being neighborly."

She shook her head. "My dinner's getting cold."

"Thank you for your time, ma'am."

She slammed the door, and the deadbolt snicked into place. Man. Seemed like she felt like a prisoner in her own home. Such a shame.

Grady started down the steps with Ainslie.

"That was nice of you." She looked up at him. "Offering to help her, that is."

"I felt bad for her. Wish she could find a safer place to live."

"Yeah. I thought the same about Ethan. But he said he had to stand on his own two feet to learn to cope with his drug addiction, and this was all he can afford."

"That's admirable."

She nodded. "I thought he was really getting things together this time, but then he started drinking and fighting. Who knows where that might've led if he hadn't been arrested."

Her anguish cut right through him, and he wanted to do something to help, but he had to know more to do so. "How long has he been struggling with drugs?"

"Started in high school. Thankfully, his love for football curtailed it, but something changed him back then. He was once this carefree kid, and then he got all sullen and moody. I often wondered if something happened or if this is just his true personality."

Speaking of changes. I know all about that, he wanted to say but clamped his mouth closed before he shared his uncle's secret.

They reached the crumbling sidewalk for the house on the other side of Ethan's place, and Grady looked down the street to be sure Drake was still standing watch. Grady located him in the shadow of a tall maple. Good. He was well hidden. If not for Grady's Delta tracking training and experience, he wouldn't have spotted him.

The harried homeowner at the next house had a baby on her hip and cursed the lack of a spouse while two other children fussed in the background. She quickly declared that she hadn't been home the night of the shooting and closed the door.

"Looked like those kids were all under five," he said, wondering how anyone could cope with that. "She could use some help, too."

Ainslie nodded. "One thing I can tell you from growing up in a very similar neighborhood is that you see a lot of suffering and misery. Which leads to drug and alcohol abuse, making things even worse."

She paused and shook her head. "My dad fell into that. He was a roughneck on oil rigs. He was gone most of the time, and by the time he got home, he'd spent most of his paycheck on booze."

Grady looked at her. "I wish you could have experienced the kind of life I had growing up. I mean, we didn't have much, but we had enough. We learned strong values from our parents. They live a life of faith, really living their commitment to God and the church I grew up in. Gave me a good foundation to base my life on. That is, when I don't get in God's way."

"I know what you mean," she said. "I was lucky enough that a girl in drill team invited me to her church youth group. The kids there were more accepting than most of the other kids in school, and I became a believer. That's when I figured out that God had a plan for my life. Problem was, I didn't much like the plan at the time." She frowned. "Don't much like it at the moment either."

He nodded. "I get that."

"You?" She tilted her head and peered at him. "Seems to me you have it all together."

"That's what I want you to think, but..." He shrugged and knocked on the next door. No answer.

They continued down the walkway, but he didn't restart the earlier conversation. Ainslie remained silent, too, a pensive look on her face. They moved down one side of the street and up the other, knocking on ten more doors in all, but came away without any witnesses.

They reached Malcolm's bungalow, and Grady hoped for Ainslie's sake that this man knew something helpful. She rang the bell. The porch light came on, illuminating crisply painted siding and window trim. A whirring noise sounded from the other side of the door, likely the wheelchair.

"Who's there?" his gravelly voice snapped out.

Ainslie moved closer to the door. "Ainslie Duncan. I'm Ethan's sister. He lives across the street from you. And I have my friend Grady with me."

The door opened, and an elderly man with a broad face and silvery gray hair stared up from his wheelchair. He had a guarded look on his wrinkled face. "How can I help you?"

Ainslie gave him a tight smile. "I was hoping you could tell me what you saw and heard the night someone shot Wade Eggen outside my brother's place."

He tsked, and his upper dentures slipped. "Didn't see much of anything except your brother standing over a man on the ground."

"Did you hear the men fighting before the gunshots?"

"Nah." He tapped his ear. "My hearing aids don't work that well."

"What about the gunshot?" Grady asked. "Hear that?"

He nodded. "Took me a minute to realize what it was. At first I thought the sound was coming from the TV next door. They like to play the dang thing so loud even the devil himself could hear it. By the time I got to the window, your brother had put his gun away and was standing over the body."

Ainslie squared her shoulders. "So, you didn't see Ethan shoot anyone, and you didn't see a gun."

"No, but—"

"There's no proof he was the shooter," she snapped, irritation finally getting the best of her. "Unless you know of someone else who actually saw the shooting."

He clenched his teeth, denture on denture sounding hollow as he raised his stooped shoulders. "No one else said anything to me, but then I didn't go around asking either. This neighborhood is going to the dogs, and it's not safe to be out and about. I stick close to home."

He stared past them and shook his head. "Should've sold this place years ago. Now I'm stuck here. With all the crime, I can't get a decent price for the house, so I can't afford to buy another."

"I just have one more question for you," Ainslie said. "Do you think it's possible that someone else shot the man, then Ethan came home and found him, and that's what you saw?"

"Like I said. I didn't see the shooting, and it took me a while to get to the window. So yeah. Sure." He shrugged his bony shoulders. "That could've happened."

Ainslie's expression perked up, and her head raised higher. "Would you be willing to testify to that?"

Malcolm nibbled on his lip, then nodded. "I guess. I mean it's just speculation is all. Not sure it's of value."

"We'll let the attorneys figure that out." Ainslie took out her business card and handed it to him.

Excitement burned in her eyes, but Grady didn't want her getting her hopes up too high. Not when they really hadn't found a strong lead to help Ethan.

8

Grady ran his gaze around the area, checking for danger as he and Ainslie approached their final house. Drake had moved down the street and squatted in the shadows of a utility box, which surprisingly hid his large body. Grady was glad to have Drake watching their backs, but Grady wouldn't lose his focus on protecting Ainslie.

She looked at him. "I hope this place pans out."

Grady checked out the house, a tiny white box with an equally tiny brick stoop out front. Without any lights on inside, he suspected they wouldn't learn anything. "At least Malcolm allowed for the possibility that Ethan might not be the shooter. A strong attorney could work that for Ethan's good in court."

She nodded. "But it would be better if we found someone who actually saw the shooting."

Grady motioned at the crumbling concrete walkway. "After you, then."

They strolled up to the house, and Grady noticed the video doorbell mounted near the door. He glanced back across the street. "Their doorbell camera might have caught the shooting."

"You think so?" Ainslie turned to stare at Ethan's place.

"It'll depend on if they have it set up to detect motion only and how sensitive the settings are." He rang the bell.

He heard the chime ring inside, and a girl, maybe twelve or thirteen, peeked out from behind a cracked open door, a chain lock holding it ajar. She was short and plump with dyed black hair chopped at her chin in a blunt cut.

Grady was about to hand her his card when Ainslie stepped forward. "Is your mom or dad home, or maybe another adult we can talk to?"

"Nu-uh," the girl said.

Grady grimaced. This girl should never have opened the door if she was alone, and she sure shouldn't have told strangers that her parents weren't here.

"What's your name?" Ainslie asked.

"Jayla."

"Nice to meet you, Jayla. My name is Ainslie." She handed her business card through the opening. "My brother Ethan lives across the street. Do you know him?"

Jayla looked at the card. "Seen him around. Don't know him."

"Did you know he was arrested for shooting a man outside his house?" Ainslie asked.

Jayla's healthy complexion paled, and she fidgeted with the card. "Nah. But heard a guy got popped."

Grady didn't like that a girl this age had to deal with a shooting near her home. It was obviously bothering her. And he disliked even more that he had to question her. "Were you home the night of the shooting?"

She didn't answer at first, then nodded. "In bed sleeping. Didn't even hear the gun go off."

"Your mom or dad home then?" Grady asked.

"Not Dad," Jayla answered quickly but shifted her focus over Grady's shoulder.

He got the feeling she was hiding something or just didn't like to talk about her dad. "And your mom?"

"She was here." Jayla shoved the card in her skinny jeans pocket. "Sleeping too."

"Do you know the man who was shot?" Ainslie asked.

Jayla gave a brief shake of her head. "Don't pay no attention to the people over there. Just mind my own business in this neighborhood."

Seemed like she was still holding something back, and they were going to have to pry it out of her. Grady knew about keeping secrets at this age—if indeed she was hiding something. "Does your doorbell camera pick up motion?"

She hesitated for a moment but then shrugged, and her expression closed down tight, like she'd bitten into a sour apple.

Grady wasn't an experienced interviewer, but he could tell this girl wasn't going to give them any more information. It was time to talk to her mother, and to ask Detective Flores if she requested video from this doorbell camera.

He handed his business card to Jayla. "Can you give our cards to your mom and ask her to call one of us?"

"Sure, but she didn't see nothing either." Card in hand, Jayla crossed her arms.

Grady searched the girl's gaze, thinking that, behind those cloaked eyes, she knew something. Maybe he just wanted her to have witnessed the shooting so he could clear Ethan for Ainslie, but he didn't want to let this lead go. "Still, have her call us."

She nodded again and slammed the door. Grady heard a deadbolt clicking in place, then a second one. "It's awful that she has to live in such a dangerous neighborhood."

Ainslie started down the walkway. "Sometimes a place like this is all a parent can afford. Especially a single parent. My mom was a good example. She did her best, but we still had to live on public assistance, and we were close to being homeless more times than I can count."

"You sound embarrassed, but there's no shame in that." Grady walked alongside her to the final house.

"Tell that to kids growing up hungry and wearing thrift store clothes. Not having the things other kids have. Using food stamps at the grocery store. It was hard." She shook her head as she started up the broken concrete walkway, a light drizzle starting to fall now. "Which is why it's also hard to understand Ethan's willingness to live in a neighborhood like this again. If only he still lived with me, maybe none of this would've happened."

Grady didn't like the look of the last place, that was dark and foreboding with tall grass and weeds in the front yard. "You can't know that. Wade would likely still have found Ethan, and whoever hurt Wade would've, too."

She looked up at him, gaze so dejected that Grady shoved his hands in his pockets so he didn't reach out to hold her. "And you might've been in the middle of it. Gotten hurt. Or killed even."

"You're right." She firmed her shoulders in a hard line and knocked on the door. "No use in speculating. I've learned that over the years, too. God doesn't explain, and questioning or thinking things should be different is wrong."

Grady knocked on the door again. "Looks like no one's home."

"Well, that's it, then. Every house and nothing much to go on." Ainslie sighed.

Grady couldn't stand to see her so down. "Not nothing. Jayla's mom might know something. Or they could have video from their doorbell camera."

She looked across the street. "Would you mind if we

went over to Ethan's place? I want to take a look inside to see if I can figure out what's been going on with him lately."

"Are you sure you want to do that?" Grady searched her gaze. "You might find something you don't want to know. You can never un-see what you might discover."

"I have to do something." She marched with purpose toward Ethan's place.

Since they were done talking to neighbors, Grady signaled for Drake to join them. She climbed the steps and dug keys from her pocket, and Grady stepped up beside her. She lifted the key toward the lock.

"Hold up." Grady waved a warning hand. "The door's cracked open."

She stared at it for a moment then pushed on it, and it swung all the way in. "Do you smell that?"

"Gas!" Grady grabbed her hand. "We need to get out of here."

He spun and bolted down the steps, pulling her along behind him, wondering if the free-flowing gas was a trap or accident. "Hurry! This place could blow."

He ran down the sidewalk, heading at top speed toward Drake, who'd stepped onto the grassy median.

"Gas!" Grady yelled.

Drake came barreling toward them. Just like him not to run from danger but toward it.

Grady picked up speed. Churning faster. Ainslie lost her footing. Stumbled. He swept her into his arms and tossed her over his shoulder without stopping. He kicked it into higher gear and ran faster.

"House is filled with gas," Grady said as he stopped in front of Drake. "We need to get Ainslie somewhere safe."

A hum overhead caught Grady's attention. A small drone carrying an object Grady couldn't make out whizzed through the sky toward Ethan's front porch. Grady squinted, trying to determine the cargo. It looked like a glass bottle.

What the heck?

Recognition set in.

"Molotov cocktail! Down!" Grady whipped Ainslie behind a large utility box and covered her with his body. Drake dropped beside them.

A loud explosion erupted in the night. Concussive waves rumbled through the ground. Debris flew through the sky, and ash cluttered the air. Flames lit up the night, the heat scorching even at their distance.

Grady coiled more tightly around Ainslie but risked looking up. Fire licked at what remained of the wood structure that had been Ethan's rental house. White hot. Burning furiously. So bright, he squinted and shifted his gaze to the house next door where the older woman lived. The house remained intact, and she came stumbling out the front and across the street to safety. But not so where the woman with three kids and no husband lived. The side of the structure closest to Ethan's house was missing, and fire greedily climbed the house. Roaring upward. Heading for the roof. No one emerged.

Grady looked at Drake. "Take Ainslie to your car and get her out of here. I have to check on the family next door."

"No, wait. Don't go!" Ainslie cried out. "It's too dangerous."

"The woman's alone with her kids."

She grabbed and squeezed his hand. "Please, be careful."

Grady gave her one last look and took off running. The heat knocked him back, and he couldn't approach from that angle. He slipped across the street to skirt Ethan's inferno and reach the other house. He ran up the walkway. The flames licked higher. Showers of sparks rained down on him, but he ignored them.

He kicked in the door.

"Fire!" he yelled and searched through the smoky haze.

The dining room to his left was toast. The blaze consumed the space and voraciously licked his way. He checked the living room. No one. It was nearly nine so they could've gone to bed.

A crying baby sounded from upstairs. Yes. Someone was alive.

He charged up the staircase in the center of the house, two steps at a time. He started in the direction of the baby's loud wails. Smoke curled up the steps, and the fire crackled closer.

A door opened. The mother bolted into the hallway from a room at the end. "My children! Help me!"

She brushed past him, and he followed.

The house was fast filling with smoke, and Grady pulled his shirt up over his face. She led him down the hallway to the first bedroom. Two children were sleep in twin beds. How on earth could they have slept through the explosion?

He scooped up the nearest child, a girl, four at most. The mother grabbed the boy, a toddler.

In the hallway, he assessed their options. "Give the boy to me and go for the baby."

She shifted her son into Grady's arms, and the soft little body cuddled against him. The girl woke up.

"Mommy," she cried out.

"Hey, hey, it's okay," Grady cooed. "Your mommy is just getting the baby, and then we're going to go outside."

She coughed, and Grady thought about taking them straight out, but he couldn't leave the mother and baby behind. She came charging back into the hallway, a blanket over the crying bundle in her arms.

"You first," he said.

She started down the steps. Grady followed. Flames now fully engulfed the dining room, and the intense heat had him lurching back for a moment. But he gained his footing and kept going. Stepping through smoke. Embers. Falling debris.

He hit the landing behind the woman, where smoke swirled around them like a living, breathing thing.

They hurried out of the house and across the road. Grady set the children on the grass, and the mother dropped down beside them and pulled them into her arms.

"Bella," the little girl cried out. "Where's Bella?"

"Who's Bella?" Grady asked.

"My doggie." Large tears spilled from her eyes and trailed through the soot clinging to her little face. "She was sleeping with me. You need to find her."

Grady looked at the house and back at the child's terrified face. He'd had a dog growing up, and Max was the most important thing in Grady's life for many years. Especially when holding onto his secret. Max was the only living thing Grady had told about his uncle.

He couldn't let this little girl lose her pet. He took off for the house and raced inside. The flames attacked the stairway now like greedy monsters. He could hardly stand the heat and thought to turn back. The face of the devastated little girl flashed before his eyes. He had to go on. For her.

He blindly took the stairs in a racing run and charged into the bedroom. Smoke trailed after him, and he coughed hard. He lifted his shirt over his mouth and ripped the covers from the bed. No dog. Went to the other bed. Tore them off there, too. Still no dog.

"Bella!" He dropped to the floor. Heard whimpering ahead.

He plunged under the bed and fumbled around in the thick smoke. He connected with the dog's snout. She chomped into his hand. His heart broke for the animal. She was obviously terrified. He gently ran his hand up the body until he could get a good hold on her. She bit him again. And again. Sharp little terrified bites.

He pulled her out and settled her in his jacket, which he zipped around her. She squirmed to get free as he bolted from the room. Flames now consumed the lower stairs. He had no choice but to go through them. He rushed down the steps, then took a flying leap, praying that God would protect him.

Gasping. Coughing. Gagging. Eyes burning from the acrid smoke, he emerged into the cool night and charged across the street.

"Where's Bella?" the little girl asked.

Grady collapsed on the ground, straining for breath as the first fire truck arrived, screaming on scene.

"Mommy?" the girl cried out.

"It's okay, baby," the mom said.

Grady finally gained a solid breath. Then another and another. The spasms in his lungs slowed, and he opened his jacket. Bella poked her tiny white head out and looked around.

The child reached for the dog.

Grady held out a warning hand, the one with tiny bite marks. "Now's probably not the best time to hold her. She might bite you."

The mother looked at Grady. "She bit you, didn't she?"

"It's okay," Grady said. "She's afraid and didn't mean to hurt me. The only thing that matters right now is that we're all safe."

He hoped anyway.

He looked down the street, searching through the chaos

of rushing firefighters. Two trucks. An ambulance arriving on scene. The smoldering smoke swirling around it all.

Had Drake moved Ainslie out of the danger zone?

Grady's gut clenched, and he wouldn't relax until he knew for sure that she was safe. Because if he knew anything right now, he knew in his gut that the bomb had been targeting her.

9

In Drake's SUV, Ainslie tried to ignore her knotted stomach. Her racing heart. She tried to will the phone she stared at in her hand to ring. Was Grady safe? Was the family safe? He'd run into flames and smoke. Disappeared before her eyes. Her heart had screamed to follow him to be sure he was okay. At the very least to shake off Drake's hand and stay nearby as he urged her toward his car. But she'd let him lead her away, because that's what Grady wanted, and she wouldn't distract him by not following his wishes. And if he was still in the flaming house, she couldn't distract him with a phone call either. Surely, he would contact her the minute he got the family to safety.

Drake glanced at her from the driver's seat. "He's okay."

"You don't know that," she said, hating how negative and fearful she sounded.

"I know Grady." Drake clicked on the blinker for the Veritas Center's parking lot. "He's a fighter, and he's smart. He'll get that family and himself out of that house in plenty of time."

Would he? Had he? She had to believe he'd succeeded because she couldn't do anything to help him other than pray, which she'd done nonstop since they'd left the blazing home.

Prayer. Why did she think it was the last resort? Minimize its importance. Likely because she didn't see a lot of answers to her requests of late. Maybe she'd been praying for the wrong things. But Grady getting out of that house safe? That was totally the right thing to be asking for.

Drake parked at the curb by the center. "Straight inside."

She nodded and climbed out, the air cooler and crisper. Free from smoke like Grady had been facing. She shivered at the thought and entered the building through the front door. The muted color scheme in the spacious lobby often brought her comfort, but tonight it was dark and quiet. She searched for the usual peace, but she was too hyped up to even think about relaxing.

Their night guard, Pete Vincent, stood by the desk watching them enter, his gaze a question mark. "Evening, Ainslie."

She swallowed hard and stepped to the desk. "This's Sierra's brother, Drake Byrd. He's a deputy with the marshals fugitive apprehension division."

"We've met before," Drake said.

Pete held out his hand. "Good to see you again. I always thought fugitive apprehension would be an interesting job."

"You know it is," Drake said, but his tone didn't reflect his enthusiastic statement, and she had to wonder if there was something going on in his job that he wasn't enjoying. Or maybe he was just worried about Grady, too.

Pete laid an iPad on the counter in front of Drake. "You know the drill. Sign in, and I'll get your security badge ready."

Pete slid a plastic card through a reader then looked up at Ainslie. "I heard about the swat."

She was going to comment, but her phone rang from her

purse. She grabbed it up. Grady's name appeared on the screen. She nearly dropped to the floor in thanks.

"Excuse me." She moved out of earshot. "Grady. Thank goodness. Are you okay?"

"Fine." One word, but she heard the raspy tone and knew he'd suffered from smoke inhalation.

She couldn't stay upright any longer and dropped onto a plush chair, her hand shaking. She'd never been so afraid for someone else in her life. Never. Tears threatened to fall.

"And you?" he asked, sounding as anxious as she'd been feeling.

She swallowed hard and looked up to stem the tears before she started blubbering in front of Pete and Drake. "We're at the center. We're good."

A long sigh traveled through the phone, and she felt his relief clear to her bones. When she had a chance to think about this event, she knew she would discover how much they both were being drawn to each other. For some odd reason, that didn't bother her right now. Maybe because she was simply relieved that he was okay. Or maybe because she really was coming to care for him more than she wanted. When he'd disappeared into the house alive with flames, her terror for his safety had told her all she needed to know.

She wished she had time to process her thoughts, but Drake started her way, and she needed to end the call. "What about the family? How are they?"

"All safe and accounted for. Even their dog. I'll be heading out shortly. I'll meet you at Sierra's place." His tone had gone back to the clipped-and-to-the-point-Mr.-Business again.

She should want that. Should want him to stick to the professional side of things. But she didn't. Right now, she wanted the man she cared for. But with Drake fast approaching, she wasn't about to go there.

"See you then." She ended the call, even though she'd wanted to keep talking. To cling to his voice to prove he was safe, but she would soon see him.

And then what? Pretend some more that she didn't have feelings for him?

"Ready?" Drake asked, unaware of her inner turmoil.

"Yes." She hurried across the wide-open lobby to give them access to the hallway. She crossed over to the condo tower and punched the elevator button.

"Grady called," she told Drake inside the car as she punched the number five. "He's fine, and so is the family."

"Good to hear." He watched her far more carefully than she found comfortable. A typical law enforcement officer who was looking for a deeper meaning. "Maybe you can relax a bit now."

She resisted nodding and looked at her feet to end the conversation. She didn't want him to know how much seeing Grady running into the fire had impacted her. And besides, she wouldn't relax. Not until she actually saw Grady —saw that he wasn't covered in burns. Then she would relax. And maybe not even then.

How could she when Ethan's house had blown up?

The explosion played in her head. The fiery ball that had rumbled under her body but she couldn't see due to Grady's protection. The raining down of wood and metal. The ash. Smoke. She shuddered.

"You coming?" Drake's voice pierced her thoughts.

She looked up to find him standing in the hallway holding the elevator door open.

She marched past him and down the hall, then used Sierra's key to let them into her condo.

"It's just me and Drake," she called out so she didn't startle Sierra.

"In the dining area," Sierra yelled.

Sierra sat next to Reed, a big strapping guy with a large nose and square jaw. He wore dress slacks and a green button-down shirt highlighting his dark coloring. Sierra was dressed more casually in jeans and a pale pink T-shirt, and they were both peering intently at a large poster board seating chart.

Sierra's head popped up, a bead of determination in her eyes, and Reed plunged his fingers into hair nearly as black as Drake's.

"Dude," Drake said. "You look like you could use a break. There's a Trail Blazers game on."

Reed glanced at Sierra, a pleading look on his face.

"Go ahead." She smiled. "You've endured this far longer than most guys would have."

He stood and grabbed her tightly in a hug. "It's official. You are the very best fiancée a guy could ask for."

"And don't you forget that when I let Bridezilla take over." She laughed.

He kissed her nose and all but ran to the sofa, where Drake had already turned on the TV.

Ainslie loved seeing Sierra and Reed's good-natured bantering. The gentle love they displayed. Something that would be amazing in any person's life. Could she have something like that with Grady? He was right about the football thing. It was no big deal. She didn't have to enjoy it. Just enjoy the fact that he did. *That* she could do.

So, what was holding her back now? Fear. That feeling from her childhood of being less-than. Oh, man, she couldn't think about this now. Not with Sierra looking up at her.

She dropped into the chair Reed had vacated. "Anything I can help with?"

Sierra searched her gaze for a moment then shook her head. "Maybe you can provide moral support while I try to figure out where to place some of our more um…well…difficult family members."

A knock sounded on the door, startling Ainslie. "That's likely Grady."

Drake got up. "I'll get it."

As he strode to the door, Ainslie told Sierra and Reed about the explosion.

Sierra clutched Ainslie's hand. "Is he okay?"

"Yes." Ainslie hoped he didn't prove her wrong when he walked in the door.

But when she heard the male voice, she knew it wasn't Grady.

Blake strode into the room. He locked gazes with her and held up a folder. "I've got information from your brother's case file."

She let out a silent breath and pasted on a smile. "Excellent. I can't wait to get a look at it."

"Let me clear the table, and we can spread out." Sierra shoved her little sticky tabs with names into the folder and moved the poster board to the kitchen island. She returned to her chair, and Blake straddled the one next to her. He opened his folder and someone else pounded on the door.

Ainslie's heart lurched. Now, this had to be Grady.

"I'll get it." Reed went to the door this time.

She kept her focus pinned on the entrance and was rewarded when Grady stepped into the room. Soot coated his face and clothing, and the caustic scent of smoke clung to him. She ran her gaze from his head to feet and back up again. His jacket was scorched, but when he took it off, his shirt wasn't charred.

She offered a prayer of thanksgiving and smiled at him. "You really are okay?"

"Inhaled a bit of smoke, but otherwise fine." His voice was raspy, but he smiled, and she had the urge to reach out and brush the soot from his face. His soft gaze lingered on her. Pulling her. Drawing her. She leaned closer. Nearly came out of her seat.

Blake cleared his throat. "You look rough, man. And I'm not even going to ask why you smell like a chimney."

Grady jerked his focus to Blake and explained the fire.

Blake looked at Ainslie, and she didn't like the concern she found there. "Sounds like you really do have someone who's trying to do you in."

"Yeah," was all she could say without breaking down. She tapped the folder on the table and looked at Grady. "Blake brought us Ethan's case file."

Grady sat in the chair next to her, the smell of smoke now permeating the air around him. He looked at Blake. "You get the CT scan for the bullet lodged in Wade's head?"

"No. That's going to be harder to come by, but I'll keep after it." Blake opened his folder and pulled out the top page, the criminal complaint form. "As you can see, they're stating that the forensic blood evidence found at the scene matches Ethan's DNA located on the body. That, plus GSR on his hands and the fact that his 9mm Beretta could have fired the bullet lodged in the victim's head, are the basis for the prosecution's charges against Ethan."

"All things we expected," Ainslie said.

"True." Blake held out the paper and pointed to a long section. "But we sure as heck didn't expect this."

Grady stared at the paper and couldn't believe what he was reading. If this document was right, Ethan was not only a liar, but he was also involved in illegal activities.

Ainslie jumped to her feet and planted her hands on her hips, her breath coming fast and furious. "Ethan is *not* a criminal. He would never sell guns." She took several long breaths and blew them out.

Blake frowned. "Says here that Wade witnessed a gun sale between Ethan and known dealers. But Wade's account is their only evidence."

"*Wade* is the dealer, not Ethan." She crossed her arms. "So it's his word against Ethan's. Just like in the shooting."

"Then we need to prove that Wade is lying," Sierra said.

"Agreed." Grady dug out his phone. "Starting with finding out what Nick has learned in his background checks on Wade and the swat call. I'll text him to join us." Grady fired off the message.

"We really need to get eyes on Wade," Blake suggested. "Hopefully, he'll lead us to his sources or buyers. Then we can put pressure on them to turn on him. I can handle the surveillance, but I can't do round-the-clock by myself. Maybe someone else will offer to spell me so I can catch a few hours of sleep."

Grady shook his head. "We need you managing the investigation. Call Gage Blackwell. Get some of his guys on the job."

"Gage?" Ainslie asked, noticing for the first time several puncture wounds on Grady's hand. She touched it. "What happened?"

"This?" He looked at his hand. "The family had a dog, and she was afraid. No big deal."

"You rescued the dog, too?"

Grady didn't want to talk about the rescue and give her more worries. "So you asked about Gage. He's a former Navy SEAL. Own's Blackwell Tactical out of Cold Harbor. They train LEOs and conduct investigations for private individuals. They're all vets or former law enforcement. Blake worked with them when he was a sheriff."

Blake nodded. "They're not cheap, but they'd do a good job."

"I'll be glad to foot the bill," Grady said. "Can you give him a call?"

"You got it." Blake took out his phone before stepping to the far side of the room.

Ainslie blinked as if her world was spinning out of control. "I can't let you pay for that."

Grady ignored Sierra, who was watching them both carefully, and planted his hands on the table. "We have to do this. Not only do we need to get eyes on this guy for the reasons Blake said, but after the explosion we need to make sure he's not the one trying to hurt you. You can't put a price on your life." He leaned closer, pinning an insistent gaze on her. "Please let me do this for you."

She glanced around the room as if looking for an answer. He didn't want to put her in a position that he knew she didn't want to be in, but he couldn't live with himself if they didn't do everything in their power to be sure she was safe. And to clear Ethan's name.

She turned back to face him, her expression resolute. She was going to say no.

"It's not charity," he whispered. "I care about you and want to make sure you're okay. A friend helping a friend. That's all."

She sighed. "I'll agree if you consider it a loan and let me pay you back with interest."

He wanted to say no. To say he had plenty of money and had no one else to spend it on, but her determined look told him to cave now and come back to the subject later. "Agreed."

"Thank you." She smiled at him, a radiant number that had his heart kicking up.

A knock sounded on the door.

"Must be Nick," Sierra said.

"I'll let him in." Phone to his ear, Blake strode to the door.

Nick plunged into the room like a bullet seeking a target and marched straight past Blake to the table. He straddled a chair across from Ainslie. "I don't have any progress to report on the swat call yet, but I've got my team working on it."

"And the background checks on Wade and Bittner?" Grady asked.

Nick slid a report across to him. "Wade's details. Nothing much to go on here. He does have arrests for illegal gun sales like Ethan said. No social media presence, though. No pictures. His legal residence is still Greenburg, Texas."

"Your hometown?" Grady asked Ainslie.

She nodded.

Blake came back to join them. "Gage's sending Coop and Jackson via their chopper. I'll get them surveilling Wade the minute they touch down." He looked at Grady. "Can they bunk at your place during their downtime? I'd ask them to stay with us, but Emory's pregnancy has her sleeping at odd hours of the day."

"Sure thing. Glad to hang with fellow army buds." Grady looked at Ainslie. "Coop served as an Army Ranger and Jackson was a Green Beret."

"Impressive credentials," she said.

He nodded. "With the way Gage has been expanding his team, I'm glad to hear two of their top operators will be handling the surveillance and not one of their new guys."

"Agreed." Blake sat.

"We interviewed Ethan's neighbors tonight," Grady said, thinking this was the right time to bring Blake up to speed. "The woman and teenage daughter across the street have a video doorbell that might've captured the shooting.

Anything in the file about them? Daughter's name is Jayla."

Blake shook his head.

"Can you follow up with Flores?" Grady asked. "See if she talked to them and recovered the video from that device?"

"Sure thing."

"I asked the girl to have her mom call me or Ainslie, so hopefully she will," Grady said. "If not, I'll go back by there to talk to her."

"Or I can do it if you need me to. Just let me know." Blake turned a page in his folder and handed a sheet to Grady. "Ethan's phone records. Flores highlighted calls made to the victim. Ethan called him twice the night of the shooting."

A deep frown marred Ainslie's face. "Ethan never mentioned that, but maybe he was too drunk to remember."

Was that the reason? Grady hoped so. Because he didn't like to think that Ethan was hiding things from them.

Nick looked at the report. "Does it say anything about tracking GPS for Ethan's phone?"

"How will that help?" Ainslie asked.

Nick's expression perked up. "Phones routinely ping off nearby cell towers, and the phone company will have a record of his whereabouts at a given time. By looking at his GPS records, we should be able to determine his movements on the night of the shooting."

Grady looked at the report. "Nothing here on that."

Blake flipped through the file. "Nothing here either. Flores gave me everything the DA authorized her to provide. If we want more, we'll need an attorney to request it."

Grady looked at Ainslie. "Do you have confidence in Ethan's attorney?"

"I don't know." Ainslie swallowed. "He hasn't come through with my last request, so I don't know how good he is. But it doesn't matter. We don't have the money to hire anyone else."

Sierra looked at Grady and Blake. "What about Malone?"

"My sister?" Reed asked from the sofa, proving he was listening in.

Sierra faced Ainslie. "She's a criminal defense attorney. A very good one."

Reed strolled over to them. "I can ask her to take on Ethan's case pro bono."

Ainslie twisted her hands together on the table. She was probably thinking about the offer of help and equating it to more charity. "You all have done so much already. I can't ask for more. The cost—"

"You want what's best for Ethan, right?" Grady didn't want to put her in a difficult position, but he knew in the long run that she would be glad they asked Malone to help. Only question was, would Ainslie forgive him for pushing her into making that decision?

She nodded slowly, looking sick to her stomach and telling Grady just how much her past still had a hold on her. He wanted to fix it for her. That's what he did. He was a fixer. Get to the problem. Attack it head on. Solve it. Well except his big secret. He opened his mouth to encourage her, but Reed stepped closer, taking her attention.

"Let's ask Malone," he said. "If she doesn't want to do it, she'll have no problem saying so."

Ainslie pressed her hands flat on the table. "I'm not saying yes, but it won't hurt to ask."

"I'll call her right now." Reed stepped away.

Ainslie trained her focus on Grady, and her terse expression said she didn't appreciate his interference. So he'd won one battle and lost another. A good trade off in his mind. Helping her brother came before winning her affections.

10

_____

The morning sun shone brightly over Ethan's rental place, and Ainslie desperately wanted to join Sierra at the house. Or what was left of it. Charred and blackened debris smoldered under Sierra's feet as she slowly walked the scene with her video camera strapped on her head, recording horrible images that screamed of a near death, and streaming the images for Ainslie.

Ainslie took a breath and watched the video play on her computer, her heart in her throat. She was safely tucked in the lab with Grady standing next to her, but the burned ruins brought back their close call, and a shiver ran over her body. Still, despite the fear, she would head over to Ethan's house in a heartbeat. Not because she had any affinity to the place. It was a furnished dump that she'd encouraged Ethan to move out of plenty of times. But to search for a much-needed lead.

Sierra passed the old recliner Ainslie had given to Ethan. The top half was blown away, the bottom charred. His favorite chair. If he'd been home...

No. Don't think that way.

"Looks bad," Grady said. "But Sierra's got this. She'll

capture it all. And if there's a lead to be found, she'll locate it."

Ainslie resisted sighing, as she was thankful for Sierra and didn't want to come across as ungrateful. "I know, but I feel like I'm adding to her workload when my job is to ease it."

"She understands. She just wants you to be safe, like we all do." Grady searched her gaze.

She struggled to look back at the screen. "I guess I also don't want to think this is because of me."

"It isn't because of you at all." His vehemence surprised her. "We have a nutjob who blew up a house in an attempt to kill you. It's all on him."

Still, she felt guilty and would record these hours along with ones she'd been trying to keep track of. "I just wish I knew why he's trying to kill me. I spent a sleepless night trying to figure it out, but didn't come up with anything."

"Maybe the person coming after you thinks Ethan told you something, and he doesn't want you to talk about it."

"But there's nothing I know about Ethan's case that isn't public knowledge." She sighed and looked at him, her mind racing for answers. "What if we're way off base here and it wasn't about killing me at all? What if it was an attempt to destroy evidence in the house?"

"I considered that, too. But if so, why wait to drop the Molotov cocktail? Why not just start the fire right after releasing the gas? Or maybe it's not about Ethan at all." Grady frowned. "I know this is way out there, but what if you accidentally captured someone in a snapshot you took, and they don't want you to have the pictures?"

She tapped her finger on the lab table to release some of her nerves and gave his comment some thought. "First, I haven't taken many photos outside of work, so it's not likely.

And second, wouldn't they target my place instead of Ethan's?"

"Yeah. Like I said. It's out there."

"I suppose it wouldn't hurt to review my files." Her phone chimed in Sierra's ringtone, and Ainslie answered.

"Thanks for doing the video," she quickly said so she could make sure Sierra knew she appreciated her help. "And I'm sorry about the extra work."

"Don't worry about it," Sierra said. "I'm glad to help. I talked to the arson investigator. The gas line for the stove was disconnected. Definitely arson. I told him I would process the scene for him. With his limited resources, he jumped on it."

After the Molotov cocktail, a ruling of arson was no surprise, but hearing it had been made official sent Ainslie's stomach clenching. She swallowed hard.

"I'll be here for most of the day, and I need a favor," Sierra continued. "Could you prepare the photos for the Randall trial? I need to get the overall photographs combined for the DA."

"Absolutely." It would feel good to repay some of Sierra's kindness.

"Thanks and let me know if you run into any problems." Sierra ended the call.

Ainslie clicked off the video and looked at Grady. "I need to get to work now."

He looked at her with a hangdog expression.

She liked that he wanted to stay with her, but that was exactly why she needed to send him away. "I'm perfectly safe here. You can go."

He searched her gaze. "Would it bother you if I said I don't want to go? That it's not about keeping you safe all the time? That I also like hanging out with you?"

A few days earlier, she'd have been bothered by his presence, but now... Now he felt comfortable. "I have to get these photos done for Sierra, so I can get over to see Ethan again."

He raised an eyebrow, likely over the fact that she didn't really answer his question. But how could she without leading him on?

"Come down when you're ready to go, okay?" he asked. "And I'll drive you."

She knew it would do no good to argue so she nodded.

A big smile crossed his face, and he seemed unreasonably happy for such a simple promise. Maybe he thought her easy acquiesce meant more. "I'm very thankful for your help. I hope you know how much. But I haven't changed my position on getting involved."

"Don't worry." He held up his hands. "Message received, but that doesn't mean I don't like being with you."

She didn't know what to say, and thankfully the door opened and Blake strode in with two other guys before she had to come up with something. Both men were dark-haired, but the first one was bigger and well over six feet tall. He was built like a tank, his powerful shoulders and biceps filling out the black jacket he wore with cargo pants. The second guy was buff too, had a short military haircut and a jaw darkened by a thick five-o'clock shadow, even though it was morning.

"Ainslie," Blake said. "Meet Coop and Jackson."

"Cooper Ashcroft." The taller guy held out his hand. "But call me Coop."

She nodded and suffered through a punishing grip as he shook her hand like a water pump that needed encouragement to produce liquid.

She extricated her hand and looked at the other guy. "You must be Jackson, then."

"Yes, ma'am," he said, his grayish-blue eyes fixed on her. "Jackson Lockhart."

"And you guys know Grady, right?" Blake asked.

"Most definitely." Coop fist bumped Grady, and Jackson followed suit.

There was so much testosterone in the room that if Sierra had been in the lab, Ainslie figured her boss would've figured out a way to collect a sample and measure it.

"We just wanted to check in with you before we start working on locating and tailing Eggen," Coop said. "Is there anything specific you want us to be watching for?"

"Assuming you find him," Ainslie said.

"Yes, ma'am, but we will," Jackson said.

"Please, I am so not a ma'am," she said, though she was admiring their precise military manners in a world where people were so informal and crass at times. "Call me Ainslie."

"Yes, ma'—Ainslie," Jackson said.

"We think Wade is into illegal arms dealing," she said. "Catch him at that so he can be arrested. Then maybe Detective Flores can make a deal in trade for the truth on his shooting."

"We'll watch for that, then," Coop said. "Once located, we'll set up twenty-four/seven surveillance rotating twelve-hour shifts."

Jackson faced Grady. "Blake says you offered to put us up in our downtime."

"Absolutely." Grady dug out his key ring and slipped one off. "I have a spare key in my lab, so you can take this one and drop your things now if you want."

Jackson took the key. "Perfect. We'll check in back home, and then get started right away."

Blake looked at Grady. "I'll serve as their point person and make sure they're escorted in the building."

Grady gave a firm nod. "I was just leaving, so I'll walk out with you."

"Nice meeting you, ma'—Ainslie," Jackson said.

"Ditto." Coop pocketed the key.

"For me, too." She smiled and watched the four men head for the door.

"Dude." Coop clapped Grady on the back. "We are definitely going to stop in your lab and take a look around before we leave town."

"Wouldn't expect anything less." Grady chuckled, his laughter ringing out behind him as the door closed.

She stared at the door after them, struck by how well Grady fit in with these tough guys. He was a real man's man. The kind of guy she'd never been particularly attracted to. And yet she found him to have a sensitive side. Caring about his friends and family seemed to come first. And in all this time, he didn't lament missing his sports. He hadn't even glanced at the TV the night before when Drake had continued to watch the Blazers play.

She wanted to keep thinking about him. To sit and just feel the emotions he evoked in her, but she had work to do and repaying Sierra was more important. She opened the Randall file containing hundreds of photos from the murder scene. Most people thought forensic photographers shot only photographs of the evidence, but they took photos of the entire scene so a defense attorney couldn't raise a question about the photographer missing a key piece of evidence. To accomplish that they stepped into the four corners of a room and took shots from each angle. Later, they combined the photos so the jury could see the entire room, which is what Sierra had tasked Ainslie with doing now.

She got out Sierra's photo log and found the numbers for the Randalls' overall photos. One by one, she opened them and lost herself in her job, glad to be doing something productive again. Hours later, she sat back to stretch and admired her work.

Grady's comment about other photos came to mind, and her moment of satisfaction evaporated. She sat forward and accessed the cloud where she stored her personal photos. In the last six months, she'd only taken two sets of pictures. The first group was from a hiking trip to Forest Park located in Portland. Park. Ha! The word park was so misleading. At over five thousand acres, it was one of the largest urban forests in the country, with miles and miles of hiking trails. It was so much more than a park.

She started through the pictures, enlarging each one to study every pixel, but she hadn't captured a single person. She moved on to the second set of photos taken in the International Rose Test Garden. The pictures revealed several visitors in the background, but she didn't recognize them.

Nothing here to help her, but one thing was suddenly obvious. Since she'd taken the job at the Veritas Center, her personal life had suffered. She'd neglected her favorite hobby. Maybe neglected Ethan. If she hadn't been working so much, might she have prevented Ethan from getting arrested for attempted murder?

That thought cut her to the quick. When she'd cleared his name, she needed to do some soul searching about the lack of a personal life. That would include finding more time for her brother, and maybe, just maybe, finding time for a relationship, too.

Ainslie clutched her hands under the table and watched the tall beautiful woman dressed in a deep green tailored pantsuit enter the conference room. She had a confident stride and held her shoulders back. Her hair rested in thick waves on her shoulders, the suit color bringing out the dark hue. Without saying a word, Malone Rice commanded the room, and when she fixed her dark gaze on Ainslie, Ainslie's old insecurities came rushing back.

"Ainslie, this is Reed's sister, Malone." Grady didn't seem to even be aware that Malone was gorgeous as he pinned his focus on Ainslie.

Malone held out a hand with pale pink manicured nails. "Good to meet you, Ainslie. I'm sorry it's under such difficult circumstances."

Ainslie quickly ran her hand down her pant leg, swiping perspiration from her palm, before shaking. "Thank you for agreeing to help. If you would please bill me, and I can pay you—"

"No," Malone said firmly. "Sierra cares about you, and that makes you family in my book, so please let me do this for you."

Her tone left no question that Malone expected Ainslie to comply. As much as she didn't want to, she was done fighting the kindness of all of these wonderful people. They genuinely wanted to help. To share their God-given talents. And she had to believe He'd put them in her life for that very reason. So saying no to Malone would be like saying no to God's plan. She took comfort in the fact that this strong woman would do a great job for Ethan.

"Good, that's settled then." Malone took a legal pad from her leather briefcase and sat. "Tell me all about your brother's situation, starting with his full name."

"Ethan Alan Duncan." Ainslie took a seat across from her and recounted the details of Ethan's predicament while Grady propped a shoulder against the wall and looked on.

Malone took notes in swift precise letters, her expression

a mask, but when Ainslie finished and sat back, Malone frowned.

"Uh-oh." Grady came off the wall and stepped to the table. "That's not a positive look."

Malone laid down her pen and folded her hands on the legal pad. "I'm not one to sugarcoat things. If the evidence has been handled and processed correctly, and if Ethan doesn't have an alibi, then it will be difficult to mount a strong defense."

Ainslie opened her mouth to say something—what, she didn't know—but Grady planted his hands on the table. "Then it's important for you to get the evidence for us so we can be sure it *was* handled right. Especially the CT scan and gun. I'm confident that they didn't find anyone with my skills to do the work. There's no one better than I am in the area."

Malone arched a perfectly plucked eyebrow. "Confident much?"

"Why wouldn't I be? Every one of us here are top in our fields." Grady's words came out between nearly clenched teeth. "We worked hard to gain those skills and experience. I'm just speaking the truth."

Malone held up her hands. "I believe you."

"All right, then. What do you have to do to get me that CT scan and Ethan's gun?"

Ainslie was surprised at how he was pushing Malone when she was volunteering her time. Ainslie would never be so insistent, and he likely knew that. Could be his very reason for stepping in.

Malone shifted her gaze to Ainslie. "First, I need to talk to Ethan and have him change his attorney of record. There won't be any problem with that, will there?"

"I haven't spoken to him about the change, but I can't see

Ethan refusing to have a talented attorney like you representing him."

She gave a sharp nod. "Then I'll interview him and talk with his PD—public defender—to ask for any work he's completed. After that, I'll need to file an order to inspect and preserve this evidence."

"Is that what it sounds like?" Grady asked.

"If you mean does it protect Ethan's right to inspect and copy or test evidence before trial and ensures that the agencies are responsible for maintaining it? Then, yes. We'll want to get the request in right away, before any evidence is lost, misplaced, or destroyed. Or even consumed or damaged by testing before we have a chance to view or test it."

"Could Ethan's PD already have filed that request?" Ainslie asked.

"He could have, which is why, after talking to Ethan, I'll need to talk to the PD."

"The police have a DNA report from Wade's shirt so they've obviously processed some of the evidence," Ainslie said.

"Then we need to get on this right away. If the PD hasn't filed it, I'll get the order written up and have my assistant serve it to the prosecutor, the medical examiner, the crime lab, and every involved law enforcement agency. I should have everything filed and delivered in a few hours. How long it takes the police to comply is another—"

"A few hours?" Ainslie asked in disbelief.

"What?" Malone tilted her head. "You think that's too long?"

"No. No. It would take the PD longer than that just to call me back if I had a question."

"Oh, right. Okay. So let's not waste any time." She offered a tight smile. "Do you want to accompany me to meet with your brother? I think he'll be more forthcoming without you, so I won't let you remain in the room when I question him. But it wouldn't be a bad idea to have you break the ice."

Feeling optimistic for the first time since Ethan's arrest, Ainslie smiled at Malone. "Then let's do this."

Grady pushed off the table. "Not without me and Drake."

Malone raised an eyebrow.

"Someone is trying to kill Ainslie." Grady quickly explained about the swat incident and fire. "Drake Byrd has been assigned to tail her in the event she might lead him to Bittner and also to keep her safe."

Malone peered at Ainslie. "Maybe it's safer for you to stay here."

"Maybe," Ainslie said. "But I'll do anything to get my brother out of jail, and I think introducing you two will move things along faster. So threat or not, I'm going."

11

Ainslie got right in to see Ethan, and he agreed to Malone's representation, but he wanted Ainslie present at the meeting. Malone agreed, albeit reluctantly. But before they could begin, he first had to wait for what the jail called walk time to call his PD and tell him of the change so he wasn't blindsided. Once that was accomplished, Ainslie and Malone stepped into the visiting area, and Ethan looked even more forlorn than he had when she'd seen him an hour ago. He didn't even perk up when he saw Malone, and what red-blooded male wouldn't notice such a beautiful woman?

"Sis." He stared blankly at her as she introduced Malone.

"Nice to meet you, Ethan." Malone offered her hand.

Ethan nodded and shook, but didn't look her in the eye.

"We have limited time so let's get right to this." Malone took a seat on a metal bench, her posture perfect. "Let me go through the plan with you. First, I'll file a motion to substitute attorneys so I'm on record as your official counsel. This form will require your PD's signature as well, but since you gave him a heads-up, the change is just a formality."

"Right." Ethan cast a distracted gaze around the room with half a dozen visitors and inmates.

Malone bent forward, probably to get his attention. "Next I need to confirm that you want my representation."

He nodded.

Malone got even closer. "I need you to verbally confirm your intentions, Ethan."

"Yeah, I want you to represent me." He sounded reluctant.

Ainslie gaped at him. She just didn't get his behavior. She wanted to cuff him upside the head and tell him to snap out of whatever was bothering him and embrace this gift Malone was offering. But maybe something bad happened in here, and if that was the case, she surely didn't want to chastise him and make things worse. So she clamped her mouth shut and sat on her hands.

"I'll file the necessary paperwork," Malone continued, sounding very professional. "And also file to be sure that all recovered evidence be preserved. I had to register as a social visitor today so Ainslie could accompany me. That's why we didn't get a private room and means I was unable to bring in a pen and can't take notes. What I would like to do is schedule a professional visit to get your side of things. Are you okay with that?"

He glanced at Ainslie and gnawed on his lip.

She couldn't stand not knowing what was bothering him any longer. "What's wrong?"

He wrung his hands on the table. "There's something I need to tell both of you. These hours of just sitting in this place. Thinking and thinking. I can't stand it anymore. I need to tell someone so I can finally get some peace."

Ainslie's heart dropped to her stomach. He was so distraught that she was terrified of what he might say and wanted to have him rethink his decision. "Are you sure you want to do it in a public setting like this?"

"I have to. Don't you see?" His grip tightened, and his fingers turned white. "It's driving me mad. Just mad."

He shoved his fingers into his hair and gave Ainslie such a pitiful look that she could hardly keep from hugging him. Except if she touched him, she'd get kicked out.

She leaned closer to him. "What's wrong?"

"It's about Wade. About how we first started hanging out as kids."

Not what she expected at all. "I always wondered if there was something that happened. He wasn't the kind of guy you would normally hang with."

"He wasn't. And I didn't want to. Honest." Ethan grimaced, and he met her gaze, his face paling. "But I saw him...I saw him murder Neil Orr."

"Neil Orr?" Ainslie's voice rose.

The nearby burly guard gave her a testy look.

"Sorry," she mouthed.

Malone was sitting, shoulders in a hard line now, eyeing Ethan, her gaze suspicious. "Who's Neil Orr?"

Ainslie waited for Ethan to answer, but when he didn't, she looked at Malone. "He was a boy we went to middle school with in Texas. He went missing when I was in eighth grade." Ainslie shifted to look at Ethan, her heart tearing over his distress and this sudden revelation. "You've known all this time Wade murdered him. Why didn't you say anything?"

"I couldn't. Wade threatened me. Then you and Mom. I was just a kid. Only eleven. I believed him. Totally. I was terrified of him."

"Tell us what happened," Malone said.

Ethan pressed his hands out flat and looked Ainslie in the eye. "I was heading to the lake for a swim and saw Wade beating Neil up. You know how mean Wade was back then. I was afraid and thought if I said something he would hit me, too."

She did remember Wade. A real bully. Tough guy. "I'm sure you're right."

"For some stupid reason, I didn't take off but hid and watched. Neil got away. Wade grabbed Neil and bit his arm. Man, Wade was mad. Madder than I've ever seen anyone. His face was so red and contorted. Scared me something fierce."

"And yet you stayed?" she asked. "How come you didn't run?"

He shook his head. "To this day, I don't know. I wish I had taken off so I didn't see Wade get Neil in a stranglehold and keep squeezing until Neil dropped to the ground." Ethan took a long shaky breath. "I knew he was dead, and I must've gasped or something because Wade looked up and saw me. That's when I ran. As fast as I could. I heard a gunshot, and thought he had a gun, too. He came after me. I made it to town before he caught up to me. There were other people around, so I thought I was safe. But he twisted my arm behind my back and dragged me into an alley. I thought he was going to kill me too."

Ainslie could see the terror lingering in his eyes as he swallowed hard.

"Did you see the gun?" she asked.

He shook his head. "But Wade got in my face and said he would kill you and Mom if I told anyone. I knew he would do it. No doubt in my mind. So I kept my mouth shut, and, as soon as I turned eighteen, I split."

Memories flooded back of the time when Ethan became more introverted, and her heart broke for what he'd endured. "This explains so much. About how you suddenly changed. Why you hung out with him and pretended to like him. Why you were always so protective of me. Why you left."

Tears formed in his eyes. "I've felt so guilty. Neil's parents... They've suffered all these years because of me. I can't even—"

His voice fell off. A sob crawled out of his mouth, and he clasped a hand over it.

"You were a kid," Malone said. "Don't beat yourself up about it."

He shook his head hard. "But I've been an adult for years. I could have said something."

"Why didn't you?" Ainslie asked, trying to be gentle with her questions. "I mean, we both moved here, and we were a couple thousand miles away from Wade."

"He knew where we'd moved and made sure I knew it. He texted pictures of you going about life here. I don't know how he got them, but they were a warning to remind me that he could still get to you."

"That's horrible," Malone said, and Ainslie had forgotten she was even with them.

Ainslie had so many questions and didn't know where to start. "When did Wade arrive in Portland?"

"Not long before he was shot." Which likely explained Ethan's recent bout with alcohol abuse. "Some detective named Paulson reopened Neil's investigation. Wade thought I would hear about it and talk. So he showed up here to keep tabs on me and prove he was close enough to kill you."

Ainslie was happy to finally put the picture together and understand her brother's behavior, but man, she was so sad for him having lived with this secret for so many years. And because of the Orr family's suffering, he'd still have to carry the burden of what he'd done for the rest of his life.

"Do you know where Neil was buried?" Malone asked.

Ethan cringed and nodded. "I went back the next day hoping it had all been a bad dream. He was gone."

"Was there blood? Like Neil had been shot?"

"I didn't see any but I did find the grave hidden in the woods. Knew it was all too real."

"We'll need to find the body," Malone stated. "And you'll need to confess to the police."

He nodded. "I'm going to do time for coming forward with this, right?"

Malone didn't answer right away. "There are extenuating circumstances and statute of limitations, so let's not worry about that until later."

Ethan gave a pitiful nod. "I'd do whatever I have to do to get this off my chest."

Malone let out a long breath. "You do realize this gives you a strong motive to kill Wade."

"I know, but I didn't do it. Still, if I end up locked up for it, it's what I deserve after not reporting Neil's murder."

"That's not true." Ainslie's heart ached over how defeated he sounded. "And I don't want to hear you say that again. You don't deserve to be locked up for a murder you didn't commit."

His narrowed eyes reflected his skepticism.

"Is there anything else you need to tell us about the night Wade was shot?" Malone asked.

He shook his head. "Everything I said is true. I don't know why Wade was waiting for me. He probably just wanted to warn me off again."

"You have two calls on your phone log to him that day. What did he say to you?"

Ethan's eyes widened. "I do? Don't even remember talking to him. Must've been half in the bag by then."

"Are you sure?" Ainslie asked.

"Look." He met her gaze and held it. "I get by telling you

about Neil that you're probably doubting everything I've ever said, but it's the truth. I don't remember talking to him."

"Did he ever send you texts or email warnings?" Malone asked.

"No. Just Ainslie's picture. No message with it. He's too smart for that."

"And you're sure you don't know any of the details of his illegal weapons sales?" Ainslie asked.

"It's like I said before. I knew he was into something at first, but not what until I looked him up."

Ainslie leaned closer to Ethan. "We have him under surveillance by a professional team."

Malone swung her gaze to Ainslie. "News to me."

"Sorry. I should have mentioned that."

"Who are you using?"

"Blackwell Tactical out of Cold Harbor."

"I've heard good things about them. Keep me in the loop."

"Of course. Is there something else we need to do here, or should we get moving on finding Neil's body?"

"I guess I need to point out the elephant in the room." Malone turned her attention back to Ethan. "Even if we find physical evidence pointing to Wade as Neil's killer, Wade can always say you killed Neil and planted the evidence."

"But I didn't!" Ethan shouted.

"Settle down." The guard eyed Ethan. "Or this visit is over."

Ethan gave him a sheepish look then stared at Malone. "I didn't even think of that."

She folded her hands on the table. "Are you willing to take the risk?"

Ethan slumped in his chair and closed his eyes.

"It's the right thing to do," Ainslie said. "God would want you to speak up."

Ethan opened his eyes. "You're right. Neil's family deserves closure. No matter what happens to me."

Ainslie thought to squeeze her brother's hand, but held back. "I'm proud of you."

"How can you be after I hid this for years? I might not have even come forward now if Wade hadn't been shot."

"With the potential consequences, it takes a lot of courage to reveal what you saw."

He gave a half-hearted smile. "Let's just move on and do this."

Malone fixed her focus on Ethan. "The first thing I need to do is contact local law enforcement on your behalf and tell them you have a statement of importance concerning an unrelated crime. Do I have your permission to do that?"

"Yes, please." He sounded almost eager now.

Malone stood. "Then I'll make that call and set up a time for an interview with the detective when I'm available."

Ethan frowned. "What about Texas law enforcement?"

"I'm sure the Portland lieutenant will contact the detective down there, and they'll probably want to interview you too. Maybe just a video interview, but they might send someone who's familiar with the original investigation to interview you in person. Or a statement from the Portland detective might be sufficient. That said, all of this could change depending on whether we can prove Wade killed Neil or not."

"I don't care what happens to me now," Ethan said. "Just get the ball rolling so Neil's parents won't have to wonder another day what happened to their boy."

12

Grady was losing patience in the detention center's waiting area. What was taking them so long just to introduce Malone to Ethan? They should've been out of there in no time.

He got up to pace and stepped over the checkerboard tile floor and past the long glass wall and video visiting machines mounted on the other wall. He pivoted and returned to the bench seating attached to the wall.

"Dude," Drake said on one of Grady's passes. "Now you're making me nervous, and there's nothing to be nervous about."

"It shouldn't take this long."

"Agreed, but you're letting your emotions get to you."

Grady stared down on Drake.

"You've got it bad for Ainslie, and I think you're the only one who can't see it."

Grady started to reply but his phone rang. Seeing Coop's name, he answered. "You find Wade?"

"Sort of. Though we don't have eyes on him yet, we're pretty sure he's holed up in a dive week-by-week apartment rental near the airport. We can't confirm he's in there without putting him on alert. Figure if he's not there now he's coming back, so Jackson's on the room, and I'm headed back to your place to get some shuteye."

"Good work." Grady hoped this surveillance would produce the lead they needed.

"You want regular reports?" Coop asked. "Or should I just let you know if something suspicious occurs?"

"Give me a heads-up when you get eyes on him, but then I only need to hear about suspicious activities. As long as you keep him in sight, that is. He skates, I want to know."

"He's not going to skate."

"Be sure to keep Blake in the loop, too." Grady disconnected the call, but before he could stow his phone, it rang in his hand. He saw the unknown number but quickly answered as it could be related to their investigation. "Grady Houston."

"Hi, this is...um...Jayla's mom." The woman sounded nervous. "She said you wanted to talk to me."

"I do, Mrs..."

"Ms. Upson. Not married. But please, it's just Heidi."

He liked her easygoing attitude. Maybe that meant she would be forthcoming. "Thanks for calling me, Heidi. I'm investigating the shooting at Ethan Duncan's house."

"Yeah, the guy who shot someone out front. Terrible thing."

"Allegedly shot someone," Grady clarified. "Were you home that night?"

"Yeah. Yeah. Sure. But I was in bed. Sound asleep and didn't hear or see a thing."

He was struck by how fast she denied any knowledge of the event before he asked, as if she'd been practicing that line. "You sure? Not even a sound?"

"Nope. Nada. I work two jobs. When I hit the hay, I zonk out and don't wake up for anything."

"And Jayla? Was she home, too?"

"Sure. Of course. It was late. She was sleeping, too."

Memories of his uncle hit Grady, and he stopped by the window to look over the busy street and clear his head. "I'm sorry for asking this, but if you're such a sound sleeper, how can you be sure Jayla was in bed, too?"

"Well, I...I guess I can't, but she said she was, and my girl doesn't lie." Her adamant tone snapped through the phone. "We might live in a dump in a rotten part of town right now, thanks to her deadbeat dad bailing on us, but we have our standards and morals. Lying is something I don't tolerate."

"I can totally respect that," he said, but he couldn't quit thinking about when he was a kid. "Is it possible she's lying to protect herself? I got the feeling when we talked to her that she might know something but was afraid to say anything."

The call fell silent for a long uncomfortable moment. "You mean like she saw the shooter, and he might come after her if she told on him?"

"Exactly. And that would be understandable, right? She's terrified, and so she clammed up."

"Hmm, well, I don't think so, but I can talk to her about it."

"Would you?" he asked, encouraged that she would even consider it. "And then get back to me?"

"Yeah, sure. I can do that. When I get a chance."

No. That wouldn't do. "Can you try to make it a priority? An innocent man is sitting behind bars, and the real suspect is running free and could strike again."

"Fine." She sighed. "Maybe tonight if she's up when I get off work."

"Thank you," he said and meant it. "I also wanted to ask about your doorbell. Might it have recorded the shooting?"

"Recorded it? Gee. I don't know. I don't pay attention to

that. Jayla's dad installed it when he lived with us. He had it set up on his phone. As far as I know, we don't even have access to it. I'd take it down, but I figure it makes people think we can see them and protects Jayla better."

Grady stifled his disappointment. "Can you give me your ex's contact info?"

"Sure. His name is Stan." She rattled off a phone number, and Grady committed it to memory.

Grady really should just leave things at that, but he couldn't. "Before we hang up, I wanted to mention that it wasn't safe for Jayla to answer the door when we came by."

"Yeah, I already let her have it for that. She said you and the lady looked okay—whatever that means—but I reminded her never to answer the door." She sighed. "Look. I gotta get back to it before they fire me. I'll let you know what Jayla says." She ended the call.

A hint of hope took hold in Grady's heart. Sure, he could be all wrong about Jayla—projecting his own past onto this investigation—but, if he was right, they had an eye witness to the shooting, and this girl could provide testimony to free Ethan. Problem was, Grady didn't know if he had the heart to push the girl. He sure wouldn't have wanted anyone to grill him back in the day. The doorbell video would be the easier option, and, if in fact the video did exist, an even better option than eye witness testimony.

He dialed Stan Zimmerman, but the call went straight to voicemail. Grady left a message and strode across the room, willing the door to open. When it finally did, Ainslie came rushing toward him, her gaze troubled.

Drake shot to his feet, his concerned expression mimicking the feelings swimming in Grady's gut.

"Where's Malone?" Grady asked.

"Still inside with Ethan. We have to get back to the center immediately." Ainslie grabbed Grady's arm and started for the door. "I'll tell you why once we get in the truck."

"Hold up." Grady planted his feet, bringing her to a stop. "We can't throw caution to the wind. We still need to be aware of our surroundings."

"Right," she said, but glanced at the door as if she might still bolt.

Grady looked at Drake. "Would you mind checking the area out front?"

"Glad to." Drake turned to leave.

"Wait." She stepped in front of him. "Before you go, I need a favor. Wade Eggen has been arrested before, and we need his DNA report."

Drake furrowed his forehead. "If they took and processed his sample at arrest, I can get a report. But that's a big if, and even then, I can't share it with you."

Ainslie frowned. "Can you at least confirm that his DNA is on file so we don't waste time requesting it if it doesn't exist?"

"That I can do." He gave a tight smile. "I'll make a call on the way to the center. Should have an answer for you by the time we get there."

"Perfect." She flashed a shining smile. "And thanks."

Drake departed through the large glass doors to the two-story lobby. Thankfully, Ainslie remained at Grady's side.

"What happened in there?" he asked, not wanting to wait until they were in the truck.

She stepped closer to him, and when she looked up at him, tears wetted her eyes. *Wow.* Whatever happened was big. Mega big.

She moved closer and lowered her voice. "When Ethan was eleven, he witnessed Wade Eggen murder one of their classmates. Ethan didn't report Wade to the police."

No. No way. Ethan was just like him. They'd both held back the truth.

The blood drained from Grady's head, and a roaring sound started in his ears. He thought he might lose it but swallowed to remain calm enough to keep watch for Ainslie's safety.

"I can't believe he didn't report it." She twisted her hands together, a sour look on her face. "I mean, he had a reason. Wade said he would kill me and Mom if Ethan said anything. And Wade's kept up the threats over the years. Most recently coming here because a detective in Texas reopened the investigation. But we both know Ethan could've found a way to turn Wade in. If Wade had been arrested, then he couldn't have gotten to Ethan from prison."

She let out a long sigh. "He's probably ruined his life over keeping this secret. It's eating away at him. Likely the reason for his drug issues."

Grady stared out the window. After all, what could he say? He knew exactly how Ethan had ruined his life. The recriminations. The fear of the secret coming to light and the fear of going to prison. The pain of knowing someone would have closure if only he'd said something. How they'd suffered from such a secret. And now—oh, man—he knew how Ainslie would react if he ever shared his past with her. If she couldn't understand how her brother—someone she'd loved for years—could do such a thing, how would she ever understand Grady's motives?

And yet, just standing next to her made him want to call the county sheriff back home and report that his uncle had killed a vagrant in a hit-and-run accident. The investigation had gone cold, and no one had ever been charged. But Grady had seen Uncle Tommy in his body shop trying to cover it up by fixing his vehicle, and Grady knew in his heart that Tommy had hit the vagrant and killed him.

Drake marched back to the door and waved them on.

Grady swallowed the need to confess, like he'd done so many times over the years, and opened the door. "Keep your eyes open for any threats."

Grady forced his mind back to his protection duties, and he didn't take a deep breath until he was cruising on the highway toward the center and was certain no one other than Drake was tailing them.

"Malone is working on notifying the detective in Texas," Ainslie said, oblivious to the sick feeling swimming in Grady's gut. "Ethan told me where he thought the body was buried, so they should be able to recover the remains. Hopefully, they'll also locate enough evidence to pin the murder on Wade."

Grady hoped so, too, but... "I'm confused as to how you think this might help Ethan. Doesn't it just give him a motive to want to kill Wade to get him off his back?"

"Yes, but if we can link Wade to the murder, we could discredit him as a witness at the very least. Then, maybe when he's arrested, he'll even admit that Ethan didn't shoot him."

"Which is why you want his DNA. To prove he killed this other kid."

"Exactly."

Okay, *this* Grady could help with. "We should have Kelsey and Sierra offer to recover the remains. We stand a better chance of locating evidence that way, and they can bring the bones back to the center for a thorough analysis."

She shot him a questioning look. "Do you think the detective will agree to their help?"

He shrugged. "Is the county you're from very large?"

"Covers a lot of land, but population is sparse."

"So the sheriff's department wouldn't have an anthropologist on staff and would have to find someone," he said. "Depending on state resources, that could be pricey. With the way law enforcement is strapped for cash, I'd think they'd jump at the chance to have free help from top experts in the country who would fly there at a moment's notice."

She nibbled on her lip. "Kelsey and Sierra would do this?"

"Of course."

"And at a moment's notice? You're exaggerating, right? I mean, we don't have an airplane hiding at the center that I don't know about." A wry smile crossed her face.

"Nick has a friend who owns a small jet. He usually lets us use it."

Her eyes widened. "Really?"

"Really."

She shook her head. "I've worked for Veritas for months, and I still don't know all the amazing things we can do."

"You're about to find out." He tapped the dashboard screen to connect a call to Nick.

"Yo, man." Nick's enthusiastic tone burst through the truck's speakers. "What's up?"

"Can you call Oren to ask if we can use his plane? Ainslie, Kelsey, Sierra, and I need to fly to Texas ASAP. We have a body to recover and could potentially clear Ethan's name."

Ainslie had been down in the Osteology Unit in the basement before—been to the room with at least one stainless steel table holding a human skeleton laid out in correct form. One that often was missing bones. Despite huge exhaust fans, there was always a strong odor emanating from the room where Kelsey boiled bones to clean them. But never had the visit been personally important like this one. So important that Ainslie's heart was beating harder than normal.

Grady held the door for her, and she stepped into the lab.

Kelsey looked up, a small drone in her hand. "Oh, good. I was just checking the battery, and then we can go."

Ainslie had never seen or heard about Kelsey using such equipment and couldn't imagine how she might employ it in her job. "You use a drone?"

Kelsey nodded. "I'm part of a new study using near infrared imaging to detect bodies above and below the ground."

Ainslie was constantly surprised at the new technology these partners employed. "That sounds fascinating."

"It's amazing actually, and I'll tell you more about it once we get going." She zipped the case and patted the hard plastic. "I'll carry this baby. If you two will roll out the carts with the other equipment, we can go meet Sierra at the SUV."

Kelsey propped open the door, and Ainslie wheeled one of the three-tiered stainless steel carts into the hallway, Grady the other. A squeaky wheel on his cart grated on her already fried nerves all the way to the elevator. As Kelsey and Grady chatted about Oren coming through and offering his plane that very afternoon, Ainslie focused on deep breathing and watching the numbers above the door climb.

Her head was spinning from the race to get ready to leave town. The minute they'd gotten the okay on the plane, Malone offered Kelsey's services to the Texas detective investigating Neil's death. Detective Paulson readily accepted the help, and the team made plans to depart. The trip was good news for sure. They could finally have something on Wade, and he could be arrested. Maybe, anyway. Unfortunately,

Drake discovered that Wade didn't have DNA on file from his earlier prison stay, so proving his guilt would be harder and take longer.

The elevator dinged on the third floor of the parking garage, and they piled out to find Sierra waiting by one of the center's vans. Her assistant, Chad, sat in the driver seat, hooking up his phone to the infotainment system for the drive to the airport.

"Let me help." Sierra grabbed one end of Ainslie's cart and started packing items in the van alongside her equipment.

The four of them quickly got things loaded, and Sierra jumped in next to Chad. Kelsey sat in the back and Ainslie was sandwiched between her and Grady who was making the trip in case the gunshot Ethan heard was related to Neil's death and they recovered a bullet from the grave. As Chad headed out of the parking garage, Ainslie was ultimately aware of every touch point of his body on her leg. So much so that she shifted toward Kelsey. That earned her a raise of Kelsey's and Grady's eyebrows.

"Thank you for letting me come along," Ainslie said to shift the focus away from her awkward movements. "I might not be able to have anything to do with the recovery due to my connection to Ethan, but thanks for letting me be there anyway."

Sierra looked over her shoulder. "Hey, if we were in your shoes, we'd want to do the same thing. We totally understand."

"Trust us on that one," Kelsey said emphatically.

Ainslie had heard rumors of Kelsey having gone through a difficult time where her stepson and she were in imminent danger, but Ainslie didn't know the details.

"Plus you're familiar with the town and the people," Sierra said. "That might come in real handy."

Sierra shifted even more. "Did Detective Paulson question if Ethan was potentially involved in the murder?"

"He did." Ainslie's stomach tightened on the thought.

"You think they'll pursue charges?" Kelsey asked.

Ainslie shrugged. "Malone was only able to talk to Paulson, not the sheriff. He's been on a fishing trip, and Paulson is trying to track him down."

Grady looked at her. "I'm guessing he'll want to cut his trip short for something this important."

"You would think so, but Paulson said he hadn't even told the sheriff that he was looking into the murder. He's new to the job and thought if he poked around in his free time he might solve the cold case and impress the sheriff."

Grady arched an eyebrow. "Not sure the sheriff's gonna be too happy about that."

"Why's that?" Ainslie asked.

"Most sheriffs I know are control freaks and don't like their minions going off in their own direction."

Could Grady be right? "I know him. The sheriff, that is. His name is Matt Murphy. We went to school together. He was the quarterback and all-star player. Mr. Squeaky Clean. I can totally see him going into law enforcement and easily getting elected sheriff."

That brought a frown from Grady. "Did you and Ethan get along with him in school?"

"Get along?" She tipped her head as memories played in her brain. "He would probably have to know I existed to get along with him. We didn't exactly run in the same circles. He knew Ethan from football, but they weren't friends or anything like that."

"What's your gut say about the sheriff pressing charges against Ethan?" Sierra asked.

Ainslie looked at her boss. "I honestly don't know. I

mean, he could be the same guy I knew or could've totally changed, right?"

"People do change," Grady said. "But in my experience, not a whole lot."

Ainslie thought his statement held a deeper meaning, but she wasn't about to ask questions and draw them into a personal discussion. Better to stick with the investigation. "Malone *did* say Detective Paulson wanted a cooperative witness more than anything. Unless evidence we uncover shows Ethan is complicit in the murder, Paulson won't push that line of questioning."

Grady met and held her gaze. "Still, that's got to be worrying you."

He didn't know the half of it. "I'm really trying to trust God, you know? Wish I was doing a better job of it. I keep thinking I've laid all of this down, and then I pick the worry back up."

"That's understandable." Kelsey squeezed her hand. "We're all still praying. Please know that."

"That's the best help you can give me." Ainslie smiled at the sweet woman. "I have to say that I thought God had tested me in life so many times before, but this is besting anything else, even losing my mom and my dad disappearing on us. I think it's hitting harder because Ethan's the only family I have left."

"God will get you through this." Grady took her hand.

The warmth of his touch, the feel of his skin, the personal connection, sent a powerful shock of awareness through her. She wanted to jerk her hand free, but didn't. She didn't want to make him think she'd changed her mind about a relationship. Leading him on wouldn't be fair to him. But he wasn't being romantic. He was offering his support as a compassionate Christian, and she would never turn down that kind of consideration.

She relaxed, took a breath, and smiled at him. "Thank you."

He held her gaze, mining for something deeper. "I'm only speaking the truth."

"I know, but it still means a lot to me." She squeezed his hand and released it before she did or said something else. She instantly felt alone again and closed her eyes to pray before she said something to make him think the moment had been more than accepting his support.

God, is this You putting Grady in my life when I can't do this alone? Are You showing me I might need him even after this difficult time ends? Or is he just here for the moment? Your love in human form when it's most needed? Or am I going to lose Ethan to prison, and You've put Grady here to help me pick up the pieces?

She couldn't think that way. She needed to be confident that this amazing team would help clear Ethan's name. And maybe now that his secret was out, he would be able to kick his drug habit once and for all and have the wonderful life that she'd always wished for him.

Please, God. Oh, please.

13

Grady had come along to the small town about an hour north of Houston to look for a boy who had been murdered. A tough assignment. One he would support for Ainslie. For Ethan. But surprisingly, as Grady walked through the tiny park toward the lake with his partners and Ainslie, he was able to relax for the first time since he'd entered Ainslie's house the night of the swatting incident.

She was safe here in Texas. Mostly. He wouldn't let his guard down completely, but whoever was trying to kill her couldn't possibly have followed them. He supposed Wade could alert someone to hurt her in Texas, but Wade wouldn't likely know they'd traveled to Greenburg unless someone in the sheriff's department let it slip and the small-town grapevine took hold. It would eventually be the talk of the town, but not that quickly.

A strong southerly wind carrying heat and dust pummeled them as they reached the two khaki uniformed deputies standing at the mouth of a path near soaring red oak trees. A similarly uniformed sheriff who Grady put in his mid-thirties unfolded his tall muscular body from an SUV parked at the path. He clapped a broadbrimmed hat over thick dark hair and stared at them. Despite the sweltering temperatures, all three officers wore long sleeves, and Grady didn't know how they handled it.

The sheriff stepped across the dusty ground with purpose in his stride. He hooked a thumb behind a large gold Texas-shaped belt buckle and took a wide stance as if defending his territory. "So you must be the dream team."

Sarcasm rumbled through his deep tone, and a smirk found its way to his face.

Okay, so it was going to be like that. Murphy's attitude didn't bode well for their visit, but Grady and his partners were professionals and exchanged introductions.

Murphy pinned his intense focus on Ainslie. "Surprised to see you here, Ainslie. I didn't know you'd become a forensic photographer."

She cocked her head, carefully watching Murphy. For a moment, Grady thought she might not answer. "Why would you when I've been gone for so many years? I'm sure there're a lot of things we don't know about each other."

He pressed his lips together in a sour look. "Still, I often hear back on what our former classmates are up to."

"I wasn't very plugged in with our class." She paused as if thinking about what to say next. "You wouldn't likely even know my name if Ethan hadn't decided to come forward."

Murphy scratched his chin, his sleeve lifting and revealing the edge of a tattoo as he eyed her.

"Oh, come on," she said. "I was invisible in high school."

The conversation was starting to get too personal, and Grady wanted to protect Ainslie from any pain this guy might inflict.

"So," Grady said, "we should get to work."

Murphy's hands tightened on the buckle, and he widened his stance. "Since I was on vacation when y'all arranged this operation, it got rushed before I could evaluate our options. Before you set foot in these woods, we discuss how this's all going to go down."

"I'm sorry you were out of the loop." Kelsey adjusted her olive green sunhat, which she'd paired with khaki shorts and a white T-shirt. "We're only here to offer our support and work within your structure."

Murphy locked gazes with her. "That's good then, because I'm in charge here."

Sierra cleared her throat, taking Murphy's attention. "We work with law enforcement all the time, and we expected nothing less."

Murphy raised his eyebrows and stood quietly. Seemed he'd expected an argument and didn't know what to do with their cooperation. "Good. Good. Glad you understand me. Next I want to clarify the role of my deputies. My men aren't some sort of glorified excavation crew who're gonna waste their time digging holes for you all to look for this boy's body."

"Oh, don't worry." Kelsey raised up on her tiptoes and rocked on her feet. "Your men won't have to lift a finger. I'll be doing the digging. And I should be able to narrow down the location without much difficulty."

Murphy pursed his lips. "And just how are you gonna do that?"

"I'll first deploy a drone that uses infrared imaging to detect bodies. It works both above and below the ground." A gleam of excitement brightened her gaze. "And if for some reason the body has been moved, the technology can also find where a corpse had been buried and removed up to two years after the removal."

"You're serious?" Murphy tilted his hat back and focused a penetrating stare on Kelsey. "You're not just yanking my chain?"

"I am *very* serious." Kelsey squinted up at him and didn't

seem the least bit intimidated. "Without the drone I can walk right by a clandestine body and not realize it's there. The drone doubles my chance of finding it, and once the technology is deployed, it's really going to revolutionize searches."

"Still sounds pretty unbelievable to me." Murphy frowned. "Can't imagine how it can work."

Kelsey lifted her shoulders. She was starting to get irritated at being questioned, and Grady didn't blame her one bit.

She inhaled deeply and let the breath out slowly. "As bodies decay, they release carbon and nitrogen into the soil. That decreases the amount of light the soil reflects. Initially, the flood of chemicals kills plants. That changes as it disperses into the soil around the body and becomes a fertilizer that reflects a ton of light. The drone's near infrared imaging can detect those light reflections."

"What happens after you launch the drone?" the sheriff asked, honestly seeming interested now.

"Once I have a hit, I use ground penetrating radar to confirm. It's only then that I start digging. So you see, it's a precise process, and we won't need to be digging holes all over the place."

Murphy cocked an eyebrow. "What are your expectations of my department?"

"Once the grave is located, I need you to cordon off the scene and keep the public away." She smiled at him. "Something I know you and your department are expert at handling."

Grady loved how she made a rather small task seem important to stroke the sheriff's obvious ego.

He gave a sharp nod. "Okay, we'll proceed right up to the digging part, when I'll want to evaluate the logistics of the area. These woods are open from all directions, and it wouldn't do to have looky-loos."

"If things are still the same as when I lived here," Ainslie said, "the locals don't want to step foot in these woods."

"Yeah, most people are still spooked by the old rumors."

"What rumors?" Sierra asked before Grady could pose the same question.

"Supposedly a family was murdered and buried back here, and they haunt the place." Murphy rolled his eyes. "But that's never been proved."

"Proof or not," Ainslie said, "most folks avoid the woods at all costs."

"Except when you're dared as a kid." Murphy's lip curled. "And depending on how brave you are, you make a quick dash to the other side. Which is why Wade was able to kill and bury someone there and get away with it."

Grady understood how the locals might react this way, but law enforcement was held to a higher standard. "Surely, the sheriff at the time searched the area."

"Yeah, sure. But if I had to guess, they didn't spend a lot of time on it," Murphy said. "Neil was a real chicken. Afraid of his own shadow. I doubt anyone thought he would go into the woods."

Grady didn't like the disparaging tone the sheriff used when describing the deceased boy, but there was nothing Grady could do about it other than to move them along. "So are we cleared to get that drone in the air, then?"

Murphy looked at him long and hard and rubbed a hand over his wide jaw. "Let me update my men, and I'll let you know when you can go for it." He ran his gaze from person to person, likely trying to reinforce his large-and-in-charge presence, then strode to his men, his worn cowboy boots leaving puffs of dry Texas dust in his wake.

"Control freak much?" Sierra rolled her eyes, adjusted

her tan sunhat, and started back for the SUV. She was dressed much like Kelsey and a similar height, allowing her to keep up with Kelsey's long strides.

They all made quick work of carrying their supplies to the path entrance, but Murphy stood near his vehicle holding a phone conversation and keeping them waiting.

As a bead of sweat trickled down Grady's back, he tipped his head at the sheriff. "A power play no doubt."

"He always did like to be in charge," Ainslie said, a frown in her voice. "And adored."

He shifted his stance and locked his piercing focus on them as if he knew they were talking about him. He ended his call and marched over, his large footfalls sounding hollow on the packed earth.

He nodded toward the park where a group of onlookers had gathered. "We're starting to draw attention. You're not to utter a word to these folks or the press. I'm the only one who will talk to them."

"Understood," Kelsey said, but Grady knew she had never intended to speak to the press. None of them would even consider it.

Murphy stepped back, giving them access to the path. "Then let's proceed."

Kelsey slung on her backpack and launched the drone. The whirring motor spiraled the device into the sky. Grady watched for a moment but then checked Ainslie out. She was winding up her long silky ponytail. Her arms raised overhead drew up her T-shirt, and he caught a look at an inch of bare skin above her shorts. His thoughts took a less than professional turn, and he shook his head to erase them.

The sheriff moved over to Kelsey. "Won't the tree canopy be a problem?"

"It'll take some skilled flying, but I've got it." She let the drone hover and glanced at Grady. "Can you bring the blue bin?"

"Sure thing." He smiled at her, hoping to ease some of the tension in her expression.

She started forward, and Murphy followed, trailing her like a hunting dog after prey.

Grady picked up the heavy tote and fell into step with Ainslie.

"This is surreal," she said, her Texas accent thicker since she'd come back home. "I always arrive at a crime scene *after* the scene has been identified. I've never participated in finding it."

"Yeah, me neither," Grady said, really visualizing for the first time what they were about to do. "I avoid scenes whenever possible. Especially murder scenes. Brings back bad memories from Delta."

"I am so thankful there are people like you who are willing to serve. So thank you for that."

If he didn't have a bin in hand, he would wave off her thanks. "And I commend people who handle crime scenes. Especially photographers like you. I don't know how you focus in on the gruesome details."

"Compartmentalize," she said quickly. "Put the job in one folder, my personal life in another, and never let them mix."

He'd never been able to do that with the horrible things he'd seen in the army. They still surfaced when he least expected it. "And that works for you?"

"Most of the time." She tilted her head as if deciding to go on or not. "A few things linger. At times, I have to work hard not to think about them. They involve babies and young children." She shook her head, and her breathing sped up. "You can't even believe the things that happened to these poor kids. It almost makes me not want to have children."

The sadness in her tone cut him to the quick, and he refused to let his mind go to the horrors she'd seen. "Almost?"

"Oh, I still want kids." She curled her hands into tight fists. "But you better believe I'll be protective."

"Me too," he said without thinking. "But I'd have to get married to have a family. That's just not in the cards for me."

She quirked an eyebrow. "Why are you still single? I mean, you're good-looking. Successful. Have a good job. You're reliable. Dependable. Fun to be with. A woman should've snapped you up by now for sure."

He loved hearing her describe how she saw him. "Is that so?"

Her face flushed red. "Guess I told you what I think about you, huh?"

He slowed to fall back behind the others and face her, locking gazes. "I think you're pretty terrific, too. And gorgeous."

A sudden rush of emotion darkened her stunning chestnut eyes. His feet stuttered to a halt, and he couldn't look away. The world seemed to stop and everything—everyone—but Ainslie disappeared. He wanted to kiss her. Now. Right here. In front of the sheriff, two of his deputies, and Grady's partners. And he knew it would be amazing. It would consume them both.

"Got something!" Kelsey's excited tone broke through his brain fog.

Ainslie gasped and snapped her focus away, releasing him from her hold.

He nodded at Kelsey. "We should go see."

"Yes," Ainslie got out on a halting breath and then gulped in air as if it were in short supply instead of the steady wind blowing steamy air. "We need to stay away from any personal discussions and keep things professional."

"Agreed," he said, but he didn't know how he was going to accomplish that. He would try. For Ainslie's sake. For Ethan's sake. For his own sake, too. Because not only would he be leading her on, something he didn't want to do, but also he was in for a world of hurt if he continued down this path with her.

They slowly tramped through the woods, fallen leaves crunching underfoot in the dry spring weather. The canopy above brought dappled shade, helping with the sheen of perspiration forming above his lip and coating his back in the eighty-plus degree weather. Today would be considered a hot day in Portland, and the fifty percent humidity didn't help.

Nearly thirty minutes of hiking later, Kelsey brought the drone in for a landing, the hum winding down and stilling. Sierra joined her, camera at the ready, and Grady thankfully set down the heavy tote.

The sheriff planted his large feet in front of Kelsey. "You sure this is the place, little lady?"

Kelsey bristled at the sheriff's comment, but Grady knew she wouldn't say anything. As a beautiful, willowy woman who frequently dressed in very feminine clothing while working in the law enforcement field, she often received sexist comments, and she'd learned to ignore them.

"I'm sure." She opened her backpack and removed a trowel. "I need your deputies to cordon off the park entrances, and I'll set the inner perimeter then get started on the dig."

He pointed at her hand and cracked a smile. "Gonna take you a good long time to get that grave dug with such an itty bitty shovel."

"Indeed," she said, not sounding put out at all. "Likely

all night. Or even longer. All depends on what I find. But digging with a handheld trowel and brushes is essential so I don't damage any of the bones or disturb evidence."

"All night?" He narrowed his gaze. "I'd like to move this along. Maybe my men can help after all."

She looked up at him with a tight smile. "Thank you for your consideration, but no. I have a process to follow, starting with removing the soil layer by layer so I can sample each layer and then put it on a tarp to be screened for evidence."

"Layer by layer?" Murphy took off his hat and swiped a handkerchief over his forehead. "Not sure what you mean by that."

"Soil is made up of layers or horizons," she explained, but Grady could tell her patience was growing thin. "I won't bore you with the details. Just know a grave will have distinct layers on the edges but the person who dug the grave will have mixed up the fill soil."

"She-ooot." He scratched his head. "Don't know why any of this matters."

Her patience finally giving out, Kelsey sucked in a sharp breath and planted her hands on her hips. "First, these layers will show me the edges of the grave so I don't miss any evidence. And then, the soil is as unique as a finger-print. If we fail to locate sufficient evidence to convict the killer, a soil scientist can compare the soil to the shovel or any soil found on a potential suspect's shoes, in his car, his house, et cetera, and place them not only on this property but specifically in this grave."

He settled his hat back on his head. "Not likely we're gonna find any evidence at the suspect's place after all these years."

"I've had it happen." She jerked her thumb over her shoulder. "Now if you'll excuse me, I have work to do."

14

Ainslie watched Kelsey pound stakes into the four corners of the grave and run string to outline the grave while Sierra snapped photo after photo of overall shots. Ainslie's fingers itched to get out her camera and take over for Sierra. To frame the photos just so, making sure the picture not only caught evidence artifacts but put the pictures in scale for the jury so they knew exactly what they were looking at.

But Sierra had everything under control. She and Kelsey moved as if in a ballet, staying out of each other's way but remaining close and doing their jobs without talking.

"They're something to watch." Grady joined her. "The way they know what to do without a word."

She glanced up at him. "I was just thinking the same thing. How long have they worked together?"

"It's a little over six years now since we opened the center." His chest puffed out.

"You all really started something special," she said with conviction. "I'm honored to be a part of it."

"And we're glad to have you. Especially Sierra. She has exacting standards, and she sings your praises all the time. Means you're exceptional at your job." His proud tone was how she'd often imagined her parents might've sounded if they'd bothered to be proud of her. His consideration warmed her heart clean through.

She opened her mouth to reply, but it would take them into the personal realm again, so she snapped it closed. The air between them filled with tension.

He ran a hand over his hair and clamped it on the back of his neck. "I should ask if there's something I can do to help."

Good idea. If... "I wish I could, too, but the conflict of interest keeps me on the sidelines."

His phone rang, and he dug it from his cargo pocket. "It's Jackson." He swiped the call to connect. "Hey, man. Ainslie's with me. I'm gonna put you on speaker so she can hear." He tapped his screen and stepped so close that she could smell the sunscreen he'd lathered on his face.

"Coop said you wanted to know when I got eyes on Eggen," Jackson said. "He emerged from his apartment looking hungover and wobbly. Went across the street to grab food and then back to the room."

"I'm glad you called." Grady shared the latest information about Wade murdering Neil.

"Murder, huh?" Jackson said.

"Since this happened back in his juvie days, I don't know if it makes him more dangerous than he already was, but you should be aware that he's capable of killing someone."

"Good to know," Jackson said, not sounding particularly fazed by the news. "I'll update Coop."

"Let me know if Wade gets up to anything." Grady ended the call.

Ainslie was again struck with the quality of partners that the Veritas team worked with. "I love how connected you all are. It's amazing."

"And you haven't seen the half of it." Shoving his phone

into his pocket, Grady grinned and nodded at Kelsey and Sierra. "Time to check in."

He stepped over to the edge of the grave, where Kelsey knelt on the far end. "Anything I can do to help?"

She swiped the back of her hand over her dirt-smudged forehead. She talked through her next steps with Grady, and Sierra stopped to look up at him.

Ainslie remained on the sidelines, listening to their conversation. Even though she knew the three of them, she felt like an outsider. Like an employee. No matter how many times they'd told her she was family, she kept looking for reasons why she shouldn't be. Couldn't be. Her past being the chief among them.

She'd taken several psychology classes in college, and was fascinated with what made people do what they did. Especially her dad. How could he one day just decide he didn't want to be a dad anymore and bail on them? She'd never come up with an answer, but she continued to search. Her past colored the way she looked at things today. Psychologists used the fancy term confirmation bias. A person believed something, either true or not, and then looked for things in everyday life to confirm the belief and make decisions based on that.

So, seeing herself as less than others from the whole charity thing as a kid, she subconsciously set out to prove it. Like thinking she wasn't good enough to be part of the Veritas partners' family, even though they'd been nothing but welcoming and encouraging. She really needed to change how she saw herself. To see herself like Jesus did. With love. Love saw perfection, not worthlessness, despite how people had made her feel growing up. And then she had to remember that she was chosen. Forgiven. Saved. Special. Not less-than. Not insignificant.

Tears formed in her eyes, and she swallowed them away

to bring her mind back to the task at hand, where it needed to stay. She could think about all of this later when she was alone with her treacherous thoughts.

Kelsey sighed and looked at Grady. "We could use some water. Gatorade, too. Think you can find a cooler and stock up?"

"Absolutely."

Sierra looked at Ainslie. "Take Ainslie with you. She knows the town."

"That was *so* not subtle." Grady didn't sound mad at Sierra exactly, just a bit annoyed.

Sierra grinned. "If I know her, and I think I do, she's struggling to find something useful to do."

Sierra was right. Ainslie wished she had a task right about now. But preferably one without Grady attached to it.

"Okay," he said, maybe thinking it made sense. "We'll be back soon."

He started back her way, and she enjoyed the way he strode so confidently in his tactical pants and combat boots. His gray T-shirt was plastered against his broad chest, giving her a better look at his muscular build. She could easily imagine him holding her, his strong arms wrapped around her. She liked the idea. Way too much.

He stopped in front of her, planting his boots in the dust. "We need to find a place to buy a cooler and grab some cold drinks."

"There's a hardware store just down the road where we can grab a cooler and a convenience store right past it."

He raised the yellow crime scene tape so she could duck under. She led the way back through the woods she'd never played in as a kid. Not because she believed the story. She didn't. But because she hadn't had friends to play with. Her fault. She always had her nose stuck in a book to avoid interacting with hurtful people.

She stepped into the park clearing, where Matt stood by his vehicle. Onlookers surrounded him. Memories of high school rushed back. She'd been a sophomore when Matt was a senior and quarterback. He could do no wrong in anyone's eyes, but he had a terrible habit of picking on others. Not a bully exactly, but subtly sending teasing barbs that held just enough truth to draw blood.

"Nothing to see here folks. Go on home." He waved at them, but they remained. "I mean it, folks. Don't make me haul you in."

"But we heard you finally found Neil Orr's body," a skinny woman in a tank top said.

"You know better than to put any stock in the town's grapevine."

Ainslie noticed he didn't actually answer the question. A hallmark of an experienced law enforcement officer with all the political savvy his elected position required.

He planted his hand on his sidearm and drew back shoulders that were even broader than they had been during his football days. "Now go on home, Velma."

The woman narrowed her eyes in a brown weather-beaten face and wiggled a finger at Grady and Ainslie. "Then who are those people?"

"Don't rightly see how that's any of your business." Matt hooked his thumbs in his belt. "Now get moving."

Grady unlocked the door of the rental SUV. "Do you know anyone in the crowd?"

Ainslie searched the faces, part of her hoping to recognize someone. The other part dreading it. "It's been too long."

She slid into the truck and caught him looking at her legs. Did he notice the pale white skin born of an Oregon winter where the people here in Texas were bronzed?

He snapped his gaze free and ran around the front of the

SUV. He climbed in and closed the door. "What's it like to be back here?"

"Honestly, I don't really feel like I'm back home. We raced from the airport straight out here, and things on the main drag have changed a lot in the time I've been gone. Especially since the casino opened a few years ago. There's even a Whataburger here now."

He gaped at her. "A what?"

She chuckled. "It's a regional burger place out of San Antonio."

"Never heard of them." He got the vehicle out of the parking lot and clicked on the air conditioning.

She adjusted the vents, and when the cool air washed over her body, she groaned. "Oh, man, this is heaven on earth."

"But you're from here."

"Doesn't mean I'm used to the heat anymore."

He swung onto the highway and rolled past the remnants of a forlorn looking old railcar, which had been turned into a restaurant and drive-in with a weathered pig on the side. It had once been the place where she dreamed of having enough money to eat.

"Back in the day, that was the only takeout diner." She stabbed her thumb in the direction of the place with a crumbled asphalt parking lot and abandoned drive-in parking spaces. "Porky's Diner."

Memories of her family heading home from a football game, the windows of their beater station wagon open, the smell of grilled burgers and onions wafting into the car. The sounds of her fellow high schoolers whooping it up outside. A crowd she didn't know very well. Not when she lived in the trailer park on the wrong side of town, and it took money to go to Porky's every week.

"Not that we could afford to get anything from there," she added without thinking.

Grady swung his head toward her, and, at his questioning look, she wished she hadn't said anything.

"We had lean times growing up," he said. "Nothing like you, I expect, but my parents had to get help from fellow farmers in the area. Many times. Everyone worked together when times were tough and shared crops, produce. Even meat and game."

She heard the love for his youth in his tone. "I always thought living on a ranch near here would be the perfect life. You'd always have your own food source. No food pantries. And you were far away from nosy busybodies in town."

"Farm living was great, but it wasn't perfect. Trust me. I couldn't wait to get away from it. Which is why I played football, hoping to get a scholarship. I wasn't good enough. So now I live vicariously through watching the game. I am an all-star at that." He laughed.

"So the sport isn't just a hobby to you then," she said as they neared the small hardware store. She remembered coming here with her father to buy supplies when she was a little kid. She pointed at the store. "Turn here."

He clicked on the blinker. "I've never given football much thought. It's just in my life. Has been forever."

"Kids in Texas start playing in preschool. Did you, too?"

He tightened his hands on the wheel, looking like she hit a nerve.

"I was nine. Started a year behind the others." He shoved the shifter into park with extra force.

She searched his face. "Something wrong?"

"Wrong?" He pulled out the keys. "Let's grab that cooler and get out of here."

She climbed out of the truck and trailed him across the grimy parking lot. She knew he was sidestepping her question. Something was bothering him about his early football days, which made little sense since he seemed to love the sport. A mystery, for sure. One she was compelled to investigate.

Grady set down their cooler with ice under a tall tree outside the crime scene tape about ten feet from the gravesite. Ainslie reached inside for a frosty bottle of water. Grady had shut down on her in the SUV, and she'd noticed. But he couldn't very well tell her he started playing football as an excuse not to hang out with Uncle Tommy anymore. And Grady wasn't about to lie to her. So the only answer was to shut his big mouth and ignore her questioning looks.

"So, you're like a hotshot weapons guy, huh?" Sheriff Murphy marched up to them. He eyed Grady, a hint of challenge in the guy's expression.

He might be pushing Grady, but it was better than pretending to ignore Ainslie's questioning glances. "Not sure I'd call myself a hotshot, but yes, I'm the weapons expert at the Veritas Center."

"Don't suppose you ever worked in law enforcement." That same challenge rode on his tone that Grady often got from law enforcement officers questioning his credentials. But this guy seemed a little over the top. Maybe compensating for something.

"Nope." Grady left it at that. If the sheriff had a chip on his shoulder, Grady wasn't going to come out on the top of any discussion with him, so what was the point of saying anything more?

His eyebrows went up toward the well-worn cowboy hat. "You into long guns?"

"Sure." Grady was glad for a question he didn't mind answering. "If it fires a bullet, I'm into it."

Murphy hooked his thumbs in his belt loops and cocked his head. "What's your take on those high priced optics?"

"Optics?"

"Yeah, I mean anyone who needs high priced optics isn't a real expert in my book." He started rocking on his boots. "A true expert can hit what he aims at with his superior marksmanship skills."

"And let me guess." Grady didn't at all try to hide his sarcasm now. "You're a real expert."

"Yeah, I've honed my skills. So no need for the pricey equipment. I can do the same job with less expensive equipment."

Grady had to bite his tongue not to respond. Murphy had no idea what he was talking about. Ainslie stood up and looked at him as if she really wanted to hear his answer. But there was no point in putting Murphy in his place and embarrassing him in front of Ainslie.

"If you'll excuse me, I need to get some water to Kelsey and Sierra." Grady pretended he didn't realize Ainslie was already taking out water bottles for the workers.

A snide grin slid across Murphy's face. "Yeah, I figured you couldn't dispute that."

Grady gritted his teeth, grabbed a sports drink for himself, and started for Sierra and Kelsey, who both looked wilted.

"You didn't answer him." Ainslie fell into step beside him. "But it looked like you were dying to say something."

"Oh, man, I was." He smiled at her. "He was wrong, but I didn't want to embarrass him."

"That was kind of you."

"Didn't see any point in it."

She stopped and turned to face him. "So tell me what

149

you would have said to him. That way you can get it out and let go of your frustration."

"It's pretty technical."

"That's okay. I'll pretend to understand." She wrinkled her freckled nose, looking like an adorable little imp.

He grinned at her. He really liked this woman. Way too much.

"Go ahead," she said. "I'm all ears."

He didn't have to be told again. "The less expensive optics —sights—that Murphy mentioned tend to have a larger dot measured by MOA—Minute Of Angle. That equals about one inch at one hundred yards. A cheaper sight could have a MOA of four or more while a more expensive sight will have either one or two, and with even higher prices comes even less MOA like one-half or less. So a one hundred yard target sighted in with a MOA of four could mean a miss by four inches. Which could mean missing the target altogether."

"You're right, super technical." She grinned again. "So what I heard is that you're more accurate with higher priced optics, and if Murphy used them, he would be more accurate at hitting his target."

"You got it. I guess I could've just said that." He chuckled.

"But then you wouldn't have explained it, and Murphy wouldn't have been schooled in optics."

He nodded. "Thanks for letting me get it out. You're right. It did help."

They shared a brief smile and moment, but Ainslie broke it off and started walking again. She stopped short of the actual grave. She would know not to let condensation from the bottles drip into the area where they were digging. She held up the water bottles. "Break time."

Kelsey stood, brushed off her knees, then ripped off her gloves. She'd removed the top layers of a rectangular area big enough to hold the body of a thirteen-year-old boy. On the near side, a skull protruded from the dirt.

"You found him." Grady's heart was heavy with the discovery.

She nodded. "Or at least I found a skull that preliminarily tells me belonged to a male."

"You can tell that from the little bit that we can see?" Ainslie held out the drinks.

"Yes, but the best way to determine sex is by looking at the pelvic bones, which are obviously not revealed yet." Kelsey took the water and cracked open the bottle. "But males tend to have larger skulls than females, and their eye sockets have a slightly blunter surface. They also have, on average, greater muscle development and more rugged muscle attachments. So this skull says a lot."

She took a long chug of the water.

Murphy trudged over and scowled at the grave. "Any way to tell if this is Neil?"

"Not yet," Kelsey said. "Ethan mentioned that Neil was strangled and that he heard a gunshot after the fact but didn't find any blood. The first thing I'll likely uncover that can give us a clue is the hyoid bone located in the anterior midline of his neck. If it's broken that would indicate strangulation. Next we should see his shirt."

"His shirt, after all these years?" Murphy asked.

"His parents said he was wearing polyester, and it takes a good twenty years to decompose."

Murphy's scowl deepened. "Neil's been missing for eighteen, so that fits the window."

Kelsey nodded. "There's a likelihood that it'll still be identifiable, and we can match it to pictures in his file."

Murphy gave a sharp nod. "Gotta love polyester."

Kelsey looked at the sheriff. "And if he had been shot,

and it wasn't a through and through, the bullet will be in the grave with him."

"I want to know the minute you find that if you do."

"I can do that. I'm assuming you either have or can get Neil's medical records."

"Got 'em in his file."

"Do you know if he sustained any broken bones?"

Murphy shrugged.

"He did," Ainslie said. "When we were in elementary school, he had a nasty compound fracture of his femur. I remember because he had a cast for a good long time."

Kelsey looked at the sheriff. "I'll need the X-rays from that break. It'll be the fastest way to officially ID him. Of course, DNA is the final test, but I'm confident in making an ID by comparing the femur I recover here to the X-ray."

"I'll head back to the office, and if we don't have the X-ray, I'll hunt it down." Murphy gestured at the grave. "How long is this gonna take?"

"A day. Maybe longer, but we'll work through the night." Kelsey took a deep breath, her nostrils flaring. "These parents have suffered long enough. Time to give them some closure."

"Agreed," Murphy said, for the first time not butting heads with someone.

"Have you talked to Mr. and Mrs. Orr yet?" Ainslie asked.

He nodded. "Just briefly to tell them they were gonna hear things on the grapevine and not to believe any of it. That I'd update them as soon as we know anything official."

Kelsey took another swig on the bottle then brushed the back of her hand against her forehead and looked at Grady. "Can you and Ainslie get the lights set up?"

He nodded.

"Okay, then" She capped the water bottle. "Time to get back to it and give those parents the answers they need."

"I'll grab the lights." Grady polished off his sports drink in a few gulps on the way to their SUV. Ainslie followed, and together they worked in silence to carry and position the large klieg lights so Kelsey and Sierra could continue working.

Which they did, through the night. Grady and Ainslie worked as minions, doing food and drink runs, and ensuring that Sierra and Kelsey took regular breaks. Grady and Ainslie took turns napping in the SUV to keep fresh.

When the morning sun glistened on the lake, Kelsey sat back on the apron surrounding the grave and stretched her back. "We have a complete skeleton. No bullets."

Sierra pointed her camera at the grave and took numerous pictures then lowered her camera and stared ahead.

The sheriff, Grady, and Ainslie silently joined them. They took a solemn moment, looking at the poor boy who lost his life way too young. His skeleton was intact, his clothing draped over the bones.

"Shirt matches," the sheriff said, sounding disappointed and relieved at the same time. "Any indication of how he was killed?"

"The hyoid bone is broken, as we suspected it would be," Kelsey replied.

"So strangulation, then?"

Kelsey faced the sheriff. "I'll have to examine all of the bones before making an official ruling. That's especially true since Ethan reported hearing that gunshot. However, the shirt appears to be intact with no sign of a bullet hole, and the skull didn't sustain a gunshot wound."

"And what about forensics?" Murphy asked. "Did you

find anything that would help us confirm Wade killed Neil or anything to point to someone else?"

Kelsey shook her head. "I'm afraid not. However, since Ethan described Neil struggling with Wade, it's possible that Neil scratched Wade, and we'll find DNA samples near the fingertips. I'll be extra careful to recover the soil in that area so Sierra can test it."

"And don't forget," Sierra said. "Ethan told us that Wade bit Neil, so we might have saliva on the shirt for DNA."

That almost perpetual scowl on Murphy's face deepened. "What are the odds of that panning out?"

"You honestly never know," Sierra said. "Not until you try to quantify the sample."

"We need to convict him." Murphy slammed a fist against his palm.

"Right. It's an election year," Grady said, dousing the words with liberal sarcasm. "Not to mention that Wade's been running free for a long time, and we don't want him to get away with murder."

"Yeah, well, that's a given." Murphy shifted to look at Kelsey. "What about the femur fracture? Can you confirm a match to that now?"

Kelsey shook her head. "I need to inventory the bones, then give them a preliminary review as I remove them from the grave, and prepare them for shipment. After that I'll take the femur to the morgue for X-ray and compare it to Neil's old records, if you've recovered them."

"I'll get the X-ray, but the morgue is located in our county seat." Murphy heaved a sigh. "That's over an hour away."

"I'm not ready to say this is Neil Orr. Not without a comparison of his femur X-ray."

The sheriff frowned. "But you got the shirt. The location. The broken bone. Femur. How can you not say it's Neil?"

Kelsey took a defensive stance. "I have professional standards that I need to abide by just like you do. As much as I hate delaying the parents' notification, it's not conclusive enough to declare this person's identity. It'll just have to take longer to get back to the parents."

The sheriff gritted his teeth and looked around as if seeking an answer to his problem. "Can you use any X-ray machine?"

Kelsey nodded. "Sure, but most medical facilities don't allow such a thing, and it would take longer to get permission than making the trip to your county seat."

"What about a vet's office?" he asked.

Kelsey nodded. "That would work."

"My wife is a vet." Murphy planted his hands on his hips. "Her practice is just down the road a piece. Now let's get moving on that inventory, and I'll give her a call."

15

Late in the afternoon, Ainslie took a seat in the sheriff's conference room, her heart so heavy it felt like an anchor was dragging it down. She'd believed Ethan when he'd said Neil had been murdered, and seeing the bones Kelsey unearthed was very real, but it wasn't until Kelsey's look of determination when she'd confirmed that the X-rays matched Neil Orr's that the horror of it all sank in. It was true. Neil Orr had been murdered, and Ethan had known for years. Ainslie could hardly wrap her head around it.

And now—oh, dear God, now—joining Neil's parents, whose weathered and tortured faces told the story of years of not knowing about their son's whereabouts, made it even sadder. They'd changed so dramatically since Ainslie had last seen them, and she wished she could do something—anything—to offer comfort. But after her brother's role in their suffering, she was the last person they would accept comfort from.

Grady sat next to her, and his knee pressed against hers. Maybe the touch was accidental, or maybe he was telling her that he was there for her, like he'd been since she'd met him. He'd even suggested she skip this meeting and not put herself through the stress. Not like she had a choice. She could never live with herself if she bolted from town and didn't face Neil's parents, offer an apology, and let them vent any anger that they might have for Ethan on her. They deserved that and so much more.

Matt propped his shoulder against the wall and introduced everyone. Sierra wasn't there, as she'd stayed behind to finish packing up the supplies and remain with Neil's bones to maintain the chain of custody.

"Go ahead, Dr. Dunbar," Matt said, surprising Ainslie at the use of Kelsey's title, especially considering that he'd given her nothing but a hard time at the crime scene. And Ainslie was still getting used to Kelsey's married last name.

Kelsey was seated next to Grady, and she explained her findings in a concise yet warm tone. "I'm very sorry for your loss."

Mrs. Orr eyed Kelsey and ran a hand over thinning hair, gray at the root and mousy brown at the stick-straight edges brushing her shoulders. "You're one hundred percent positive this is my boy?"

"The only way we can make a one hundred percent positive identification is through DNA," Kelsey explained gently. "And that will take at least twenty-four hours to process."

She eyed Kelsey. "But you're sure enough to sit across the table from me and tell me it's Neil?"

"I've compared the broken femur X-rays from his doctor to X-rays of the recovered femur," Kelsey said. "It's a perfect match. Plus, he's wearing the clothing you described. So, yes, I am certain enough to tell you that we have recovered your son's remains."

Mrs. Orr crossed her arms over a frail and thin body. "I've been expecting this for years, but I never knew it would hurt like the dickens."

Kelsey pressed her hand on the woman's wrinkled hand.

"I'm so sorry for your loss, Mrs. Orr."

She jerked her hand free and looked at her husband. "I can't believe it's real."

He sat slumped in his chair. Just the opposite of her, he was plump and round with a large nose and glossy smooth skin.

"We finally know," she said, tears streaking her cheeks and bringing a trail of black mascara with them. "We finally know where our boy is."

Ainslie remembered Neil got his timid personality from his father, and today the man nodded but didn't speak.

Mrs. Orr swiped a streak of mascara across her face and swung her focus to Kelsey. "What happens next?"

"I'll take Neil's remains back to the Veritas Center in Oregon to review all the bones and work with the medical examiner to determine his cause of death."

Mrs. Orr shot up in her seat, and her bony shoulders created peaks in her worn black T-shirt. "Oregon? Can't you do that here?"

"I'm sorry," Kelsey said softly. "I don't have the tools I need here."

Mrs. Orr sighed. "How long will that take?"

"I'll work as fast as I can, but it will take a couple of days at a minimum."

Mrs. Orr planted her palms on the table and leaned toward Kelsey, her irritated glare deepening. "And then I can bury my boy the right way?"

Kelsey was taking the brunt of this woman's frustration, and, bless her heart, she remained calm and in control and simply took the woman's wrath with the patience and kindness she was known for. "The medical examiner will have to sign off and release his remains, but yes, then we can return them to you, and you can arrange for proper burial."

Mrs. Orr gave a firm nod and fell back in her chair. "Do

you have a guess as to how he died?"

"I'd rather not speculate."

Ainslie wished Kelsey could mention the broken hyoid bone so the woman had even more closure, but Ainslie understood that Kelsey needed to keep that information to herself at this point.

Mrs. Orr looked up at Matt. "What about finding his killer, Sheriff? What are you gonna do about that?"

Matt came to his feet and rested his hands on his waist. "The Veritas Center staff will be processing forensics leads found with Neil. When those results are back, we'll compare them to a known suspect and hopefully close this investigation."

Mrs. Orr's painted-on eyebrows shot up. "This is the first time I'm hearing about a suspect. Who are you looking at?"

"It's too early in the investigation to discuss that."

"Come on, Sheriff." She slammed a fist on the table. "We're Neil's parents. We have a right to know."

"I'm sorry," Matt said sounding sincere for the first time since they'd arrived in Texas. "I wish I could loop you in on this, but I just can't. I promise though, when the results come in, if we have a match to this suspect and make an arrest, you will be the first to know."

Mrs. Orr frowned at him. "Thanks for nothing."

Matt cringed, and Ainslie almost felt sorry for him.

Mrs. Orr shifted her focus to Ainslie. "And tell that brother of yours thanks for nothing from us, too. We could've had closure years ago if he would've only stepped up and reported what he saw."

"I'm sorry," Ainslie said, making sure to infuse her tone with her deepest regret. "I know that Ethan is very sorry, too. It won't make up for all of these years that you have suffered, but please know that he wishes he'd told you."

"That's not good enough." She glanced at Matt. "I want

him to be punished."

"He was just a boy at the time," Grady said.

Ainslie appreciated his support, but at Mrs. Orr's sharpening glare, it was obvious that she didn't plan to cut Ethan any slack.

"So?" She stared at Matt. "What are you gonna do about him?"

"Unless evidence proves he had a part in Neil's death, there's nothing I can legally do."

"Then we might as well forget about that." She glared at Matt and waved a hand to encompass the Veritas team. "It's not like Ainslie's buddies here are going to tell you if they find evidence on her loser of a brother."

Kelsey jutted out her chin. "We're bound by ethics and the law to report all evidence we locate. We would never withhold a thing. Not for any reason."

"And before you mention it," Grady said. "Ainslie hasn't participated in recovering Neil's remains, and she won't have access to any of the evidence."

"Right." Mrs. Orr suddenly pushed her chair back and looked at her husband. "C'mon. Let's get out of here."

She stormed toward the door and looked back at Matt. "See that you call me the minute you know anything."

"Yes, ma'am," Matt said. "You can count on me."

"To be able to count on law enforcement in this town— that'll be a first." She marched through the doorway, her slight frame making the pointed stomping of her feet a meaningless gesture.

Her husband gave them all an apologetic look and trailed her.

"That didn't go so well," Grady stated.

It went better than Ainslie had expected. "Her anger is understandable."

"She could have cut Ethan some slack due to his age,"

Grady muttered.

"I'm not sure I would if I were in her shoes." Ainslie wished more than anything that she could travel back in time and make sure Ethan reported the murder when it happened.

"Speaking of Ethan, I need to interview him," Matt said. "In person. It would be helpful if I could fly back with y'all and take care of it right away."

After his lack of cooperation since they'd arrived in town, Ainslie had to work hard not to gape at his request.

"Unless of course you want it to take longer for me to rule out his participating in Neil's murder." He flashed a cold smile in Ainslie's direction.

Here he was, playing them again, but she wanted Ethan cleared, so she looked at the others. "Is that okay with you all?"

"Fine by me," Grady said, but he didn't sound like he liked it.

Kelsey nodded.

"Then it's settled," Matt said. "Y'all hang here while I run home to pack a bag and let my wife know I'm leaving." He charged out of the room.

Ainslie sighed.

"Hey," Grady said. "None of us wants him on the plane, but he'll talk to Ethan, and that issue will be put to rest."

Ainslie nodded, but she was still unsettled. She prayed that her brother hadn't lied about Neil's death, that he'd had no part in it. Matt was a determined sheriff and would ferret out any lie.

Grady could get used to flying in a private jet, even if the surly sheriff was along for the ride. The plush leather seats were so comfortable that Grady struggled to keep his eyes open after a nearly sleepless night. Shortly after they reached cruising altitude, Sierra and Kelsey moved to the back of the plane and climbed into the twin-sized beds so they'd be ready to begin work the minute they hit the lab. Murphy sat in a corner seat, and Grady and Ainslie took a seating group as far away from him as possible. Their chairs faced each other, and a small table was mounted in between.

Ainslie was looking at her phone, and Grady couldn't just sit and stare at her—enjoy the new golden tint to her skin and the flush of red on her high cheeks, a few new freckles joining it.

Stop. Focus.

He got out his computer and checked his email. The machine sounded an alert.

"Video call from Blake," he told Ainslie and answered.

Blake's face appeared on the screen. "Looks like you're on the way back."

"We are," Grady said, reminding himself not to say anything that might gain Murphy's attention. "Kelsey located the remains, and she's confident it's Neil Orr. Sheriff Murphy is with us, coming back to interview Ethan."

Blake cocked his head and gave a nod. He was a sharp guy and also knew he needed to watch what he said. "I was hoping to update Ainslie on my conversation with Ethan, but that can wait."

"Just a second." Grady motioned for Ainslie to join him, but then he got out his Bluetooth earbuds and gave a pointed look at Murphy, who was overtly watching them before offering one of the earbuds to Ainslie. He looked back at the screen.

Ainslie slipped into the chair next to Grady and plugged the bud into her ear. "Please don't tell me there's a problem."

"You look tired," Blake said.

"Gee. Just what a girl wants to hear." She chuckled and smoothed her hair back.

"Sorry." He winced. "Emory's always telling me I'm too blunt."

"Little bit?" Grady laughed and cast a look at Murphy to see if he was still listening in and he was.

"Ethan told me he helped Wade with a weapons purchase," Blake said.

"He what?" Ainslie's voice rose. "Was it illegal?"

"Borderline, I'd say. He carried cash from Wade to a supplier. But he didn't handle the weapons or even see them so he's not complicit in the gun sales. Though, he admits to knowing what he was doing."

"Why on earth did he do that?" Ainslie asked.

"He said he needed the cash."

Ainslie's shoulders slumped. "I would've given him money."

"He said he's really trying to stand on his own two feet and can't keep running to you when he needs help."

"Better to run to me than do something he might get into trouble for," she grumbled.

"Again, he didn't actually break the law," Blake said. "At least not if he's telling the truth."

"Did you believe him?" she asked.

"I did."

Grady looked at Ainslie. "Blake is a great judge of character, and you can trust his assessment."

She nodded and looked back at the screen. "Did Ethan say why he told you?"

"He thinks the guy he met with might be the person who shot Wade and did it outside of Ethan's place to try to set him up for the murder."

"And he didn't mention this earlier because he thought he would get in trouble, is that it?" Grady asked.

"Pretty much, but also he doesn't know this guy's name so he couldn't turn him in, and Ethan thought there was no point in getting in trouble if it didn't help." Blake frowned. "I'm not sure why he confessed to me, because nothing has changed."

"Um, hello," Grady said. "All you have to do is look at someone, and they're going to spill their guts."

Blake rolled his eyes. "He gave me the location for the money handoff, and I'm looking for CCTV footage in the area. I'll let you know if I find anything."

"Thanks, Blake," Ainslie said.

He gave a perceptive nod. "Also, I interviewed the bar staff where Ethan got into the fight the night Wade was shot. None of the staff remembered anyone who was beaten up that night. Looks like the guy was on his way out when Ethan fought with him."

"You sound suspicious," Ainslie said.

"Just frustrated. The bar doesn't have video cameras." Blake shifted in his chair. "Ethan hit on one of the waitresses a few times, so she remembers him, but she didn't notice when he left."

Ainslie tightly clutched her hands in her lap. "We really need to catch a break."

"Agreed. I talked to Detective Flores, and she wasn't able to share anything we didn't already know. She *did* say that Malone had gotten in contact with her about getting the gun to you, Grady, so you can test it. Malone pointed out that it would be good for the prosecution to have a second opinion. Flores agreed and referred Malone to her lieutenant."

"Sounds promising," Grady said.

"Yeah, keep your fingers crossed on that." Blake flipped the pages in a small notebook. "Malone has also filed the necessary paperwork with the DA to get Wade's phone and computer records. Flores said that it seems like Malone is well-connected and should be able to get everything we need. Flores also said Heidi and Jayla weren't home when she canvassed the neighborhood. She had them on her follow up list. I encouraged her to make them a priority and to try to get the video."

"Let's hope she does," Grady said.

"What about Bittner?" Ainslie asked. "Any news on him and how he fits in this?"

"Oh, right." Blake tilted his head. "I guess you haven't heard. The marshals brought him in. They questioned him, and he claims to know nothing about the swat."

Ainslie sat forward. "But he really can't be trusted, right?"

"Right," Blake said. "Still, we need to be thinking about who else might be behind the swatting incident. I talked to Ethan, and he has no idea."

"I guess we need to ask what the point of the swat might be," Ainslie said. "Could the caller have been hoping that I would somehow have been killed in the incident? Might they think I know something that they're trying to stop me from revealing? Just trying to warn me off investigating Ethan's part in the shooting?"

"All good questions," Blake said. "But we don't know enough right now to form a hypothesis."

Grady faced Ainslie. "What about the recent photographs you've taken? Did you look back at those to see if you might've captured someone you shouldn't have?"

Blake's eyes widened. "You think that happened?"

She shook her head. "I reviewed them. There was nothing. At least I didn't see anything."

"Maybe you should send them to me to review," Blake suggested.

"I can do that."

Blake looked down at his notebook. "Okay, two other things. The police did do a GSR swab for Ethan. As we expected, it came back positive. Malone can do her thing and call this test into question, so I wouldn't worry too much about it. And second, Wade didn't suffer any broken bones from the beating, so there's no way to determine if the assailant was right or left handed."

"Has Nick been able to trace the swat call yet?" Grady asked.

"No, and let me tell you, he's in a foul mood. It's very rare when he fails, and he doesn't like it. But he'll keep after it."

Ainslie let out a long breath. "I am so incredibly blessed by all of your support, and I don't know what I'd do without you."

Grady gave her a pointed look. "You should never have to find out what it would be like."

She raised an eyebrow, and it was clear that she was catching his double meaning, something he was surprised at thinking much less saying out loud. She grew more and more important to him with every minute he spent with her. Shoot, he might be half in love with her already, and he didn't know what to do about it.

"One thing's for sure," she said. "I'm going to have a good long talk with Ethan and get him set on the right path of telling the truth at all times. I don't like secrets. Don't like that he's withheld things. That's not the kind of man I want my brother to be. Not at all."

Right. For a moment, Grady had forgotten about his past. He might have feelings for Ainslie even wondering what to do about them, but there was nothing *to be* done. Not when the minute his secret came out, she would turn the other way.

16

Nearing ten p.m., Ainslie wheeled the equipment cart toward the trace evidence lab, glad that Matt had gone straight to a hotel when she'd half expected him to ask for a tour of the Veritas Center. It had surprised her, since most law enforcement officers visiting the big city would likely have requested a tour. But he didn't seem at all interested. Maybe his monster-sized ego wouldn't let him admit that they might be good at what they did. Or maybe he just didn't care about forensics. Either way, they wouldn't have to tiptoe around him anymore.

Grady opened the door, and she pushed the cart inside, fatigue dragging her shoulders down. She just wanted to crash, but that wouldn't happen yet. She might not be able to help with the investigation, but she could at least take care of the equipment to free up Sierra to do the important work.

Sierra was just closing an evidence locker and turned to join them. "I'm going to grab a shower and a quick bite and then get to work."

"I'll clean up and put the equipment away," Ainslie said.

"I'll help," Grady said.

Sierra smiled at them. "Thank you. Then you should both get some sleep."

"Sure," Ainslie said. "But if you need anything let me know, okay? I want to help where I can."

"Of course." Sierra started for the door, but it swung open before she got there, and Nick entered.

"Hi, Nick. Bye, Nick." Sierra laughed as she exited.

Nick rolled his eyes. "Glad you guys finally got back."

Ainslie trained her gaze on him. "Sounds like you have something for us."

"I do." He frowned and propped his shoulder against the wall. "We finally traced the swat call, but I'm not holding out hope that it'll lead to anything actionable."

Grady narrowed his eyes. "How can that be?"

"It was a VoIP call like we thought. The user configured the displayed number for the call."

"Meaning?" Grady asked before Ainslie could.

"Meaning they chose to display your cell number, Ainslie."

"How can that be?" she asked.

"Often these accounts don't require proper identification, and users can do whatever they want. And that's the problem. Since they're so sketchy, they rarely lead anywhere."

"But it at least proves I didn't make the call," she said.

"Actually, no," Nick said. "It proves you didn't do it via your cell, but not that you didn't do it via the VoIP call."

Grady narrowed his eyes. "So it's a dead end, then."

"Didn't say that." Nick grinned. "VoIP calls are made via computers or other internet access devices. So there's a trail to where the call originated. We're narrowing down the point of origin for this call, and if it doesn't lead to a personal address, hopefully it's a public location with security cameras."

"Then we can see the person who made the call," Grady clarified.

Nick shook his head. "Not necessarily. If it's a public place, we can see all the people who were present when the call was made, but we may not be able to tie it to a specific person. I'm not going to go into details here but just know it has to do with the wireless router and the device used to make the call."

"So what you're saying is that we're no closer to knowing who made the call." Frustration traveled through Grady's tone.

"Not what I'm saying at all," Nick said. "We're lightyears ahead of where we were when we started. It just might take a few more of those years to bring it home. And FYI, Malone obtained Ethan's phone and computer files for me. We're starting to review those now, especially looking at his GPS. I'll let you know if it produces a lead."

"Excellent," Ainslie said.

"Malone didn't happen to mention the gun and CT scan, did she?" Grady asked.

"Sort of. She said she was having a harder time obtaining the physical evidence than the electronics because they can't make copies and hand them over."

Grady frowned. "Figured as much."

"Don't get down." Nick pushed off the wall. "She's still optimistic."

"I have a question for you," Grady said. "The family who lives across the street from Ethan has a video doorbell. The husband configured it then split, and they claim not to have access to the files. I've got a call in to the guy, but he's not calling back."

Nick cocked an eyebrow. "And let me guess. You want me to get their video from the night of the shooting in case it recorded something."

Grady nodded. "Can you do it?"

"Sure, but it'll be on the down-low and won't be admissible in court."

"Then don't do it!" Ainslie took a step toward Nick. "That video, if it exists, could be one of the keys to freeing Ethan, and we can't mess with that."

"Yeah, she's right," Grady said. "But what if I got the wife to give you permission to access the information."

"Sounds like a loophole that might work." Nick scratched his bearded jaw. "I should run it past Malone first, though. Just to be sure. I'll let you know if she gives me the okay."

Grady nodded. "Keep us updated on what you find in Ethan's electronic files."

"You got it." Nick strode to the door.

"Thank you," Ainslie called after him. "I appreciate all your hard work."

He looked back at her. "Hold that thanks until I actually make a difference. Then go for it. Heap on all the praises you want." He grinned and exited the lab.

"I love his attitude." Ainslie rolled the cart into their storage room. "I need to learn to lighten up."

"I don't know." Grady trailed her. "I like you just as you are."

Personal. He'd gotten personal again. She wouldn't go down that path. She looked back at him. "I can handle this if you want to grab some sleep."

"It'll go faster with the two of us." He stepped past her, grabbing a muddy case and walking to a small sink on the far wall to start washing off the dirt. "When I'm done with this, I'll wipe down the cart and then walk you up to Sierra's place."

She picked up a tote. "I can find my own way, you know."

"I know." He set to work cleaning the cart.

She stowed a large tackle box kind of case that held evidence recovery supplies and watched him work. He stroked the stainless steel with a wet paper towel, and she watched the muscles in his shoulders bunch and release. Watched the fluidity of movement, his body lithe and fit. She focused on the handgun strapped to his belt and imagined him on the front lines as a Delta Force operator. He'd likely been splendid at the job, but all she could imagine was a sniper bullet piercing that broad chest and taking him down.

The room suddenly felt small and airless. Shocked at her response, she took deep breaths. She wasn't just attracted to Grady. She cared about him. Big time. She'd been running from that, but why? Sure she wanted to focus on Ethan only, but obviously she'd failed at that. If she hadn't, she wouldn't have developed feelings for Grady.

He looked up. "You okay?"

"Fine. Just a bit tired. We should go." She hurried to the door and stepped into the hallway, not waiting for him, but marching to the elevator. They rode in silence, his focus pinned to her, but she kept quiet before she said something about her discovery.

She raced across the skybridge, barely noticing the sparkling stars above.

"Hey," he called after her. "What's the hurry?"

"Tired," was all she said and dug in her pocket for the condo key. She turned the corner and slammed into her boss.

Ainslie righted herself. "Sorry."

Sierra looked at Grady over Ainslie's shoulder. "You running from something? Or someone?"

Ainslie wasn't about to talk about Grady right now. "You look refreshed."

"The shower did wonders." Sierra smiled. "Oh, and Reed

stopped by to stock the fridge for us. Help yourself. Maybe feed Grady, too."

"I'm sure he'll want to head to his place for some sleep," Ainslie gave him a pointed look.

"Yeah, what she said," he replied but didn't sound convinced.

"I'll catch you both later." Sierra hugged Ainslie and whispered, "Sweet dreams. At least they will be if they're of Grady."

Ainslie shook her head as she watched Sierra depart. She was really trying to throw Ainslie together with Grady, but that was not going to happen.

Ainslie marched down the hall, got the condo door unlocked, and turned to Grady. "Good night. Thanks for walking me."

"You're welcome." He studied her face. "If you need anything in the night, just call me."

She sighed.

"You know you can accept our help. It's different. It's from people who care about you. In the same way you help Ethan. You do it because you care. So do we. I..." He shrugged.

She was moved by his insecurity in sharing and didn't think but let her feelings dictate for once and reached out to touch his shoulder. "And I do appreciate it. It's just going to take me some time to learn when to accept help and when to go it alone."

He nodded, but his eyes glazed over as if he'd mentally traveled somewhere else. "It's hard to forget the past. To let it go. We get labeled or pigeon-holed, and we believe the labels, even if they're not the truth. I know God wants us to forget all of that. Not to live under the weight of 'should haves' that stop us from believing in who God wants us to be and embracing His plans for us."

Grady took a breath and shook his head. "Listen to me preaching to you when I don't have things together *at all*."

"I don't know, mister." She gently poked his shoulder. "You seem like a pretty together guy to me."

"If you only knew." He took her hands. Drew her closer. He smelled like sunscreen and the outdoors, and she wanted to free her hands and slide her fingers into his hair. Draw his head down and kiss him. Hug him. Hold tight to him and let him offer any kind of help he wanted. To give in. Finally give in and let go of her past. Of her need to be in charge. To be in control.

And just be who God wanted her to be.

He looked deep into her eyes, and she stood mesmerized by his power over her emotions. He gently touched the side of her face. Opened his mouth as if to speak, then planted a quick kiss on her forehead and walked away.

She watched him go, wondering. Wondering. What had he been alluding to? What had happened to change his mood so abruptly?

He was nearly to the corner when he looked back. His face was a mask, and she couldn't read his emotions before he disappeared around the corner.

She went inside and closed the door. She wanted nothing but to collapse in bed, but after that strange encounter she wouldn't be able to sleep. Besides, she needed to wash the day from her body. Wash off the Texas dust. Maybe wash off the old feelings of less-than that had intensified on their trip to Texas.

She headed to the shower and willed her mind to let go of thoughts of her past, letting them wash down the drain with the water.

Is Grady right, God? Did You put him in my life, make this all play out, to help me see how much I'm clinging to the belief that

I'm somehow less? But I'm not, am I? You chose me. Have a plan for me. For my future. To prosper me.

She turned off the water and stepped into a heated towel. "Question is, does that plan include Grady?"

～

Grady quietly entered his condo so he wouldn't wake Jackson if he was asleep, but Grady found him sitting on the couch watching ESPN.

"You're back." Jackson pointed the remote at the TV as if he planned to turn it off.

"Nah, leave it on." Grady dropped down on the other end of the couch. "I haven't heard a sports report since the swat on Ainslie."

Jackson looked at him, held his gaze for a moment, then looked back at the TV. "So you have a thing for her or what?"

Grady's mouth fell open. "What are you talking about?"

"Come on, man, Coop and I aren't blind. It's pretty obvious."

"Yeah," was all Grady felt like saying.

"Sounds like you're not happy about it."

Grady didn't know Jackson well enough to have this conversation and was shocked that he'd brought it up. Time to shut him down. "We aren't in a place to take it anywhere. End of story."

"Hey, I get it. Trust me." He shifted to look at Grady. "When I met Maggie, we were in the same situation. But man, working it out was a very good thing. Now, I'm a dad, and wow. That's like...I mean, wow. Can't even put it into words."

A pang of jealousy stabbed at Grady. "Noah, right?"

Jackson nodded enthusiastically. "He just turned one. He's super inquisitive, getting into everything, and I love it."

A broad smile on his face, he dug out his phone and showed Grady the lock screen photo of Maggie holding a chubby toddler with Jackson's dark coloring. Reminded Grady of his siblings who frequently sent pictures of his nieces and nephews, followed by nagging him to get married and have a few kids of his own.

He wanted to. Now even more than before he'd met Ainslie. But again, he wasn't going to have that conversation with Jackson.

"Cute kid," Grady said. "And Maggie looks really happy."

"She loves being a mom." Jackson leaned back, a contented smile on his face. "You should totally work out your issues with Ainslie. I promise you'll be glad you did."

"I'll think about it." Grady got up. "I'm gonna hit the hay."

He left the room, knowing he was running from Jackson just like he'd nearly run from Ainslie. If he'd learned anything in his time with her, it was that he now wanted more out of life and couldn't keep carrying this secret. He had to report his uncle. Even if revealing his past made her think less of him. Even if it meant they wouldn't be together. Even if the uncle he loved had to go to prison. It was time to end this once and for all. Time to rectify a wrong. He needed to take care of his issues. Take responsibility. Report his uncle.

How, though? That was the question. What did he do? Call up his mom and dad and say, "Oh, by the way, Uncle Tommy killed someone. I know because I saw his damaged vehicle before he fixed it."

Grady plopped down on his bed. He couldn't resolve this issue over the phone. He had to handle it in person. Which meant it would have to wait until after Ethan was released, Wade was in prison, and Ainslie was safe.

Yeah, he had to wait to tell his parents, but he didn't have to wait to tell Ainslie. He could break the news to her whenever the opportunity presented itself. He'd look for that time, man up, and confess. Then, everything would be in her hands. Hers and God's.

17

Ainslie fumbled for her ringing cell phone in the dark and glanced at the time. Three a.m. And the screen displayed Sierra's name.

News on Ethan? Had something bad happened?

Ainslie answered.

"Sorry to wake you," Sierra said. "But we've been called out for a drive-by shooting that killed two people. I'm still in the lab so if you'd come down we can ride together."

Far worse than Ainslie expected, and her heart dropped. She thought about arriving on scene to find two people who'd had their lives cut short, and she swung her feet out from under the covers so she could get to the job of helping find the person who gunned them down.

She slid out of bed. "I'll be right down."

Ainslie slipped into jeans and a T-shirt, pulled her hair back in a ponytail, and brushed her teeth. She grabbed a jacket and her camera bag and started for the door, then came to a sudden stop. Should she call Grady and tell him she was leaving the building? He would want her to, but did he really need to be disturbed?

Nah. She was headed to a crime scene with copious

police officers. She would be perfectly safe. She would let him sleep. Drake, too, who was passed out on the couch, his face buried in a big pillow, and she tiptoed past him and into the hallway.

Sierra was waiting at the lab door, a navy blue Veritas Center windbreaker on, keys in hand. Without a word, they hurried to the parking garage and climbed into the crime scene van that was loaded with all the equipment they would need, minus Ainslie's cameras.

Sierra got behind the wheel and cranked the engine. It roared to life in the quiet of the night.

"You should know," she said pressing her fingers on the reader to open the security gate. "The victim is a mother and young child."

Ainslie's stomach clenched. "How young?"

"Toddler."

Tears wetted Ainslie's eyes, and she looked up at the roof of the van to stem them. Being tired didn't help her gain control of her emotions, but she couldn't very well arrive in an official capacity at a crime scene blubbering like a baby.

Sierra plugged the digits into the GPS for a northeast Portland address and got them on the road while Ainslie looked out the window. The night was clear and rain-free. That meant it would be cold at the scene, and she would be glad for the warmth that the Tyvek suit added. Not that she would notice the cold once she got to work. She would have to devote her entire concentration to the scene because there was no way she was going to let someone get away with murdering a toddler and mother. No way.

Sierra merged the van into the light morning traffic on the Sunset Highway. "I've made some progress on Neil's shirt."

Ainslie faced her boss. "Does that mean you found something to help?"

"Not sure if it will help. At least not yet. But not only did I find saliva on Neil's shirt, I also found blood. I don't know if it's his or the killer's yet, but it could be a strong lead."

"Sounds wonderful."

Sierra nodded. "Emory's already processing the DNA."

"Then hopefully we'll know something by this time tomorrow."

"Could take longer. She said she was having some issues with quantifying the samples."

"That doesn't sound good."

"She doesn't think it'll be a problem. It'll just take her a bit longer."

Ainslie shook her head. "Before I came to work at Veritas, I thought processing DNA was so easy. You popped the sample into a machine and presto. DNA. And I always wondered why it took so long. I had no idea how much human involvement it takes to run it."

"That's true of a lot of the forensics, isn't it? Gives a whole new meaning to job security." Sierra tapped her thumb on the wheel. "I didn't get to the soil samples yet, but I want to start as soon as possible. Once I walk this scene, if I think Chad can handle processing it, I'll give him a call."

Ainslie's mind went to the upcoming job, where there would be a great deal of evidence to recover. Especially ballistic evidence from the drive-by. "Do we know anything about the family or the shooting?"

"Just that the woman was the girlfriend of a gang member who's known for his brutality." Sierra shook her head. "Of course, he wasn't home at the time, so he didn't get hurt. The police are looking for him."

"Any witnesses?"

"None that they know of yet, but it's early in the investigation." She frowned, not speaking for the longest time. "So, you and Grady? I thought you were moving right along when we were in Texas, but when I bumped into you in the hallway, things seemed tense."

Ainslie had to work hard not to let her mouth drop open at the sudden change in subject. She didn't know what to say, so she didn't say anything.

Sierra glanced at her. "Am I being too nosey?"

"Maybe just a little."

Sierra grinned. "It's okay. You can tell me to mind my own business. It's just that, when you fall in love and are deliriously happy, you want everyone to find the same happiness. And you're such a special person, you really deserve it."

Ainslie's heart melted at her kind words. "You're so sweet to say that, but I don't know about the deserving part."

"What?" Sierra gawked at her. "Why would you think that?"

"I've got a lot of baggage from growing up poor and having others judging me and my family."

"I see."

"In fact, that's what Grady and I were talking about before he left for the night." She took a breath. "Something's holding him back, too. He hasn't said what, so I figure it's a big deal."

"Would explain why a great guy like him is still single." She gave Ainslie a pointed look. "Why not come right out and ask?"

That answer was simple. If she asked, he might tell her something they could work through, and then what would keep her from falling head over heels for him?

"Okay, I get it." Sierra mocked zipping her lips. "I'll let it go. For now."

"Thanks for understanding."

They made the rest of the drive in silence, the air growing tense the closer they got to the home. Sierra pulled up to the scene, and parked while Ainslie mentally prepared herself to see the victims. She scanned the area. Three patrol cars blocked the street outside a forsaken duplex hunkered in the shadows from nearby commercial buildings. An unmarked detective's car was parked at the curb, and an older man with a sagging suit jacket stood on the sidewalk and stared at the house. Ainslie looked for the medical examiner's vehicle, but they hadn't arrived yet.

"Let's do this." Sierra sounded like she needed to motivate herself to face such a tough task.

Ainslie totally got it. When children were involved, the work was far more difficult, but also more motivating. She jumped down from the van, and strong winds that were rippling the yellow tape cordoning off the area hit her head-on. She went straight to the back of the vehicle, as did Sierra. They dressed in protective clothing in silence and approached the cordoned off area.

The detective lifted the tape for them to duck under.

"Sierra," he said and looked at Ainslie with a question mark in his eyes.

"Richard, meet my photographer, Ainslie Duncan," Sierra said. "She joined us a few months ago, a real asset to the team."

"Detective Richard Gaines." He looked back at the house.

Sierra moved next to him and frowned.

He glanced at her. "You see it, too, right?"

"Bullet spray is all wrong for a drive-by."

Ainslie joined them. "Too high for a car. Maybe a truck or van. Or they were on foot."

"Exactly," Gaines said.

"Let's not take any chances on getting this wrong." Sierra got out her phone. "Time to call in an expert. Time to call Grady."

Grady stared at the chipped white paint flaking from the dilapidated duplex in the strong wind barreling in from the Gorge. This duplex was located in a known drug area, and Grady wasn't surprised by the drive-by shooting at all.

He *was* surprised by the callout though. As far as he was concerned, it came at the worst time. He didn't like getting hauled out of bed to go to a crime scene when he desperately needed a good night's sleep. Especially with the thought that he might get Ethan's gun and the CT scan soon. He wanted to do his very best for Ainslie, who was busy snapping photos outside the home.

Despite being woken up, he didn't mind having the chance to keep an eye on her. With the police presence here, she should be safe. Didn't mean Grady would let down his guard. He would do his job and do it well for this slain family once Ainslie cleared him to access the scene. But he'd also keep an eye out for imminent danger, too. He'd learned to combine tasks with that sixth sense in Delta, and that was something you never lost.

He planted his hand on his sidearm as a reminder while he waited and watched her work alone under bright klieg lights, the only nearby person the officer of record. She moved through the scene with effortless ease, clearly comfortable with her camera. She'd put on a baggy Tyvek suit like all the forensic staff in the house were wearing, including him, but he could still imagine the curves hidden under the shapeless fabric. Could imagine going back in time to her home invasion and holding her instead of walking away. Maybe back to earlier tonight. Instead of kissing her on the forehead and running like the chicken that he was, telling her about his uncle, and her saying it was all okay and she didn't think less of him because he'd hidden such a big thing for all those years.

She lowered her camera and crooked a finger at him. He stepped over the crunchy brown grass to where she stood near the building.

She squatted and set a tent marker near a dried out shrub with leaves desperately clinging for life, then tipped her head at the wall above. "Thought you'd like to get a look at this spray pattern."

He crouched next to her and glanced at the deformed brass that had cut into a rotting landscape beam. Then he took a long look above at the wall peppered with bullets, each one embedded in decayed siding, the window shattered.

"Pattern definitely suggests a submachine gun. I'll need to get my tools to do some calculations and maybe I can weigh in on the weapon used." He rose.

"You'll have to wait until I have my final overall shots taken care of." She stood and looked at him.

He'd never really paid attention to when Sierra had taken her own crime scene photos and had only once been on a scene since Ainslie had been hired, so he didn't know the correct terminology for her work. "Overall?"

"I shoot evidence from a distance, mid-range, and close-up perspective."

"So this slug for example. You'll take two different views of it?"

"At least two, but yeah. Getting the closeup is important for many reasons I won't bore you with, but also capturing the artifacts in a mid-range shot helps put the item in perspective for detectives and a potential jury."

He got it now. "You give them a background reference so they can put it in context and know where you found the item."

She nodded vigorously. "And at times, it also helps them identify the item. Without documentation like that, getting a conviction using evidence can be problematic."

"And here I thought you just showed up and took pictures." He grinned.

She raised an eyebrow, the hint of a smile on her face. "You mean like anyone can do my job?"

"Well, anyone with a cell phone."

"Right...yeah. You got it. Just like you show up and glance at holes in the walls."

He laughed. "Touché."

Her smile widened, and her high cheekbones rose. He couldn't stop looking at her, and she locked gazes with him. He wanted to weave his fingers into her hair. Pull out the tight ponytail and release her thick locks. Then kiss her and never stop.

Oh, man. He was in so deep. Acting like a lovesick fool, and at a crime scene no less. He stepped back and shoved his hand into his own hair. "I'll just get those tools."

"Um. Yeah. Good." She spun and raised her camera, but he saw a slight tremble in her hand. She was as affected by their shared moment as he was.

Chastising himself for not keeping a professional demeanor, he marched back to his truck parked on the far side of the fluttering crime scene tape. He reached inside for his gear, and the hair on the back of his neck rose. He knew this feeling. Knew it well. They were being watched. And not in a good way.

He dropped the tools and whipped his body out of the truck. He wouldn't put it past the thugs who riddled this house with bullets finding out they missed their target to come back and go all kamikaze on them.

He scanned the property. Then across the street. Down the street. His eye caught on a glint in the window of an apartment building. Movement. Something poking out, highlighted by a nearby streetlight. A rifle barrel? Maybe.

"Sniper. Everyone down!" He drew his sidearm, but the distance prohibited getting off an accurate shot.

Ainslie spun to look at him as if in slow motion. Her eyes wide, terror dawning in them.

His heart shredded. "Down!"

She dropped.

Crack. A bullet fractured the air. Thudded. Dirt puffed up next to her head. Grady didn't think but charged across the lawn. He hurled his body in her direction. Landing hard, taking his weight on his arms, before cocooning her in them and rolling toward a broken-down pickup truck.

Pfft. A bullet whizzed past his ear, pierced the open lid of Ainslie's kit and lodged in the steps. Grady held Ainslie tight and put his back to the shooter to insulate her from danger. He let out a breath of thanks when they made it behind the truck.

Her body shook in his arms. "Were those bullets meant for me?"

"Either that or someone is hunting crime scene workers." Grady listened for additional reports, but all he heard was the closest police officer's radio squawking from his car.

"What are the odds of that?" she asked.

"Not high," he said, but regretted it when her trembling increased. "We're good until the officer gets help out here. Besides, the shooting stopped and the shooter likely took off."

"Is it safe for you to let me go now?"

"Safe. Probably." *Do I want to? No.*

He relaxed his arms. Instead of slipping away, she curled to face him. She rested her fingertips gently on his face, the touch like a butterfly, sending a million points of awareness through his body. He waited for her to speak. To say something—anything—she didn't, and he couldn't stop the emotions flowing through his body. He couldn't stop himself, and he leaned closer. Her gaze heated up. He lowered his head. Kissed her. Her warm lips sending a fire racing through him.

She leaned back. "You saved my life. I could have died out there. I'll forever be indebted to you."

Not what he'd expected her to say. Not at all, and he didn't know how to respond. Here he thought she was feeling the same racing emotions he was. The desire to take this thing between them to the next step. To admitting they had feelings. Strong feelings. Her wanting the same thing. But did she?

She slid her hand behind his neck. Drew him closer.

"I want..." she said, her voice breathy as the words fell off and those lips that had enticed him for months connected with his again.

He didn't care who saw them. Who walked up. He tightened his arms. Lost himself in the feel of her. Drawing her against his body and throwing himself into the kiss. Kissing Ainslie. Here in his arms. Finally. What he wanted. He was home. Totally home and at peace.

"Is everyone okay?" Sierra shouted from inside the house, and Grady heard the raw fear in her voice, snapping him free from his emotions. Bringing him back like a plunge into an icy river.

Ainslie had almost been killed. He'd barely warned her in time. And kissing her, here or anywhere was wrong after her comment. She was feeling vulnerable. Thankful for his rescue.

Was she now going to confuse her feelings of gratitude with the raw, aching emotions that traveled between them? How could he ever know if she was expressing gratitude for saving her life, or if she truly did have feelings for him?

18

Ainslie looked at the warring emotions in Grady's expression before scooting away, her face hot with emotions morphing into embarrassment. She wished she could read what he was thinking. She couldn't. He was hiding his feelings well. But more importantly, what had *she* been thinking? Kissing him. Here at a crime scene. At work. She'd lost her mind. Her ever-loving mind. Gone. In a flash as quick as the bullets.

"Ainslie? Grady?" Sierra called out again.

"We're fine," Ainslie shouted, but she didn't know if Sierra could hear her above police sirens screaming down the street, the cars racing closer.

Ainslie looked around the truck, checking for what she didn't know, but she had to quit touching Grady before she told him about those feelings that swamped her at the lab and surfaced again when she was in his arms.

"We'll wait here until we get the all clear," Grady yelled back to Sierra, his voice rising over the wailing. "You do the same."

"I'm going to call you."

Ainslie's phone rang, and she shifted to get it out of

her pocket inside the Tyvek suit. Her shaky hand made it more difficult, but she finally grasped it and answered. "No one was injured, right? The bullets didn't pierce the house."

"Right." Sierra let out a long breath. "And you're sure you're both fine?"

"I suspect Grady will have some bruises from protecting me, but I'm good." She looked at him, but he was avoiding eye contact. Maybe he didn't like that she'd kissed him. Nah, she knew that wasn't true. Fire lit in his eyes, and he'd returned the kiss with zeal. Man. It was amazing. Super amazing and incredible. Something like she'd never experienced before. Never. Her heart burst with emotion. Love? Maybe.

But it didn't matter. Not until she found out what was making him hold back from a relationship. She needed to have that conversation that Sierra had suggested and have it soon, because she was falling hard for him, and her reasons for not pursuing a relationship just didn't make any sense anymore.

But now, she needed to focus on this incident. To stow her feelings. To stay alive. "His warning call saved me."

"Yeah, I heard that." Sierra's long exhaled breath whispered through the phone. "Thank God he was here."

Yes, thank You, God! Thank You. Thank You. Thank You.

"Can you put me on speaker?" Sierra asked.

"Sure." Ainslie stabbed the screen and held out her phone. "Go ahead."

"Your thoughts on if this shooter was targeting Ainslie or if it's related to the drive-by?" Sierra asked.

"Based on where the bullets hit..." He paused, his tone holding a lingering tremor of adrenaline. "I'd say targeting her."

Hearing him confirm the directed attack again nearly

brought a gasp from deep inside, but Ainslie swallowed it. "If so, that means I'm being watched or tracked."

Grady grimaced. "Agreed. We need to get the team and Drake together to see if we can figure out how."

"Maybe someone put a tracker on your phone," Sierra suggested.

Was that possible? "I don't see when that could've happened. I have a password and don't leave my phone lying around where others can access it."

"Still, we can have Nick review it," Sierra said. "For now, though, once the police take your statement, I need you to head back to the center and stay there."

"I'll make sure that happens," Grady said.

She thought to tell him that, though she might have feelings for him—that though she might honestly be falling for him—she was still her own person and in charge of her life. She decided when to stay and when to leave. But his behavior was fueled in part by lingering adrenaline and in other part by his fierce need to protect those he cared about. He'd just saved her life because of the second trait. How could she not at least listen to him and do what he suggested if it made sense?

"If I know you, Ainslie, and I think I do," Sierra said. "You're trying to think about how to stay and finish the job here. But even if I would let you stay—which I won't—if you're the target, then your objectivity is compromised, and you can't shoot the new evidence anyway."

Ainslie hadn't thought of that.

"Besides, if you head back to the lab now, you can get everyone together quicker to figure this out."

Ainslie gaped at her phone. "You want me to call a meeting of the partners at this time of night?"

"No, I'm going to call Maya and have her arrange it."

"But it's the middle of the night."

"Time is of no consequence when someone tries to take out a family member," Sierra said with vehemence.

Ainslie knew they thought of her as family, but man, their care and consideration went beyond any family support she'd experienced, and she was so deeply touched that tears sprung to her eyes.

She suddenly got God's plan here. He was showing His love through these people. Showing her that she mattered. That He did indeed choose her. She wasn't just some lost cause like so many people had told her. She was loved by Him. By others. And she could in return love others, too. Other people like Grady.

"I'd like to run the trajectory for these sniper shots and search the shooter's hide before I go," Grady said,

"Didn't you see the gun?" Sierra asked.

"I saw a flash. About a hundred or so yards down the road. Then a gun barrel. Second story window. But that's not enough to hold up in court, and there is no way I'll let anyone get away with taking potshots at Ainslie. No way."

"Of course," Sierra said. "I would expect no less from you."

He made firm eye contact with Ainslie. "While I run this down, will you wait in the house in an interior room?"

"You don't think the shooter will come back, do you?" Ainslie asked.

"We can't be too careful." He curled his fingers into fists.

"And I'll get Drake out here, too," Sierra said." He can help escort Ainslie back to the center."

"I hate to bother him," Ainslie said.

"He won't think it's a bother," Sierra stated. "In fact, he'll be mad that you didn't wake him up in the first place."

"You know he will." Grady's attention switched to movement on the street. "Detective Gaines is heading toward the house. Looks like we're clear. I'll get right on that trajectory to confirm the hide and get a look at the slugs."

"Good. I'll get an update from him, and we can move forward from there." Sierra ended the call.

Grady started to stow his phone, but it rang.

"It's Coop." Grady quickly answered using his speaker.

"Eggen ditched me," Coop said by way of greeting. "He's in the wind, and you need to take precautions."

Grady flashed his gaze to Ainslie, whose face had paled, then looked back at his phone. He didn't even know how to respond to Coop's announcement. Grady first needed details to take any action. "What happened?"

"Eggen was sleeping when a light came on in his room, and I saw shadows," Coop said. "Looked suspicious but movement stopped before I could determine if it was two people. I kept watching and got a hinky feeling. So decided to go check it out."

He paused and sucked in a long breath. "I couldn't see through the front window so I went around back. Bathroom window was wide open. Figured he climbed out. I busted down the door. Guy was gone. Not sure if he was alone or with someone. His rental car's still here, so I cruised the area looking for him on foot. Didn't find him. Seems like someone came in that window and they left together."

"How long ago did this happen?" Grady tried hard to keep his disappointment from his tone so he wouldn't make Coop feel even worse.

"Ninety minutes. Maybe more."

Grady ran the logistics in his head. Plenty of time for Wade to get over here and take a few shots at Ainslie. Grady told Coop about the shooting, and Ainslie glanced around the area, maybe looking for another threat.

"Aw, man is she okay?" Coop sounded even more distressed.

Grady honestly didn't know how she was doing.

"Shaken up, but fine," he said and hoped it was the truth.

"You think it was our guy?" Coop asked.

"I don't know what to think," Grady replied. "But I'll update the detective in charge here and get him to put an alert out on Wade."

"Sounds good." Coop let out a long breath. "I'll hang here and let you know if he shows up again. And I'll get Jackson out here to scour the area. If Eggen's nearby, we'll find him."

"Thanks, man." Grady tried to sound appreciative and not upset.

"Don't thank me. I blew it."

"Coulda happened to anyone."

"I'm not just anyone," Coop snapped and hung up. He took this situation personally.

Grady got it. Totally. He would feel the same way if he were in Coop's shoes. He stowed his phone and looked at Ainslie and found her staring at him.

She blinked a few times as if trying to process the news. "You think Wade knew where I was somehow, and he was the one who shot at me?"

"Honestly, I don't know what to think." Grady had to work hard to keep his frustration from his voice so he wouldn't make this situation harder for her. "Let me get working on the trajectory and maybe we can figure that out. First, we talk to Gaines."

She turned toward the house, where Gaines had gone, and Grady escorted her inside.

Gaines stood by the door talking to Sierra. He looked at Grady. "I'll need to interview you both."

"Then you'll have to join us in an interior room. There's no way I'll allow Ainslie to remain out here." Grady motioned for her to keep going, and they stepped into a narrow hallway that led to an outdated but clean bathroom.

Gaines trailed behind and lingered at the doorway. Grady didn't waste any time telling the detective about Wade.

Gaines tugged on the lapels of his ill-fitting suit jacket, pulling it closed. "From what you're saying, you really don't have any solid connections here. Still, it wouldn't hurt to put an alert out on the guy."

"While you do that and interview Ainslie," Grady said. "I'm going to run trajectory on the slugs."

Gaines gave a clipped nod. "I was hoping you'd offer to do that so Sierra has the right scene to process."

"Should have the information for you in an hour or so." Grady changed his focus to Ainslie. "You'll stay here until I come back to get you, right?"

She nodded.

He gave her a tight smile and went to his truck to retrieve his equipment bag from the jump seat and took it to the location where the bullets had landed. He squatted and aimed a flashlight on the slug embedded in the step. He couldn't be positive of the caliber until the bullet was removed and he could take a better look at it, but at first glance, he thought it was a .223 caliber, commonly used in the very popular AR-15. The semi-automatic rifle was used by many law enforcement agencies and was one of the top ten popular guns sold in America. A weapon that Wade would have no trouble getting his hands on. But it was also chambered for other caliber ammunition, so Grady was only making an educated guess.

Now to figure out if the slug actually came from the suspected window. A precise measurement required a bullet to pass through two fixed objects. The second shot fired fit that requirement. It had pierced Ainslie's kit and then lodged in the steps. Perfect for his needs.

He took a longer look at it. Even with his naked eye, he could tell the shot had come from above, as the hole in the kit wasn't perfectly circular like a straight-on shot would create. But he still needed details for when the shooter was called to account in a court of law. And he would pay. Grady would see to that personally. No matter how long it took or what he had to do.

He set up his tripod holding a trajectory rod mount with an inclinometer—a device that measured angles and slopes. He passed a fiberglass rod through the hole and fixed it in place with an O-ring, then added additional lengths of rod to reach the step.

He took his time and worked carefully, even with a clock ticking down in his brain, warning him to work fast and locate this shooter before he tried to take Ainslie out again. Even with the adrenaline still hyping up his actions. He breathed deeply to ward off the urge to hurry. He checked each step and measurement. Then double-checked. No way would he risk making a mistake and waste valuable time going to the wrong building just because he saw a flash, and then have to start over again. He had to forget about what he'd seen. Work the facts.

He passed the rod through the stairs and started recording the measurements.

"What did you find?" Drake asked from behind.

Grady spun in surprise. With his focus fixed on his task, he'd missed hearing Drake approach. Big mistake that could've been deadly.

"I've got the angle," Grady said. "I'll do my final calcula-

194

tions, and then we'll know for sure where the cowardly shooter hunkered down for the kill."

"Not sure he's all that cowardly," Drake said, locking gazes with Grady. "If he's willing to take shots with multiple police officers around, that makes him even more dangerous than we first thought. Starting now, we need to up our protection game, or the consequences could be fatal."

19

The moment Ainslie hit the Veritas Center conference room to sit down with Drake and the partners—minus Sierra—the adrenaline flooded from her body. Grady still seemed hyped though. He didn't talk about the bullet trajectory, and she was surprised he didn't go to the shooter's hide but had instead told Gaines where to find it.

She'd asked Grady about it, and he'd said he wanted to get her to a safe location, then he would go back to the hide later. But it seemed like he was holding something back, and she hoped he would bring it up in this meeting.

He stepped to the head of the table and ran his gaze over the others, who Ainslie was surprised to see that, despite the time of night, were alert and ready to work. He held up a marker. "Okay, so...ideas on how this shooter found Ainslie. Go."

"Before we start with that." Nick set down his can of Dr. Pepper. "I just found something in Ethan's computer files that you should know about."

"Go ahead," Grady said.

"There's a vulnerability in Google Calendar when the calendar is shared with others. The information can be indexed by Google search engines and become public, leaking sensitive details like email IDs, event details, location, meeting links, and a whole lot more."

"Wait, what?" Blake gaped at Nick. "You're saying that shared calendars are viewable on the internet?"

Nick gave a solemn nod. "Anyone who has the skills to run the search or knows someone who does could know Ethan was attending the going-away party for his co-worker the night of the shooting."

Grady's eyes widened. "And if they did indeed get his calendar information and knew where he was, they could set him up to take the fall for murder."

"Exactly." Nick looked at Ainslie. "That wouldn't be true for how the shooter found you tonight because the callout wasn't on your calendar, but it's a reminder that we could have a breach in your security. Like maybe the GPS in an app on your phone."

"Wait, back to the calendar," Maya said, looking shocked. "Is Google offering a fix?"

"Actually, a fix isn't needed." Nick leaned back in his chair. "If you share calendars, just set the calendar sharing to only say Free/Busy."

Maya shook her head. "Would've been nice of Google to tell people that."

"Yeah. This problem isn't new and many experts have been issuing warnings for some time." Nick frowned. "I should've thought to warn you all, but I didn't because I didn't think anyone uses it."

Grady stared at Nick. "So you think there might be a vulnerability on Ainslie's phone?"

"Not sure, but it's possible." He looked at Ainslie. "I can review your phone if you'd like."

"Yes, please!" She dug it from her purse.

"I need you to turn off the password."

She nodded and navigated through the screens to turn it off then slid her phone across the table to him.

Drake swiveled his chair to face her. "We might be complicating all of this when it could be as simple as someone followed you and Sierra to the scene."

"To be fair, we weren't watching for a tail," Ainslie admitted. "I should have, I guess, but..."

Drake waved a hand. "I doubt you would've seen them anyway. Someone who can fire off a few rounds with officers around and get away has to have some evasion skills."

Grady scowled and wrote the two ideas on the board. "What else?"

"Tracker on the van, but that's very unlikely," Blake said. "Still, I'll check it out."

Kelsey looked at Ainslie. "You didn't tell anyone where you were going, did you?"

Ainslie shook her head. "I just took Sierra's call and headed down to the lab."

Emory looked at her husband. "Could an officer have broadcast over their radio that Veritas Center staff were on scene?"

"Hmm." Blake tilted his head. "That would be odd, but it would make the information public on scanners."

He looked at Ainslie. "Who called Sierra?"

"I took the initial call," Maya said, taking his attention. "I'll follow up to see what I can find out."

"So if we're dealing with the same person who might've found Ethan's calendar, then we should consider the person has computer skills." Nick shifted to face Ainslie. "Do you have an app on your phone that helps you locate it if you lose it?"

She nodded. "Find my iPhone."

"If that account is compromised, it'll tell a hacker your exact position at all times."

She shivered and held his gaze. "Like right now he'd know I was here."

He gave a serious nod. "If you have GPS turned on, that is."

Ainslie shivered. "Gross."

"And scary," Maya said.

"I'll make sure it's turned off." Nick picked up her phone and tapped the screen. "Yeah. You had GPS on. It's off now." He looked up at the others. "FYI, I want to remind everyone never to globally set the GPS to on."

"But I use it all the time for my maps app," Ainslie said.

"That's okay. Just fine tune your settings to allow only the apps you use to access GPS when you're using them." He smiled. "After I make sure your phone is clean, I'll give you a crash course in security like I do for the partners."

"Yeah, he even reviews our phones monthly to make sure we haven't managed to screw things up too badly." Maya chuckled, but underneath the humor, Ainslie could see she was thankful for Nick's help.

"I can do that for you, too," he said. "That is, if you want me to. These guys have to say yes because they have corporate phones and I don't want to compromise center security, but your phone is personal so—"

"I'd be glad for your help to keep on the straight and narrow." She smiled at Nick.

He laughed. "Hey, I can take care of your phone, but the rest is up to you."

Ainslie laughed with him and was glad for the moment of lightness. Grady on the other hand didn't look so happy.

"Any additional ideas here?" he asked, but received only head shakes in return.

"Sounds like we need to get to work on figuring out how he found her." Emory yawned and rubbed her belly.

"I'm sorry that we got you up when you need sleep for the baby," Ainslie said.

Emory waved a hand. "I wasn't sleeping. I was in the lab running DNA samples from Neil's shirt. I hope to have results by this time tomorrow."

Guilt over having gotten a few hours of sleep when this pregnant woman had been working weighed heavily on Ainslie. "Thank you so much. It's exciting to think we might be able to prove Wade bit Neil or his blood was on Neil's shirt."

"There was blood?" Grady asked at the same time as Blake.

Emory nodded. "Sierra found a few tiny drops on the shirt. Could be Neil's blood. We won't know until the process completes."

Grady faced Kelsey. "Any thoughts on this?"

She shook her head. "I didn't find any injuries to suggest that Neil had bled, but I'm only dealing with the bones and the shirt."

"So, it's strangulation then?" Maya asked.

"As of now, yes." Kelsey rested her hands on the table and formed a steeple with her fingertips. "But I'm not done examining the bones and have no official ruling."

"Since we've moved on to Neil." Grady slashed a bright red line under Neil's name on the whiteboard. "Blake, can you put pressure on the police to get Ethan's gun and Wade's CT scan?"

Blake frowned. "Pressure isn't going to help in this situation, and I don't want to step on Malone's toes. But I can follow up with her."

"That would be great," Ainslie said, wanting to encourage him when he was looking so frustrated.

"Okay, are there any other updates while we're together?" Grady asked, scanning his partners.

Blake nodded and told everyone about the cash payoff Ethan made for Wade. "Unfortunately, I struck out on getting any video, so that's a bust."

Ainslie was honestly glad for that, as she didn't want to see her brother walk the fine line of committing a crime. And she sure didn't want these wonderful men and women to see it either.

Nick's phone dinged. He looked at it and pumped his fist. "Yes! The swat call came from the same bar where Ethan attended the going-away party."

Ainslie didn't see why he was so excited. "That's not good news, right? They don't have security cameras, so we can't possibly see who made the call."

"We can interview the staff, though," Blake said, the frustration in his expression lifting a fraction. "If one of them saw our caller, we can have them work with a sketch artist."

"I'd be glad to do the sketch," Kelsey offered. "Assuming of course that I'm done examining Neil's bones. He takes priority."

"Let's not get ahead of ourselves," Grady warned. "We first have to find someone who saw the caller."

"I'll need to get a look at the bar's router." Excitement lingered in Nick's tone. "That way I can see the MAC address of the device that made the VoIP call."

"MAC as in an Apple device?" Ainslie asked.

Nick shook his head. "MAC stands for Media Access Control. It's a hardware identification number that's manufactured into every network card and uniquely identifies each device on a network. Means I can see each device that accessed the bar's Wi-Fi that night."

"Is there a database of these MAC addresses so we can trace the device to the owner?" she asked.

"Unfortunately, no. But the trail left by the device might take me to another lead."

Ainslie wished they had more to go on, but it was still a solid lead. She looked at her watch. "We should head over there the minute they open."

"Not we," Grady stated. "You need to stay here where you're safe."

"We'll see." She didn't want to argue with him in front of his team, but when the meeting broke up, she went straight to him. "I really want to go to the bar with you."

He folded his arms over his broad chest. "Putting your life in danger isn't necessary when I can take care of it."

"I can't just sit here and do nothing. I need to do this. To help Ethan. I just have to." She put as much force into her words as she could, but he stood rigid and unyielding.

She needed an ally. She turned to Drake. "Can you join us for a minute?"

He headed their way. He looked at them, and his steps turned hesitant. "How can I help?"

"I want to go to the bar to interview the staff," she said. "Grady thinks I might be putting myself in danger if I go."

"He's right."

Not the answer she wanted. "You're an expert in safely transporting people. Is there a way that the risk can be minimized so it's safe for me to go?"

"Yeah, sure," he replied. "We could use a vehicle the shooter wouldn't connect to you. Have you lie down on the floor in the backseat and proceed that way. Should be a piece of cake. As long as Grady doesn't drive. The shooter's likely connected him to you by now, and that would be a dead giveaway."

Grady tightened his arms. "I'm not letting her go without me."

"Sorry." Drake widened his stance. "If you want her to be safe, then you need to meet her at the bar."

Grady eyed her. "I don't want her to go at all, but what I want doesn't seem to matter."

Ainslie didn't want to force Drake to endure this argument any longer. "Can you make the arrangements and let me know when we'll be ready to go?"

"I'm sure I can get a couple of my brothers to help." Drake offered Grady an apologetic look and strode to the other side of the room, taking out his phone as he went.

She moved closer to Grady. "I don't want to go against your wishes. I hope you know that."

"Yeah, I do."

"I just feel compelled to do this. I can't explain it. It's almost like needing to breathe. I've had to sit on the sidelines for most of this investigation. If I can do something here and do it safely, then I need to." She rested a hand on his arm. "Please try to understand."

"I'm trying."

She sought a way to better explain. "You have siblings. What if one of them was in Ethan's situation? Would you sit by?"

"No, but then I carry a gun and can protect myself."

"Can you?" She removed her hand and peered up at him. "From everything? What about that sniper shot? Could you protect yourself if someone wanted to take you out that way?"

"No," he admitted and shifted his feet. "Not if it was a long distance shot."

She didn't like to cause him to admit his vulnerability when it clearly didn't sit well with him. "You trust Drake's assessment of the situation and his transport skills, right?"

"Yes."

"And Nick has my phone, so I can't be tracked that way.

There really is no way anyone will know where I'm going except you, Drake, and whoever he brings in to help."

"Okay." Grady let his arms fall to his sides. "I don't like it, but I get it. Just promise me you'll listen to Drake and not take any chances."

"I promise," she said and meant it. After all, she didn't have a death wish. She just had a wish to free her brother from jail.

Grady climbed the rickety stairs in the apartment building where the shooter had hunkered down to take shots at Ainslie. He stepped down a hallway that carried a mixed odor of human filth and coffee. Near an open door, he spotted syringes discarded in the corner. Clearly not a quality establishment.

He continued to the location he'd identified in his trajectory calculations and stepped through the door to a one room apartment. Sierra, still dressed in her Tyvek suit, was squatting in front of an open window, long tweezers in hand.

"Find anything?" he asked, really hoping she had a strong lead for him.

She spun, her gloved hand going to her chest. "You scared me."

"Sorry," he said. "I should've given you a warning call-out."

She stood and took a long breath then blew it out and took another, her Tyvek suit ballooning with the effort. She grabbed a capped vial that looked empty and held it up. "I found a single strand of hair. Curly. Black. Was caught in a rough gouge on the window frame. Unfortunately, no follicle so no DNA."

"But you can do something with it, right?"

"Maybe." He'd never heard her sound so hesitant.

"Maybe what?"

She stowed the vial in her kit. "This is a real long shot."

"Doesn't matter. We're at the point where we need to do everything we can."

She rested her hands on her hips. "Researchers I know have developed a method that can identify a person from as little as one centimeter of a single strand of hair."

Impressive. "How?"

"They're analyzing proteins in the hair itself. Like keratin. Sequences of amino acids in proteins vary based on a person's genetic code. So this information can be used as accurately as DNA to identify people."

He eyed her. "What's the catch?"

She arched her eyebrows. "What makes you think there's a catch?"

"If there wasn't one, you'd be using it and not just talking about researchers."

"Oh, right. Most methods used today require several steps of grinding and heating the hair. This destroys much of the protein, and we might not detect enough variation in the remaining proteins to make a confident identification."

He wouldn't even pretend to say he understood her answer. "So how does this help us, then?"

"The researchers I mentioned did away with grinding and are heating the hair in a detergent solution. When they used mass spectrometry analysis to analyze their extractions, they discovered they'd recovered more proteins with that method. So, if we have a strong suspect whose hair appears to match, then we can get a sample of the suspect's hair and send it, along with this hair, to the experts for analysis."

"Strong suspect is the key, and our only lead right now is

the swat caller." He shared the news about the caller at the bar. "I'm headed over there next."

She gave a quick nod. "Let's hope someone saw him, and he has curly black hair."

"If we have a suspect, can't you just compare it using other techniques?"

She bobbed her head. "I can do a visual analysis, but this technique has been called into question of late, and I suspect soon it won't be of any value in court."

Odd. "But why not, if it matches?"

"We don't know the proportion of people in the general population who might have the same hair characteristics as the hair I'm evaluating. Or even the probability of a coincidental match of two hairs. So we can't offer probabilities of a match. Really, I can only rule on an exclusion—no conclusion, or association. Does that make sense?"

"Unfortunately, it does." He looked at the window where she'd recovered the hair. He could easily imagine the shooter hunkered down there. Grady estimated the distance to the crime scene and mentally lined up the shot. A hundred yards give or take a few. His conversation with Murphy came back.

"You're thinking so hard I can almost hear the words," Sierra said. "What's up?"

"These days, shooters think of a hundred yards almost as the minimum distance for modern rifle shooting and hunting. And we insist on a gun, scope, and cartridge combination capable of at least two or three times that distance at the very least."

"Makes sense."

"So why did our shooter miss at a hundred yards? Isn't he familiar with guns? Not a good shooter, or like Sheriff Murphy, too proud to use high price optics?" He told her about his conversation with the sheriff.

She narrowed her eyes. "Sounds like we're not looking at a trained sniper or sharpshooter."

"Yeah, that's my take, and I've been liking Wade Eggen for this since the shooting."

"Really?" She eyed him. "Why's that when we have zero evidence pointing to him?"

"He's an arms dealer. I figured that meant he knew his way around a gun, and from what Nick's report on him said, he's cocky enough to try a shot like this with cops around."

"But now you don't think so."

"Exactly. If an arm's dealer is going to take someone out this way, he'd get his hands on the right equipment to succeed. Top of the line optics for sure."

She turned to stare out the window. "Makes sense."

"So I'm back to square one on suspects," he said trying to hide his disappointment. "Which is no one. Absolutely no one."

20

Grady waited for Ainslie in the bar that smelled like stale beer and cigarette smoke that had permeated the walls years ago and still lingered. Nick had been given access to the small closet in the back housing the network equipment and was hard at work reviewing the wireless router.

Grady wanted to be doing something productive, too, but he'd promised to wait to question anyone until Ainslie arrived, so he paced the floor near the gleaming wood bar top. His boots stuck to the tile each time the soles connected. The bartender and the owner had filled a big yellow bucket with sudsy water and a tall mop but had started wiping down tables first.

Grady tuned the two men out and went to the window to look out on the lot. Drake had arranged for help from his brothers Aiden, the ATF agent, and Brendan, a Multnomah County deputy with SWAT experience. Both were very experienced law enforcement officers, and Ainslie was in good hands with them. Didn't mean Grady could relax. Not one bit.

He heard the back door open and steps coming his way. He spun and waited. Ainslie stepped into the room in front of Aiden, and Grady watched her come in. She'd taken the time to change out of her soiled jeans and T-shirt from the crime scene dirt dive that had ripped her Tyvek suit and stained her knees. She wore skinny black jeans, a beige high-necked sweater, and short boots with very high heels, stretching out those amazing legs.

He let out a slow breath and took in a clean one. With the angst he'd been experiencing the last hour, it was time for him to admit he had some serious feelings for this woman.

"Thanks for waiting for me." She gave him a dazzling smile.

Any angst, unease, worry, whatever he felt, melted from his body, and his only thought was to sweep her into his arms.

Aiden stepped up to them, his piercing gaze breaking the mood. He had the same blue eyes as Drake, and they seemed to cut right to the quick when pinned your way. Dressed in tactical pants and a long-sleeved T-shirt, he was an inch or so shorter than Grady and in great shape, even after recently recovering from donating his kidney to his father.

"I'm gonna keep an eye on things from the parking lot." He tipped his head at the door. "Brendan has the back. I'll take the front."

"Hey, man, thanks for doing this," Grady said, thinking it would be great to have guys like the Byrd brothers around to help with Veritas clients who found themselves in danger. "Tell Brendan thanks, too."

"Sure thing." He looked at Ainslie. "Just give a shout out when you're ready to leave."

She smiled at Aiden, and a bolt of jealousy hit Grady.

Her gaze remained on Aiden as he strode off, his boots thudding on the floor, and Grady didn't like the fact that she was watching another guy. There wasn't any interest burning in her eyes like when she looked at him, but man, he wanted all of her attention.

"We should get started," he said, more for himself than anything. He gestured at the owner, who was squeezing water out of the mop in a large wringer.

She flashed that smile at Grady again, gave a nod, and crossed the room. "I'm Ainslie Duncan, and I have some questions for you."

The owner—a short, stout guy in his fifties with buzzed salt and pepper hair—swiped his hand down his pant leg then stuck it out. "Donald Quincy. Owner. Bartender. Flunky." He laughed, but he had a nervous glint to his expression as he lifted a chair off a nearby table. "Why don't we sit down?"

"Sure." She dropped into the chair.

"C'mon, Freddy, sit with us," Donald said. "She might need to talk to you, too."

The string-bean of a guy with shaggy dark hair, baggy T-shirt, and sloppy jeans hiked up his pants and sauntered to a chair.

"This is Freddy." Donald straddled a chair, his short legs stretched to the max. "Been working here a few years now. Good bartender, and despite the hair hanging in his eyes, a keen observer of what goes on here."

"Nice to meet you, Freddy." Ainslie smiled, but Freddy didn't respond. "So we're here because on Monday night around nine, a guy used your Wi-Fi to make an internet phone call from this location."

"Yeah, so the guy in the back told me," Donald said. "But he made it sound far more complicated than that with all the technical details he gave."

Grady leaned against a wood support post by the table

where he could see both entrances. "Nick likes to be thorough in his explanations."

"Yeah, well, I got the gist of it." Donald rested his arms on the back of the worn wooden chair. "And I been thinking about that night. I was here. But I don't remember anyone with a computer." He looked at Freddy. "You were here. Did you see someone with a computer?"

He shook his head.

"It wouldn't need to be a computer," Grady said. "Could be a phone or tablet."

Donald furrowed his forehead. "People are using their phones all the time in here, so that wouldn't even stand out."

"I get that there'd be a lot of texting," Ainslie said. "Maybe internet access. But how many people actually make calls these days?"

"Yeah." Donald tapped his chin. "Yeah. That might narrow things down, I suppose."

Ainslie nodded. "And he wouldn't want to be overheard, so he probably stepped away from other people."

"Could've gone to the john to make the call," Freddy said.

Grady shook his head. "He'd risk someone walking in and overhearing him. If it was me, I'd step outside or take up a spot near the door where I could bail if I needed to."

Freddy tilted his head, and his eyes suddenly brightened. "Yeah. Yeah. I saw a guy like that. Rita probably saw him too cause it was her area that night."

Ainslie sat forward. "Do you remember him well enough to describe him to a sketch artist?"

"Sure, yeah. Sure. He was kind of odd looking. He had this really curly black hair that stuck up on top and was cut in a mullet in the back."

A bolt of excitement shot through Grady. "You're sure about his hair being black and curly?"

"Positive. It's a look you don't forget." Freddy shook his head. "What kind of guy still has a mullet? I hate those things."

Ainslie's eyes brightened and she motioned for Grady to join her by the door. "Wade has curly black hair. Not sure if it's a mullet, but we can ask Ethan."

"He does?" Grady's excitement over the lead built in his gut. "You're sure?"

"Yeah, I talked to him at the hospital, remember?"

He stepped closer and lowered his voice. "Sierra recovered a curly black hair in the shooter's hide."

"Wade? Wade shot at me?" Her tone shot up.

Grady wanted to say yeah, it had to be him, but his gut still said the guy should've made the shot.

"You don't look like you believe it's him," she said.

"It could be. But if it is, I'd be surprised. He has access to quality weapons, and he missed the shot. Still, if he is lying about Ethan shooting him, he must be hiding the real shooter's ID for some reason. Maybe he doesn't want you to find out who it is and is trying to stop you."

She wrung her hands together. "I wish we had a picture of him to show to Freddy and Rita."

"Blake can probably get his mugshot."

"But that was from several years ago. He could look different now." She frowned, but it evaporated in a burst of excitement. "Wait. Can Kelsey sit with Freddy to do the sketch? Then, I can look at it and see if it's Wade."

Grady caught her sudden enthusiasm and nodded. "Let me check in with Nick to see what he's finding, too. If he located that MAC address, then Flores can compare the number to Wade's phone, and we'll have him."

"This could be it. It could really be it." Ainslie grabbed Grady's arm. "Not only will we likely have Wade for Neil's murder when the DNA comes in, but we'll be able to prove he's behind the threats to my life. And then, hopefully Flores will have enough ammo on him to get him to admit to who really shot him, and Ethan can go free."

～

Ainslie gaped at Blake from a table in the trace evidence lab. "Are you serious? Wade confessed and turned himself in?"

"Yes," Blake replied. "Flores just called to say Wade Eggen came in and confessed to killing Neil Orr."

Still unable to believe the news, she shook her head and dropped onto the nearest stool.

Grady fixed his narrowed gaze on Blake and took a seat next to Ainslie. He seemed as confused as Ainslie by the turn of events.

"This makes no sense," she said. "There's no evidence against Wade at this point. Just Ethan's word against his. So why confess after all these years?"

Blake shook his head. "That I can't tell you. He's being processed, and Flores hasn't interviewed him yet."

"Maybe the guilt finally got to him, and he had to say something," Ainslie said. "You know, like Ethan did. I mean if I kept something like that a secret for all that time, I'd want to get it off my chest. Not that I could ever imagine myself keeping such a thing secret."

Grady met her gaze. "You have no idea what you will or won't do unless faced with that kind of situation."

"I suppose." She sat back and crossed her arms. "But I couldn't live like that and can't understand anyone who could. I'm still trying to come to grips with Ethan having done it."

Grady's face went slack, but he didn't speak. He clearly didn't agree with her. Maybe he was disappointed in her rigid statement.

Didn't mean she would back down from her opinion. "Maybe I'm being close-minded here, but keeping secrets that others have a right to know about is just plain wrong."

Grady winced. "And yet good people do it all the time."

She flashed him a look. "You're saying Wade's a good person?"

He held up his hands. "Just speaking hypothetically."

Blake leaned forward. "Let's not get off track here."

She continued to watch Grady for a moment longer then swung her focus to Blake. "With Wade in custody, can we get his current mug shot to show Freddy?"

Blake nodded. "Flores has agreed to text it to me when they're done processing him."

"And what about the MAC address Nick found?" Grady asked.

"Flores will get Wade's phone information, too. Hopefully, that will connect him to the swat."

Grady planted his hands on the table. "If he *was* behind it, then I hope Flores will try to pin all attempts on Ainslie's life on him."

Blake nodded. "She'll do her best, but her top priority is working with Sheriff Murphy to nail down Wade's confession so they can get murder charges brought."

"I never thought I'd say this." Ainslie shook her head. "But it's a good thing Matt came back with us. Charging Wade can move forward faster."

"Might Flores get a hair sample from Wade for comparison to the one found in the shooter's hide?"

"And what about a weapon?" Grady asked. "Can't Flores get a warrant for his apartment and car and look for the rifle?"

Blake looked like he wanted to sigh over all their questions. "Yes to both, but, like I said, she has her priorities.

Means we need to keep working this investigation as if Wade hadn't turned himself in."

Ainslie thought about the implications of Wade's arrest. "But one thing's changed. I'm safer. I mean, it really looks like he's the one who's trying to take me out."

"It does indeed," Blake replied. "But I still urge caution."

"So I can't go home just yet."

"No!" Grady's voice shot up. "You'll stay here until we prove Wade's involvement."

Blake gave Grady a careful study before he stood. "For what it's worth, I agree. Maybe we'll know more once you get a chance to evaluate the slugs Sierra recovered at the scene. She's back, and I'm heading to her lab to distribute the evidence."

"Good." Grady looked uncomfortable under Blake's scrutiny. "I want to get my eyes on those slugs."

"I'll drop them in an evidence locker for you and keep you updated on Flores's progress."

Ainslie smiled up at Blake. "Thank you for all your help."

"Almost forgot." He reached into his pocket and pulled out Ainslie's phone. "Ran into Nick in the hallway. Your phone is clean—no tracking apps installed—and ready to use again."

She took it from him. "Thanks."

After a sharp nod, he marched out of the room.

Ainslie looked at Grady. "I hate knowing Wade's in custody, and yet we still have to wait for so much to move forward with freeing Ethan."

"Justice doesn't always move swiftly."

"I wish we could at least prove Wade's the one who's been trying to hurt me." She shifted on the stool, trying to find a comfortable position, but it was her jangled nerves that were keeping her from settling down, so she stood.

"Couldn't we have Coop go back inside Wade's apartment and look for hair in the bed?"

"He could." Grady's eyes narrowed as he looked up at her. "But it wouldn't be legal, and he might contaminate the scene. I can't recommend that. It's too risky if you want your brother to be cleared. We have to follow the letter of the law."

She sighed. "It's just that we basically know it's him coming after me, right? And we only need a silly little hair to prove it."

"We'll need more than that for a trial, but yes, the hair could be a key piece of evidence if Sierra can confirm the match." Grady stood. "I'm going to process those slugs then give Malone a call. See if I can light a fire under her on getting that CT scan and Ethan's gun."

Ainslie nodded, but he didn't move to leave.

"Is there something else before you go?" she asked.

He shook his head. "Just don't want to leave you."

"I'm safe here."

"It's not about your safety." He pressed his lips together and looked over her shoulder, his gaze uncertain for the usually confident man. "I meant about just being with you."

Not at all what she'd expected him to say, and she didn't know how to respond.

"It's okay," he said and started for the door. "You don't have to say anything."

"Grady," she called after him.

He came to a stop, his hand on the door, and he turned to look at her.

The heavy weight of his expectant gaze nearly swamped her, but she wouldn't run from the feeling. Not this time. "I like being with you, too."

A wide smile crossed his face, and he gave a quick nod. Then without a word, he stepped out the door.

She sat for a few more minutes, her thoughts jumbled, then opened the photos for the drive-by that Sierra had completed after Ainslie had left the crime scene. Ainslie wanted to look at the pictures to see if she could learn anything from Sierra's work. She started with reviewing the copious shots of bullet holes in the wall where Sierra had added labels and scales before snapping the pictures. A bullet hole looked like a bullet hole to a jury. Same with blood spatter and stains. To differentiate them, they used road-mapping, placing a series of labels and scales on the surfaces being photographed to expose patterns or defects.

She was just about to begin this process outside the house when the sniper fired and she dove to the ground. She almost felt the bullet hitting the dirt inches from her head. Her hands coming over her head to protect her. Involuntary, she knew. And then the panic. Oh, the panic. She'd been terrified. Frozen in place. Until Grady. A quick thinker and protector.

Her palms started to sweat, and she released her mouse to sit back, staring at the screen.

She'd almost died. Could be dead. And here she was fighting the best thing that had happened to her in a long while. Grady Houston. A fine man who'd just clearly expressed his interest in her. A man who she knew deep in her heart would be a great partner in life. Someone to share a life with. To have children with. To grow old with.

Her phone rang. Seeing his name, she quickly answered. "Grady?"

"Ethan's gun and Wade's CT scan were waiting down here for me." His excited tone raced through the phone. "Grab your cameras and come down to my lab. I need your help to record the process of proving your brother's innocence."

21

Ainslie slung the camera case straps over her shoulder and bolted from the lab. She was so pumped, her hand shook as she punched the first floor elevator button. She had to settle down or she wouldn't be able to take clear pictures and video. She closed her eyes and imagined a tranquil day at the Oregon beach, a place she'd always found relaxing as the waves rushed onto the smooth wet sand. Clouds hung overhead in her mind, since the coast was often cloudy with fog stubbornly clinging to the water.

She concentrated on easing out the stress with each imagined wave so that, by the time she got to the firearms lab, she felt calm and centered.

The first room held display cases filled with different weapons and ammunition neatly labeled with their details. Long tables sat in the middle. The space was empty, but she heard movement in the back area. She found Grady standing near a table by a big stainless steel box near the far wall. She remembered he'd called the box a bullet recovery containment system. It was filled with water, and the caustic smell of gunpowder from the steady stream of bullets fired into this system lingered in the space.

He turned to look at her. "Great. I was just getting things set up. While I finish, can you photograph the weapon and ammo I laid out on the table."

"Of course." She set down her bags and grabbed a pair of latex gloves. "You sure it's okay that I'm taking these pictures, what with the conflict of interest and all?"

He nodded. "It's not like you can change any of the outcomes."

"True." She took out a few markers and a ruler from her bag and placed them near the evidence to show scale. She took copious pictures to be sure she captured everything.

"By the way, I processed the slugs fired at you. They were .223 caliber as I'd thought. There are a few rifles chambered for the .223. I think he was using an AR-15."

"And does that tell you anything?"

"Only that, if he'd used the right optics, he wouldn't likely have missed. So we need to be thankful that he was cocky or dumb enough to think he could make the shot without it."

"Is that common?"

"Common?" He tipped his head and looked at her. "I guess. Yeah. A lot of guys think more highly of their marksmanship than they should. But then again, a lot of guys like all the toys, too. Could be he just didn't have a sight or couldn't get his hands on one quickly. He sure wasn't going to walk into a Cabela's and buy one to use to murder someone."

"I guess not." She snapped the last picture and stepped back. "Done."

He joined her and picked up Ethan's gun. "Did you get a close up of the serial number on the frame?" He pointed to the number engraved on the body of the weapon.

"I did."

He tipped up a box of ammunition. "I need to show the ammo specs as well."

She arranged the box for best lighting and snapped the pictures.

"Okay." He tapped a block of thick gel mounted on another table. "I'm going to load and fire the gun into this ballistic gel from the same trajectory as at the scene."

She had to admit surprise that he wasn't using that water containment unit, but he was the expert. "Why the gel instead of the water?"

"It will better simulate the actual shooting and damage to the bullet." He picked up the magazine. "I want you to video this procedure. I'll do an introduction, load the gun, and then fire into the gel. I'd like you to zoom in to capture the bullets, et cetera while I load and when I retrieve the slugs from the gel. I'll talk through the whole thing, giving my step-by-step procedures."

"I'll get the camera out." She reached for the bag and withdrew the small but pricey video camera. "Will you start at the table?"

He nodded. "And then move to the mini range I set up."

She positioned herself on the far side of the room and looked through the viewfinder until she found the perfect spot. "I'm ready when you are."

He gave a firm nod and met her gaze, a look of determination on his face. "This could be it, you know? One of the things that could clear Ethan's name."

"Then, let's get to it." She smiled.

He smiled back at her, letting it linger, warming her heart. If she weren't already smitten, this ease between them would take her over the edge. "Tell me when to start the camera rolling."

He grabbed a pair of hearing protectors. "Put these on, and then go ahead."

She slipped them over her head and started the camera. "Rolling."

"I'm Grady Houston, weapons expert and partner at the Veritas Center." He stated his qualifications and experience, and Ainslie had to admit she was impressed and knew a jury would be, too.

He picked up the gun. "Today I am test firing a Beretta 92 FS found in the possession of Ethan Duncan on the day of Wade Eggen's shooting." He held out the gun and read the serial number then pointed at the ammo box. "The gun was loaded with American Eagle 9mm Luger 115 Grain Full Metal Jacket bullets, and I will be test firing bullets from the recovered magazine and ones from the box of the same manufacturing batch located in Mr. Duncan's home."

He put on his own pair of hearing protectors and slid the magazine into the gun, looked at the camera, a glint in his eyes, and said, "Fire in the hole."

He fired the gun. Once. Twice. The muffled sound was still loud, despite the ear protection. He ejected the magazine. "And we're clear."

She loved watching how certain he was in his movements and how firmly he held the gun when firing. She'd known he was an expert at this, but seeing him perform the tests brought his work to life for her.

He moved to the end of the table. She kept the video rolling with one hand and removed the bulky ear protectors with the other. He extracted the bullets from the wobbly gel and went to a machine on the far wall. "The machine you're looking at is called BULLETTRAX. I'm mounting one of the fired bullets into the holder, and the machine will digitally capture the surface of a bullet in 2D and 3D, providing a topographic model of the marks around the bullet's circumference. I can then measure it and make comparisons to the bullet on the CT scan taken of Wade Eggen's head. I will follow this procedure with each bullet."

He started the machine running, and it rotated the bullet three-hundred-sixty degrees. He repeated the process for each bullet then grabbed a large manila envelope and held it up to the camera. "You should know that other experts have suggested the bullet in Eggen's head could be an American Eagle 9mm Luger 115 Grain Full Metal Jacket bullet. I have requested those findings be provided in a sealed envelope so I can't see their results before beginning my measurements to keep from biasing my results. Once I have concluded my tests, I will open the envelope on camera and make the comparisons."

He set down the envelope. "But for now, we're going to stop recording. I'll be taking the fired bullets to a nearby facility to run a CT scan of additional bullets for exact comparison to the scan of Mr. Eggen's head."

He nodded at Ainslie, and she turned off the camera. "This is all very interesting, but how soon can we get that CT scan of the bullets."

"Not we." He frowned. "I should go alone. There's nothing for you to do there, and I don't want to risk taking you out into potential danger again."

"But with Wade in custody it should..." She shook her head. "Never mind. I don't want to have to bother anyone else to escort me when it's just to run some bullets through a CT scanner."

"Just some bullets?" He mocked pulling a knife from his chest. "This is my life's work we're talking about here."

She swatted her hand at him. "I didn't mean anything by it. What you do is very important."

"I know that. I was just messing with you."

"Oh," she said, liking the fact that he'd been joking

when so much of their time had been serious and tension filled.

She suddenly wondered what it might be like to be on a date with him. To go to a movie. Dinner. For a walk. Even just watch TV together. At the moment she honestly wouldn't even mind sitting with him while he watched football. Putting a sports game between them now seemed so foolish when, if she could get beyond that and her feelings of inadequacy, she could have a much richer life. Maybe with Grady. Or without. Doing the work to improve herself would return rewards beyond what she'd once been able to imagine. And that was thanks to her feelings for Grady. So, no matter the outcome, knowing him had forever changed her life.

"You look a million miles away."

"Sorry. Just distracted."

"By what?"

Should she tell him? Dare she open the subject? Yes, it was time to lay everything out there once and for all. "You really want to know?"

"I do."

"I was thinking what it might be like to go on a date with you."

His mouth dropped open.

She should ignore his stunned surprise, but she lifted his jaw with her finger.

He grabbed her hand and tugged her against his chest, then wrapped his arms around her back to hold her close. She reveled in his touch and circled her arms around his trim waist to move even closer.

He took a halting breath. "I would very much like to find out what it would be like to go on a date with you."

Her turn for stunned surprise. "You would? I thought you didn't want to get involved."

"That's not it at all. I just…" His expression hardened for a flash before he washed it away. "There's something I need to tell you before we can move forward."

She watched him, and he looked so conflicted that a bead of worry took hold in her heart. "Sounds serious."

"It is. And complicated. And not something I want to talk to you about in my lab with my team in the other room."

Now he really had her attention, and her curiosity was burning a hole in her brain. She couldn't wait to know what he'd been keeping from her. But when? Where? Her brain raced with ideas, but she was muddled by his nearness.

"Tonight," she said, fleshing out an idea even as she spoke. "I'll make dinner, and we can talk then."

"Sure. Good." He leaned back. "Wait. We can't do my place. Jackson will be there. How about Sierra's condo?"

"Maybe. But if she's not working, Reed could be with her."

"Then it will have to wait," he said, almost sounding relieved.

"No," she said. "Sierra wants us to get together. I'll just tell her I need her condo to cook you dinner. She'll gladly do it for me."

His eyebrows shot up. "And you'll actually ask?"

"I will." And she wasn't even going to feel guilty about it.

"Then, until then." Grady pressed a kiss on her forehead and released her.

She had the urge to settle back into his arms and get a proper kiss. Not that little peck or even one that was fueled by adrenaline. Or by fear. Like at the crime scene.

Oh, she knew it wouldn't be hard to get him to kiss her. But not here. When he kissed her again, she wanted it to be private and romantic, not in a stark ballistics lab where it would feel all clinical.

Grady slipped the bullet CT film onto a light box table and paused before beginning work. He wanted to call Ainslie down to the lab so she was present the moment he had the results from the scans, but he still had work to do before he could rule on the findings. She would only serve as a distraction.

He started working on the first of fifteen scanned bullets from the box found in Ethan's house. He measured the bullet base diameter and length using a calibrated vernier caliper—VC. He took his time measuring each one, making sure he recorded precise physical measurements and used both the VC and CT scan to assess accuracy and precision.

He'd also chosen bullets of similar caliber and had them scanned for comparison. This was for effect for the jury, as the differences could easily be seen in the scan.

He mounted the scan of Wade's head in the lightbox and placed the 9mm 115 grain bullet scan next to it. The slug was very similar to the one in situ, but the measurements didn't work out, and his heart soared for Ainslie.

It was official. Finally. The 115 grain bullet was too small to be the slug in Wade's head. Grady knew he would be asked to identify the specific caliber of the bullet lodged by Wade's eye, but if both bullets were the same design type, a higher mass bullet in 9mm may have similar values to a lower mass bullet in a .357 caliber. So he couldn't answer that. No ballistics expert could. What he could do was look at the state expert's findings to see where they went wrong, but he needed Ainslie to film the opening of the envelope.

He grabbed his phone. Satisfaction burning in his gut, he punched her number.

"Do you have something?" she asked sounding breathless.

"I do. Come down and bring the video camera again."

"Can't you just tell me on the phone?"

"It's better in person. Plus, I need you to film the opening of the envelope from the state expert."

"On my way." She ended the call.

Envelope in hand, he sat back to wait, his mind focused on Ainslie. His analysis could finally cast doubt that a bullet from Ethan's gun sat in Wade's head. That, plus the other information they'd gathered, could finally help to free him. Which meant Grady would have no reason to spend time with Ainslie. Probably didn't matter anyway. Not after they met for dinner tonight and he told her about Uncle Tommy.

Grady's palms started sweating at the thought of it. He imagined what it was going to be like to sit next to her. Maybe across from her. And spit out a decades-old secret.

He heard the lock on the lab door release, and he let out his anxiety in a long breath so he didn't seem stressed for Ainslie or the video.

She rushed into the room, her gaze expectant. "Well?"

He held up the envelope. "This guy was all wrong. I won't know why until I see his findings, but the bullet lodged in Wade's head most likely wasn't fired from Ethan's gun."

Ainslie locked gazes with him, excitement burning in her eyes. "So you have the proof, then? Ethan didn't shoot Wade?"

He wanted to simply say yes, but absolute proof never existed in ballistic comparisons. "Not one hundred percent proof, no. There are mitigating factors that could've come into play."

She dropped onto a stool, her eyes narrowing. "Like what?"

"First, the expert and I both had to make assumptions," he said.

Her eyes narrowed. "I don't understand."

"We both assumed that Ethan's magazine had once been loaded with all American Eagle 9mm Luger 115 Grain Full Metal Jacket bullets, when in fact the magazine had four open slots. He could've accidentally, or on purpose, loaded a different bullet in these slots. Or he could have a separate magazine that he used to shoot Wade then discarded it and put the 115 grain magazine back in the gun."

"But that's not likely, right? Because the police only found those 115 grain bullets in his house. Nothing else."

"Right, and I don't think any of these scenarios are accurate, but I'm telling you this because it shows that it's a strong start, but we'll still need more to clear Ethan's name." He paused. "And there's one other statistic that's in his favor as well. The larger grain bullet on average has a deeper penetration level than the 115 grain, so it would likely have traveled deeper into Wade's head. I can't fire a larger round into his head to compare, so I can't quantify that, but it's a logical conclusion based on where the bullet is located and on my ballistic tests."

"So we still need more." She sighed. "And here I thought this was going to be it."

"Hey," he said going over to her. "I don't mean to downplay the importance of this discovery. It's huge. And we need to look at it in that light. But I didn't want you to think we could stop working just quite yet."

"I don't like it, but I get it."

He tapped the envelope. "Time to get out the camera."

She set it up and gestured for him to start. He smiled at the camera and eagerly ripped open the envelope. "I'm back with the earlier findings."

He withdrew the sheet of paper and read down the page. "Ah-ha. The expert simply didn't do a thorough job, but assumed all 9mm Luger bullets were of the same length when in fact they vary. Even ones coming off the same manufacturing line. For example, the diameters of the bullets I scanned from the box located at Mr. Duncan's house ranged from 8.95 mm to 9.01 mm."

Grady took a long breath and checked the page again. "The report says our expert determined the bullet in Mr. Eggen's head had a diameter between 9.03 and 9.19 mm at the base, which the expert said was in line with the general dimensions of a 9 mm Luger bullet. He's incorrect. Luger bullets don't exceed 9.02 mm. But the dimensions he quoted could fit a wide range of 9 mm varieties, and even .38 Special or .357 round types. Any one of these bullets could be lodged in Mr. Eggen's head but not the bullets found in Mr. Duncan's gun. This concludes my video report, and I thank you for listening to the technical details."

He looked at Ainslie to end the video.

"Wow," she said. "You really know what you're doing."

He was about to comment when his phone rang. "It's Sierra."

"Is Ainslie still with you?" Sierra asked.

"Yes."

"Put me on speaker, please."

He tapped the speaker icon.

"What's up?"

"Two things. Detective Flores just had a hair sample messengered over to me."

"Wade's?" Ainslie asked excitedly.

"Yes. And I've done a preliminary analysis. The hair I recovered at the shooter's hide matches this sample."

"So, Wade is the person who's been trying to kill me?"

"Looks like it."

"Is this enough to charge him with attempted murder?" Grady asked.

"That, I'm not sure of, but Flores has asked our team to

process his apartment with her, and I'm hoping we'll locate additional evidence to point to him."

"Can I join you?" Ainslie asked.

"That's not a good idea," Sierra said.

"Will you video it so I can watch? I mean I hate to ask—"

"Of course I will," Sierra said. "But before I go, I'm going to give my buddy a call to get him out here ASAP. He's the guy who can complete a more thorough analysis of the hair. An analysis that will stand up in court."

"Thank you, Sierra," Ainslie said.

"You're welcome." Sierra's tone was warm and genuine. "And as a bonus, since I'll be at Wade's apartment, my condo will totally be free for your dinner with Grady."

22

Grady had to admit that he'd hoped dinner would be more intimate and romantic. Instead, it was a simple meal with salad, lasagna from the freezer, and the laptop sitting on the island standing by for Sierra's video call.

"I'm sorry I didn't have more to choose from for dinner," she said, putting a bowl with rosy red tomatoes and crisp cucumbers resting on fresh green lettuce in front of him

"I don't care what we eat," he said. "Besides I like rabbit food."

"What's your favorite meal?" she asked, seeming to want to know more about him, which he took as a good sign.

"Steak, baked potato, and my mom's garden peas." He stabbed a fork into his salad and held it midair. "Or actually pretty much anything my mom makes."

Ainslie sat at the island and poured ranch dressing on her salad. "Sounds like your family is close."

Good. She'd brought up his family. It would be a good segue to tell her about Uncle Tommy.

He looked at her. "Yeah, we are. I don't get back to Nebraska nearly often enough to eat her cooking, but I usually attend Sunday family dinner via Skype and drool over the food. She's not able to grow as much produce as she did on the farm, but she uses every inch of the space she has available."

"Losing the farm must've been hard on them." Ainslie stabbed her fork into a tomato.

He watched it squirt against the bowl before responding. "It *was* hard until Dad got a sales rep job for a seed company. Turns out he really likes the work, and he's good at it. They miss farming, but don't miss the uncertainty of crop failures. Or weather disasters and lean years. He likes that regular paycheck and big bonuses."

She took a sip of water. "Did you ever consider farming?"

He shook his head. "You see your parents go through the struggle of working so hard only to have the government interfere with pricing and screw things up. Or a drought takes a crop. Or even a tornado. You don't get any time off, working pretty much twenty-four/seven, seven days a week, three hundred sixty-five days a year. That wasn't the life I wanted."

"How did you get into weapons?" she asked. "I mean, you're not born an expert at that."

"True that. Takes time. I went to visit my older brother at college for a big game. His roommate's dad was there, and he was a ballistics expert at the FBI's Quantico lab. I was a big hunter and belonged to a gun club for competitive shooting. I was totally into it, and once I heard you could make a living doing something like that, I decided that was the job for me."

She cocked her head, a cute quizzical look on her face. "But then you went into the military."

He nodded. "We didn't have money for college, so that was out. And there's no better place to shoot tons of guns and gain practical experience than in the military. So I enlisted. Got my bachelor's in forensic science. Then as I worked on my master's, I did an internship program with the FBI lab."

"That's a lot to cram into a short period of time." She sat back and carefully watched him. "I don't know when you could possibly have had time for a personal life."

"I don't have much of one. I go to games and watch sports when I get a chance, but that's about it." The more personal the discussion got, the more he was losing his appetite and set down his fork.

"No dating?" she asked.

"Very little." He folded his hands on the counter and met her gaze head-on. "But that's not about having the time. It's about my past."

She didn't say anything for the longest time just continued to watch him. "What you were alluding to in the lab, and the reason we're having dinner."

He nodded. "I have something in common with Ethan."

Her eyes widened. "Don't tell me you had a drug problem."

"No. I have a secret. And until I notify the right people, I'll always be a slave to it. Like Ethan was. I didn't turn to drugs to forget, but it's haunted me for a long time." He took a deep breath and thought about the words to say so she would understand. "I was nine, and it's something I should have told someone back then, or in all the years since, but I couldn't be the one to destroy my family. Then the years slipped away. I stayed busy to avoid it. You know, became a workaholic, which is why I was able to achieve so much. But now, because of everything that's happened with you and Ethan, I know I have to tell my parents and the sheriff back home."

"Go on." Her expression was unreadable when he desperately wanted to know what she was thinking.

"You've said you can't understand keeping a secret, and if

you don't want to have anything to do with me after you hear about this, I'll understand."

She slid closer. "Don't think about that. Just tell me."

"Our farm was near a small town where my Uncle Tommy lives and owns a body shop. A vagrant had been wandering around town for a week or so, panhandling. Church folks helped him out, but the local businesses didn't like having him around. Said he was bad for business. Uncle Tommy kept finding the guy sleeping near his place when he'd open shop in the morning. He didn't like it. Not one bit."

Grady paused, his heart pounding at the telling. "At one of our Sunday night dinners, Uncle Tommy was angrier than I'd ever seen him. He'd just run the guy off again."

Grady shook his head. "Uncle Tommy's this crusty bachelor. Former military. Kind of rough around the edges and not the kind of guy who found compassion in his heart for a homeless guy. He said often enough that he believed people should pick themselves up by their bootstraps and make something of themselves."

"So what happened?" She looked mesmerized by the story, but what was she feeling about it?

He wouldn't stop to ask. "One night this vagrant was killed in a hit-and-run on the highway. The sheriff didn't have any leads other than that the guy was likely hit with a large pickup that potentially had white paint. That described half the vehicles in the county and didn't narrow things down a lot. I listened to all the gossip, but being nine, I didn't think much about it. Until I went to see Uncle Tommy late one night. He was teaching me how to play poker without my parents knowing about it. I would sneak out of the house on Friday night and ride my bike to Uncle Tommy's apartment above his garage. But this particular night, he must've forgotten I was coming, because he was in his shop working.

"He didn't hear me come in." The painful memory twisted Grady's gut. "He was working on his truck. The front end was all bashed in. Like he'd hit something." He paused on the next word, which he could barely get out over a tightening throat. "Someone."

"The vagrant," she said, sounding breathless.

"Yeah," he said. "I paid more attention to the gossip after that night, and the damage fit the details that people were talking about."

She leaned even closer. "What did you do?"

"I ran to my bike and hightailed it home. I didn't know what to do next, so I did nothing. Funny enough, the next day Uncle Tommy came by driving his old Jeep and asked why I didn't show up for poker. I lied and said I was sick. He bought the story, and all was well with us. Or at least from his side of things. Except it kept bugging me. Badly. I wasn't sleeping much, and when I did, I had bad dreams about Uncle Tommy running the guy down. I tried to tell my mom a few times, but Uncle Tommy's her brother, and I just couldn't hurt her. So I didn't say anything to anyone. And here we are. All these years later. Uncle Tommy's a free man. As far as I know, they never identified the vagrant and never figured out who hit him."

She sat back and eyed him, but he couldn't read her reaction. "I'm sorry you had to go through that."

He had to work hard not to gape at her response, so different than he'd expected. "Thank you. I thought you'd be disgusted."

"I totally get how a nine-year-old would keep that to himself. But I won't pretend to understand how you could continue to stay quiet. Only you can really understand that." Her tone was flat. Her face devoid of any expression.

Yeah, but what was she thinking about him? About a possible future with him? He was desperate to know, but his pride wouldn't let him come right out and ask.

But he could try to explain. "I don't think even I understand my continued silence. It's just one of those things that seems less real as time passes. Like it happened to someone else, and I can push it into the back of my mind. Try to forget about it. But then something happens and it comes flooding back."

She pursed her lips and watched him for a long uncomfortable moment. "So what are you going to do about it?"

Yeah, what? "After we clear Ethan and Wade is charged with trying to kill you, I'm going back home to tell my parents then go to the sheriff."

She gave a sharp nod as if she approved, yet her expression remained blank. "That's good. I'm sure you'll feel much better after you do."

"Honestly, I'm not sure how I'll forgive myself for not doing it all this time, but I'm gonna try. Because I want more than work in my life. I want a wife and family. And to be the best husband and father I can be, I can't keep carrying this heavy guilt." He waited for her to say something but she just continued to watch him. "I don't mean to sound like I'm trivializing my actions, and that I think I should just get over it. It's serious, and I take full responsibility for my part in staying silent."

She opened her mouth like she was going to say something. Maybe tell him how she felt, but her computer chimed, and she clamped her mouth closed.

He let out a breath. "That will be Sierra, right?"

Ainslie nodded and accepted the call, leaving Grady to wonder what she thought about him and the secret he'd kept for so many years.

She got the video running, her mood somber, but it

could be because they were looking at Wade's apartment. Or it could be because she was so disappointed in him that she couldn't even talk about what he'd done. He'd expected to feel relieved, but he didn't. Not one bit. He still had a long way to go, but, like he'd told Ainslie, he would put in his best effort to let go of his guilt.

He shifted his focus from the video, where Sierra systematically worked her way through the apartment, to Ainslie. Maybe once they parted ways for the night, she'd think about what he'd done, really think about it, and then decide she couldn't be with a guy who'd hidden such a big thing for so many years. Or she could even be thinking that right now.

He would totally understand. Totally.

"Well, would you look at this." Sierra pulled a box out from under the bed covered in a worn floral bedspread.

The camera focused in on the box holding a small drone and supplies to make Molotov cocktails.

"The drone that started the fire." Ainslie shot Grady an excited look.

"Sure seems like it, and there's more." Sierra dove back under the bed, the camera feed going dark.

Ainslie's gaze was pinned to the screen, and she slid to the edge of her stool.

He could feel her excitement, and his heart lifted over the fact that they were finally getting somewhere in clearing Ethan's name.

Sierra scooted back out, and the camera caught a clear shot of a black semi-automatic rifle.

Grady leaned in for a better look. "It's an M&P15. Chambered for .223 cal like the slugs recovered at the crime scene." Grady looked at Ainslie. "Likely the gun that was used to try to kill you."

"Something about it looks so deadly." She stared at the

screen and shivered. "The black frame. That stock. It doesn't look like a hunting rifle you see on TV or movies. More like the kind of gun that bad guys and cops use. So it's a people hunting gun."

He'd never heard it called that before, but she was right. "Yeah, it's more of a personal protection gun. And it's popular with law enforcement agencies. But don't confuse it with automatics that the real bad guys use. It's not like that at all and wouldn't have been used for the drive-by you were working."

Ainslie's phone rang, and she grabbed it from the counter. "It's Matt Murphy."

She answered and pursed her lips as she listened. "Sure, I guess, but couldn't you just wait for her to call you back?"

She frowned and tapped a finger on the counter as if irritated. Not that Grady was surprised she was getting frustrated when talking to Murphy. The guy might know how to do his job, but he sure didn't know how to play nice.

"Okay. Fine." She sighed. "Text me when you arrive, and I'll come down to get you."

She slammed her phone on the counter. "He's really something, you know that?"

"What's up?"

"Emory called him and left a message saying she had Neil's DNA results. She told him to call her back, but she's not answering, so he wants to come over here and talk to her in person."

Interesting. "Why in person?"

"He didn't really explain, but he never was a patient sort."

"I don't want to see the cranky sheriff, but it's good news that the DNA is done." He smiled at her and tried not to think about the fact that he still didn't know how she felt about his secret. In any event, it didn't seem to be interfering with her ability to focus on the investigation.

"It's odd that Emory called him first," Ainslie said. "But she'll let us know as soon as she thinks we need to know anything."

"Nothing else to see here," Sierra announced grabbing their attention.

"Thanks for letting us watch," Ainslie said.

"Can you get that gun back here ASAP?" Grady asked. "I want to confirm it's the one used at the crime scene."

"I can have Chad finish up here, and I'll bring it back to the lab."

"Perfect."

She stood facing the door. "So how'd dinner go? Are you two dating now?"

Grady groaned. "Hanging up now, Sierra. See you in the lab."

He closed the computer, and his phone rang. "It's Emory."

He put her on speaker. "Sheriff Murphy's looking for you."

"I know. I went to my condo to put my feet up and have dinner with Blake, and Murphy left me four messages. I'll call him back after I hang up with you."

"No need to. He called Ainslie. He's on his way here, and she's going to let him in."

"Then I guess we all might as well just meet in my lab, and I'll review the DNA results with everyone at once."

By the time Ainslie and Grady got down to the lobby to escort Matt to the DNA lab, he'd already managed to annoy their night guard. Pete's tight expression as Ainslie walked through the lobby toward him proved it.

"You may be a sheriff, but we don't make exceptions for anyone." Pete gritted his teeth. "Everyone signs in and needs an escort. Everyone."

Matt planted his hands on his hips and stared at the iPad on the counter.

She stopped at the desk and gave Pete an *I'm sorry* look. "Is there a problem, Matt?"

He fired her a testy look. "Other than you don't trust anybody here, you mean? Where we're from, we have a little faith in people."

"It's not a matter of trust," Grady said. "It's a matter of chain of custody and protection of evidence. I'm sure you employ similar security standards at your office."

"Nothing this stringent, as you know from your visit. And I sure don't have a fancy place like you all got here." Matt waved a hand and looked around. "Pretty dang frou-frou for people who cater to law enforcement."

Grady crossed his arms, obviously taking offense at the comment. "Our main DNA clientele allows us to provide reasonably priced services to law enforcement and do pro bono work, too. You know, like how we're providing our services to you for free. And DNA testing can be stressful, so we like our clients to feel relaxed."

Ainslie wished Grady didn't need to defend such an amazing place to Matt. She glared at him. "Sign the iPad, grab your badge, and come with me."

Ainslie didn't wait for Matt to agree but headed back to the door and pressed her fingers on the print reader to open it. Grady joined her.

"I want to wring his neck," she whispered.

"You'll have to get in line." Grady grinned. "The guy sure has a need to feel important."

"Probably comes from his quarterback days, when he was revered and developed such a big head. Obviously, that hasn't changed." She tapped her foot until Matt joined them.

"Behind these walls you'll find a state-of-the-art lab like none you've ever seen." She stepped through the door and marched straight for the elevator, then got them headed up for the quick trip to the second floor. She opened the lab door and stepped back to let Matt enter. She expected him to look impressed, but honestly, her irritation continued to mar his handsome face.

Emory got up from behind her desk and tugged her lab coat closed over her burgeoning belly. She stuck out her hand. "Emory Jenkins."

Matt shook hands. "Tried calling you back."

"I was taking a little break, but thank you for coming out here. I know that must've been inconvenient for you."

"It was. Hope the trip was worth it."

Emory looked like she wanted to sigh, and Ainslie wanted to deck Matt for his insensitivity.

Emory picked up a folder and pressed it open on the lab table. "You'll find the results for the DNA recovered from Neil's shirt. This first profile came from the saliva on his sleeve, and it's a match for Wade Eggen."

Matt stared at the paper. "That's good news."

"Yes." She turned the page. "This second profile is from blood located on the front of Neil's shirt."

Matt's head popped up. "Blood? I didn't know you found blood."

"We did."

"Neil's?"

"No, and it isn't a match for Wade either."

"A third person?" Ainslie asked fearing it might be Ethan.

Matt locked onto Ainslie's gaze. "Your brother?"

"No, it's not Ethan's DNA," Emory said. "I also ran the results through CODIS. Didn't find a match there either. The subject is unknown."

"So someone else was involved in the murder," Grady stated.

"Could be, or could be blood from something else that happened in Neil's day. Or could be from a person who helped bury him. So many possibilities of how that blood got on his shirt that there's really no way to narrow it down."

Matt looked at Emory. "Other than finding out who the blood belongs to."

"Yes," Emory said. "Find that person, and you could find an accomplice to murder."

Grady could hardly comprehend that the DNA results not only didn't answer all the questions but brought up another mystery to solve before freeing Ethan.

"A good lawyer could have a field day with this blood in court," Murphy said. "Could raise enough questions as to Wade's guilt."

"But he confessed," Ainslie argued.

Murphy scowled. "Doesn't mean the prosecution's a slam dunk. He could always recant."

She shook her head. "I can't even imagine this could happen. Not after all the work it's taken to prove he was involved."

Grady didn't want to point out that the best cases could be lost in court over one forensic item. OJ's glove came to mind as a good example, but Grady wouldn't bring it up and make her feel worse.

Grady's phone rang, and he grabbed it. "It's Jayla's mother."

"Jayla?" Emory asked.

"A girl who lives across the street from Ethan. I think she witnessed Wade's shooting or at least knows something about it." He stepped away from the others and answered.

"I talked to my girl," Heidi said. "She still says she was asleep and didn't see or hear a thing."

Grady thought for sure he was right about this girl, but it was looking like he'd let his personal life color his opinions. "Do you believe her?"

"I don't know." She paused, and Grady let the silence linger to encourage her to talk. "Something's up with her. Not sure what. I asked her about the doorbell video. She's kind of tech savvy, you know. So I thought she might be able to figure out how to find the account. She acted kinda weird. Could just be about her dad splitting on us. Could be more, I guess."

Okay, so maybe he *had* been right. "Do you think if I talked to her again, she might tell me more?"

"Maybe. But I don't want her to be pressured. She's going through a tough enough time with her dad and all."

"When would be a good time for us to come by to see her?"

"I'll have to get back to you on that."

Grady looked at Ainslie, who only wanted her brother out of jail and to be safe herself. Was that too much to ask? He didn't think so. "I don't mean to put pressure on you either, but this is important. Very important."

"Okay, fine." Her frustration with him flowed through the phone, and he felt like he was acting like Murphy had just behaved with Ainslie. "You can come over after dinner tomorrow. Seven works for us."

"Thank you," he said earnestly. "I'll see you then."

He hung up and went back to the group. Ainslie looked up at him.

"Heidi thinks Jayla is hiding something, and she might talk to us. So I made an appointment to talk to her."

Ainslie frowned. "Poor girl being put in the middle of this. I'd rather not bug her, but I'll do it for Ethan."

Matt snorted. "Would serve him right if she kept quiet after what he did to Neil's parents."

Grady had to shove his hands in his pockets before he decked the guy for his insensitivity. Grady looked at Emory. "I assume you all are done here, and I can escort the good sheriff to the door."

"We are," Emory said.

Grady pointed at the door. "This way, Sheriff."

He looked at Grady. "I'd like to talk to the little lady in charge of the bones."

"She's not here, tonight," Grady said, though he had no idea if Kelsey was in her lab or not. He suspected she was, but if she'd needed to talk to Murphy, she'd have contacted him. "But I can have her call you."

"What about the woman in charge of the other forensics? I'd like an update on that, too."

"I'll have her call you as well." Grady went to the door and tugged it open, giving the sheriff such a pointed look that even a guy like Murphy couldn't refuse to leave.

23

The team gathered in the conference room, Grady once again at the head of the table while they waited for Maya and Malone to arrive. He noted their outstanding leads on the whiteboard, and Ainslie snuck a quick look at him. She hadn't seen him since last night, and she was still conflicted over his big reveal. She understood that a nine-year-old would be afraid to tell on his uncle. She even got that Grady might've kept the secret for a few years. But it had been twenty-five years now, and she couldn't understand that, any more than she'd understood Ethan doing the same thing.

She knew Grady wanted her to tell him she didn't think badly of him, but she couldn't. Not when she couldn't grasp his motives. Maybe she didn't understand because she didn't have the kind of close-knit family he'd had growing up and couldn't fathom the repercussions that would ripple through his family. From what he'd said, his parents had been pillars in their community.

That kind of family she could only comprehend from an outsider's point of view. From looking at families like his over the years and seeing them lead the community and set standards for everyone, standards that her family could never follow. Matt Murphy's family was like that. His dad owned the local car dealership and was a deacon at the Baptist church. His mom was the church secretary, his sister head cheerleader. He was the quarterback and basketball star, too. Both prom and homecoming king. Class president. On and on. She could easily imagine the shockwaves that would travel through the community if one of their family members had hit and killed someone. It would destroy them.

But she didn't think Grady was motivated to keep quiet due to social standing. At least not the Grady she'd come to know. This seemed to be just about his family unit. But then she could be all wrong.

She imagined visiting his parents. What would they think of her and her humble beginnings? They'd been hard-working farmers. She imagined salt of the earth kind of people. Maybe they weren't like the social leaders in the Murphy family. Country club members.

She sighed, drawing his attention. He arched a brow, and she shook her head, telling him it was nothing. Or more likely communicating her confusion.

Maya clipped into the room in her no-nonsense way with Malone right behind her. Maya still wore her lab coat, and Malone was dressed in a black suit with a crisp white blouse, and she had her hair wrapped up in a bun. She looked regal and intimidating, and Ainslie had no problem imagining her in a courtroom wowing a jury.

Grady clapped his hands to still the conversations being held around the table. "Let's get started."

Malone dropped into a chair near the head of the table. "I'd like to go first, if I can. I have big news."

"Sure," Ainslie said eagerly, though it wasn't her call.

"You'll be happy to know the DA has reviewed the evidence from the swat call and sniper shooting at the crime scene and has brought two counts of attempted murder charges against Wade Eggen."

Ainslie let out a long breath. "Thank goodness."

"This is, of course, in addition to the murder charge for Neil Orr."

Grady gave a thumbs up and smiled at Ainslie. "So that guy's not getting out anytime soon."

"Have they questioned him again about who shot him?" Grady asked.

Malone nodded and frowned. "Unfortunately, despite the evidence suggesting it's not Ethan, Wade remains adamant that Ethan fired the gun."

"Wait, what?" Ainslie gaped at Malone. "How can he keep lying about it?"

"I can help with that," Nick said, drawing everyone's attention. "I used a Cellebrite software program called Cloud Analyzer to research Ethan's phone data on Google's servers. They logged several location points with latitude and longitude for his phone during the time when he supposedly shot Wade. The points show him on the road from the bar to his place when the witness reported hearing the gunshot."

"Excellent work." Malone gave Nick a dazzling smile. "That, coupled with Grady's bullet analysis, and we're making good progress in getting Ethan released."

"Progress? Are you kidding?" Ainslie asked. "We still need more?"

Malone gave a concise nod. "Wade's claim still trumps almost everything. Unless we can prove he's lying."

"But both of these things *do* prove that," Ainslie argued.

"Not really," Malone said. "More like they poke holes in

his statement. Sure, it might put doubt in a jury's mind, but if you sat on this jury, who would you believe? The man who is accused of attempted murder, or the victim who now has to live with a bullet in his head for the rest of his life?"

"But Wade is a criminal himself. A killer. It wouldn't be hard for me to believe he was also a liar."

"The problem is"—Malone sat forward—"there's no apparent reason for Wade to lie. No motive. No reasonable explanation for the jury."

She paused and locked gazes with Ainslie. "And without that or concrete proof that Ethan didn't pull the trigger, I'm sorry to say, he's still facing a stretch in prison."

Just after six-thirty, Grady drove the company SUV down the highway toward Heidi and Jayla's house. Ainslie was tucked into the passenger seat, and Nick loomed large in the back. He'd come along in case Heidi gave them permission to access the doorbell videos.

Despite Malone's dire tone at the meeting, Grady was feeling optimistic about this visit. If Jayla had witnessed the shooting, and if the doorbell camera recorded the incident, they would have everything needed to free Ethan. And with Wade behind bars, Ainslie could return to her normal routine. So could Grady. Until he had to go to Nebraska and ruin the lives of his family members. *No. Stow it.* No point in even thinking about the upcoming event when he could do nothing about it.

He looked at the mostly clear sky with bright reds and yellows as the sunset took the light with it, a hint of predicted rain in forming clouds. He liked that the days were getting longer, but as they neared Ethan's desolate neighborhood, he was glad for the darkness so he wouldn't have to see the dire conditions Jayla and Heidi were living in.

He clicked on his blinker and exited the freeway. "I wonder if there's anything we can do to find a safer neighborhood for Jayla and Heidi."

"I'm glad to help you try, but it'll be tough," Ainslie said. "I know when Ethan was looking, there was nothing reasonably priced anywhere but out here. The way property values shot up in the metro area again, rent has skyrocketed."

Grady rarely considered how blessed he was with his housing situation. "With my condo, I don't even think about rent or property values. But there's got to be something we can do, right? Maybe find housing assistance."

She frowned at him. "Maybe they don't want assistance. Maybe Heidi wants to stand on her own two feet."

Right. The whole charity thing again. "I only want to help."

"Yeah, I get that. People said that when I was a kid, too, but it was often followed by judgment."

He looked at her for longer than he should have and swerved into the next lane. A horn honked, and he jerked the SUV back.

"Drive much?" Nick asked, his sarcasm traveling over the seat.

Grady resisted rolling his eyes. He'd wanted to see if there was more behind Ainslie's comment. Like maybe something to do with him telling her about Uncle Tommy. She still hadn't said a word about the secret, and it was eating away at Grady's gut. But right now, he thought her comment was all about the way she was raised.

He'd told her how he felt about it several times, but it was so important to her that he needed to make sure she understood his point of view. He glanced at her again. "You know there's no judgment from me, right?"

She gave a swift nod, and his gut relaxed a fraction. "Still, if you decide to mention finding a place for Heidi, be sensitive to her responses."

Nick snorted.

Grady looked in the mirror at him. "What?"

"Sensitive and you don't go hand in hand, bro." Nick chuckled.

Ainslie looked over her shoulder. "Grady has a sensitive side. He just doesn't show it very often."

Grady didn't know how to take that. Was she complaining? Stating a fact? Noncommittal and didn't really care one way or the other?

He wished he wasn't driving. Or at the very least that Nick wasn't along for the drive so he could talk about Uncle Tommy. But did he really want to know what she thought? There'd been a coolness directed his way ever since the big reveal, and that didn't bode well for him.

His phone rang, and Heidi's name flashed on his dashboard screen.

"I hope she isn't calling to cancel." He accepted the call. "What's up, Heidi?"

"She's gone. Jayla...someone took her...I saw him." The words barreled through the phone, tripping over each other in a complete panic. "He dragged her into a big SUV and drove off."

Ainslie shot out a hand and grabbed Grady's arm in a tight hold, her frightened gaze locked on him.

Grady took a breath. "Slow down, Heidi. Tell me what happened."

"I got home from work late. The front door was busted in. I ran inside. Saw a big guy dragging Jayla out of her room. I ran after them. Jumped on his back." A deep, heart-wrenching sob came over the speakers.

Ainslie gasped, her hand tightening.

"He bucked me off," Heidi stated. "Socked me in the mouth and shoved me down. Now he has her. Hurry. Please help. I need help."

They were still a few minutes out, and Grady grappled with how to handle this. "Did you call 911?"

"No. I thought you could help."

The pressure of finding Jayla without law enforcement nearly swamped Grady. He had many skills, the center many resources, but the police were trained and ready to handle an abduction. "Hang up now and call 911. We'll be there in three minutes."

"But I..."

"Do it, Heidi! They can get there faster." At least Grady hoped they could, but police response these days with budget constraints was slower than in the past. "And they'll put out an alert on the man and his vehicle."

"Okay. Hurry, though." The call ended.

Ainslie faced him. "Hurry! Hurry! She needs us. Please hurry. Oh, God." Her hand fell off and she closed her eyes.

Grady pressed harder on the gas, and the SUV shot forward.

"She said he broke in the front door," Nick said. "The doorbell camera might've recorded it. If I can get onto their network, I should be able to figure out where the files are being stored and might be able to get a look at this guy."

"Good thinking." Grady's heart thundered in his ears as he whipped onto Heidi's street. "Do that the minute we get inside."

Grady screeched to a stop at the curb, the vehicle rocking like an earthquake rumbled below. A short woman with dark hair and a split lip bolted from the house and barreled down the sidewalk.

Grady jumped out and introduced himself. Heidi clutched his arm. "Help! Oh, help. My baby. I need to find her."

"Did you call 911?"

"Yes. Yes. Police are on the way." She tightened her grip, and Grady resisted wincing at the vice-like pressure. "But we can't wait. You need to do something now. Now!"

"This is Nick," Grady said as calmly as he could when he felt the poor woman's panic clear to his soul. "He can check the network for a video from the doorbell of the break-in. Where's your computer equipment?"

"In Jayla's room."

"Show me," Nick said urgently.

She spun and ran back inside. The three of them charged after her and through a tiny combo living/dining room, then down a dingy hall to the bedroom at the end.

A laptop and wireless router sat on a small white desk with chipping paint next to a twin bed with a pink bedspread. A metal folding chair was tipped over by the desk.

Nick righted the chair and dropped into it, waking up the laptop at the same time. "Good. Good. No password."

Heidi moved behind Nick. "I wouldn't let her have one. Told her I needed to be able to see everything she got up to."

"Excellent," Nick said without looking up.

Grady made eye contact with Heidi. "Tell me again what happened. Don't leave out any detail."

"The man." She clutched her hands together. "When I came in, he was dragging Jayla toward the back of the house. She screamed at me. 'Help me, Mom. Help me. He shot the guy. He's the one. I saw him. He's going to kill me.'"

So she *had* seen something, and now it had put her in

danger. Grady feared this guy had planned to kill Jayla but her mother interrupted, and now he might've killed her after leaving the house. "Did you recognize the man?"

She shook her head, hair dyed an inky black slapping at the air. "He was wearing a ski mask."

"Did he speak?" Ainslie asked. "Maybe you recognized his voice."

"No. No. He didn't say a word." She clamped a hand on her mouth then let it drop. "But his eyes. They were vicious. He'll kill my baby. I know it."

"What was he wearing?" Grady asked to keep her from panicking. "His size?"

"He was big. Tall. Over six feet. Built solid. Strong. He held Jayla like a rag doll and still shoved me off."

"Found the files," Nick said, his voice calm in an ocean of panic.

Grady gaped at Heidi. "You lied to us? You did have access to the doorbell files?"

"No. No." Heidi's eyes glistened with tears. "I didn't know. Honest. Jayla's a computer nerd so she must've gotten the login from her dad or something. I had no idea."

"Whatever happened," Nick said. "We have a recording from about ten minutes ago."

"Play it." Grady charged behind Nick, and Ainslie joined him.

Nick clicked play. A tall man wearing a ski mask, just like Heidi described, approached the door. He wore black pants and jacket. He reached out for the doorbell and ripped it from the wall. The video died.

"Oh. My. Gosh!" Ainslie gaped at the screen. "Did you see it?"

Grady shot her a look. "No, what?"

"Play it again, Nick," she demanded.

Nick restarted the video.

She stabbed a finger at the screen. "There. Stop."

He froze the video as the intruder's hand twisted, revealing on his wrist a tattoo of a horse head in black, the mane looking like flames of yellow and orange.

"I know that tattoo." She shot Grady a tortured look. "There's only one like it. It belongs to Matt. Matt Murphy."

24

Despite the sound of sirens screaming toward the house, Ainslie couldn't take her focus from the tattoo as a wave of shock traveled through her body. Matt was involved in this. The sheriff. The man people trusted. Matt Murphy. How could that be?

"How can you be so sure it's Murphy's tattoo?" Grady asked.

She could barely think but swung her gaze to Grady. "Our high school team is called the Broncos, but our logo had green hair as a nod to the town's name. Matt wanted to be different. Said the yellowy-orange reflected the fire in his passing abilities."

Grady still looked confused. "Why would Matt take Jayla? What does he have to do with all of this? Is he involved?"

"What's going on?" Heidi cried out. "Who's this Matt guy?"

Ainslie glanced over his shoulder at her. "He's a sheriff from Texas, and it's too complicated to explain."

"Maybe he shot Wade." Grady shifted his focus to Nick. "Look for video on the night Wade was shot."

"Already on it." Nick's gaze remained on the screen, and his fingers flew over the keyboard.

"Police," a male called out from the front door. "Ms. Upson."

"Coming," Heidi replied but didn't move.

"Go meet them," Grady encouraged. "Tell them what happened and what we're doing."

Grady gave her a gentle push to get her going, and she raced off.

"I don't get this." Ainslie faced him. "Why do you think Matt would shoot Wade?"

Grady tilted his head, his hand clamped on the back of his neck. "Maybe Murphy has something to do with Neil's murder, too."

"Matt? No. He was a model kid. Perfect. He wouldn't kill someone."

"There was that blood on Neil's shirt. It could be Murphy's DNA."

Could it? "He's a law enforcement officer. Wouldn't his DNA be in the database?"

"Not necessarily. It's not mandatory and it's up to local agencies to decide if they add the information. And as the sheriff, Murphy could easily keep his profile out of the database."

"Found footage," Nick announced. "The file was deleted from the hard drive not more than fifteen minutes ago, but it's backed up to Google's Cloud."

"You think Matt deleted it, or made Jayla do it?" Ainslie asked.

"Sounds likely, but no way to tell." Nick started the footage playing.

Ainslie had to squint to make out the events across the street, but the camera did capture a tall man approach Wade, who was sitting on Ethan's stoop.

"That guy's way too big to be Ethan," she said. "But his build fits Matt."

Grady leaned closer to the monitor. "Too bad his back is to us."

In the video, Wade shot to his feet and planted his cowboy boots on the sidewalk and his hands on his slender hips. The two men's curt jerking of hands and terse body language played out for several minutes, the exchange seeming to get more and more heated.

"They're arguing," Ainslie stated the obvious, but she'd felt a need to say something.

The guy raised his fists to Wade and slammed one into his face.

Wade stumbled, but then roared back at his assailant.

The man dodged the hit and pummeled Wade until he slumped, hands on his knees. The man said something then turned toward the camera.

Ainslie searched his face. "It's Matt. It *is* him. It really is. Oh my gosh. Wow. Just wow!"

He started to walk away. Sauntering. Taking his time as if having punched Wade was no big deal. At the sidewalk, he spun. Drew a handgun from his holster.

Ainslie grabbed Grady's arm. "Matt's going to shoot him."

Matt raised the weapon. Fired. A reddish spark lit the night.

"Muzzle flash," Grady said.

Wade dropped.

"That's the proof we need to free Ethan." Ainslie continued to hold Grady's arm. She'd waited for this moment for over a week and expected to feel relief, but an innocent teenager had been abducted, and they had no idea where she might be.

All they knew now was that a killer had her.

She stared at Grady. "We have to find Jayla. We just have to."

He nodded. Just once, but it held a heavy weight. "I have no idea where to begin to locate them."

Nick swiveled on the chair. "Murphy's driving a rental, right? Most rentals have GPS trackers on them. We find the rental company, we find the tracker."

"But there are how many car rental companies?" Grady asked. "That's going to take some time."

"Not really," Nick said. "Murphy is going to be his own downfall."

"Explain," Grady demanded.

"He insisted on stopping by the lab last night, so his SUV will be on the lab's security feed. We just have to hope the camera got a clear look at the rental company logo. Then I hack into their system, and presto, we're tracking the dude."

"That's not legal, is it?" Ainslie asked, worried Nick would get into trouble.

"No," he said. "But a kid's life could depend on it, so I don't much care."

Grady gritted his teeth. "The police can get a warrant to get the same information."

"But that will take time." Nick stood. "Time Jayla might not have."

"Do it," Grady said. "I'll coordinate with the responding officers. If they get the warrant before you hack the rental site, then you can hold off."

"No can do from here. I set the lab's router for local access only. Means I need to go back to the lab."

"Can't you get someone else to look?" Ainslie asked.

"Yeah, sure, if I wasn't so paranoid about network security and hadn't set it up with a retina scan." He held up his hands. "I know, I know. If I croaked no one else has access, and I should do something about that, but—"

"Forget about that for now. Let me get the officer's contact info, and we'll get out of here." Grady marched out the door.

With Jayla missing, Ainslie didn't want to leave Heidi alone, so she followed Grady to the other room. Nick was hot on her heels.

Heidi sat on the tattered sofa, and three officers huddled by the door. Grady quickly brought them up to speed on their role and shared their plan but stopped short of telling them about the impending hack.

Ainslie sat next to Heidi. "You heard Grady, right? We need to go back to the Veritas Center. But I want to make sure you'll be okay here."

She pressed her palms on the knees of her worn jeans. "One of the officers said she'd stay with me."

"Perfect." Ainslie touched Heidi's hand. "We're going to find Jayla. I promise."

Heidi met Ainslie's gaze, the woman's eyes tortured. "You can't promise that. No one can."

Grady didn't care what the speed limit sign read. He did ninety on the highway and held the needle near fifty on side streets to reach the center in record time. He didn't even come to a complete stop before Nick bolted from the vehicle and raced through the lobby.

Grady shifted into park and killed the engine. Sierra had arranged for her brother Erik to serve as liaison between the team and his agency, but he remained on scene with Heidi.

Grady got out his phone. "I'm going to call Erik for an update before we head inside."

"Officer Byrd," he answered.

"We're at the center," Grady said. "Any updates?"

"Murphy's vehicle was spotted crossing the Ross Island Bridge. Jayla in the front seat with him."

"So he's headed west." Grady was surprised at the sheriff's direction and that he hadn't already killed Jayla. Did he need her alive for something? "If he planned to kill Jayla, I thought he'd go somewhere remote. Head east out into the Gorge or Mount Hood National Forest. And then he'd also be close to the airport."

"He'd know we could've captured his vehicle on nearby CCTV and would be monitoring the airport," Erik said.

Grady thought about it while watching a car pull into the lot. Nick's best tech, Zach, who sported a man bun, sloppy T-shirt, and torn jeans, jumped out and raced for the lobby. Nick had called him in on the way over, and it was always refreshing to see when their staff dropped everything to help.

"You still there?" Erik asked.

Grady focused. "Murphy has no reason to think we know he's the guy who took Jayla."

"What about the doorbell video?"

"He kept his head down when he arrived so we couldn't ID him." Grady looked at Ainslie. "Did we ever mention in front of him that we were looking for the video feed of the shooting?"

She squinted her eyes. "I don't think so."

"Still, he ripped it from the wall," Erik said. "And has to be smart enough to have wondered if it recorded the shooting, right?"

Ainslie nodded, though Erik couldn't possibly see her. "Maybe he's the one who deleted the file."

"But again, he didn't touch the cloud file," Grady said.

"And as a sheriff, he would have to know about backups like that."

Ainslie fired a questioning look at Grady. "What if Heidi interrupted him before he could delete that file?"

"Yeah, yeah. Could be." Grady was liking the idea the more he thought about it.

Ainslie's eyes widened. "If he knows about the cloud file, then he needs to keep Jayla alive to gain access to it."

"And we should be watching for him to try to delete it." Grady whipped open his car door. "Gotta go tell Nick. I'll call you back."

He bolted from the SUV into rain now spitting from the sky, the change from the glowing sunset quick, as often happened in Oregon. Ainslie followed and they charged past a surprised Pete but didn't stop to explain. They took the stairs to Nick's lab on the third floor. Grady burst into a cold room, where Nick sat at one of the many computers lined up against the wall. Zach sat at the last one. Neither of them looked up.

Grady quickly updated them. "We need to monitor the cloud—"

"Yeah," Nick said calmly. "Already have Zack working on it. Perfect timing. I'm just pulling up Murphy's vehicle so you can get the plate number to the police." Nick tapped the monitor as a picture of a still shot of an Escalade's bumper loaded.

Grady took in the white vehicle's details, dialed Erik, and reported the information.

"I'll get that added to the alert," Erik said, and it sounded like he'd taken off running. "And we'll contact the rental agency."

"Let me know the minute you have the information." Grady disconnected the call and stood expectantly behind

Nick. "What do you think? Is it time to hack the rental agency?"

"Yeah," Nick said.

"Can you do it without being traced?" Worry for Nick darkened Ainslie's eyes.

"I'm the best and can hide my tracks well, but..." He shrugged.

"I can't tell you to do something that risks you going to prison," Grady said.

"No one's telling me to do anything." Nick looked up. "Plus, with the exigent circumstances, I doubt I'd get much more than a slap on the wrist."

"But you might still have a record, and worse, you could be banned from computer use."

"Yeah, that could happen." Nick looked like the thought made him physically ill. "But a girl's life is at stake, so we move forward." He started typing.

"Someone is accessing the cloud file right now," Zach said. "It's the phone assigned to the kid, Jayla."

Nick whipped his head to look at his tech. "You have a location?"

"Yep. Coffee shop." He rattled off an address not far from their location.

Grady looked at Nick "That's not in PPB's jurisdiction so Erik can't respond. And I sure as heck don't want to risk some rookie responding to a hostage scene. We'll call Erik to have him liaison with the locals. While he does that, we'll get eyes on Murphy before he changes location."

"Let's go." Nick jumped up and faced Zack. "Keep your eyes on this and keep me updated on any changes."

Grady looked at Ainslie.

She waved a hand. "Before you tell me to stay here, forget it. I'm coming with you."

She ran for the door, and Grady had no time to argue. If

they found themselves in danger, he would insist she stay in the car.

He got them on the road headed toward the coffee shop less than a mile away and used his car's infotainment system to call and update Erik.

"I'll get someone out there ASAP," Erik said. "If you get there first, it would be good if you sent me pictures of the vehicle to help with planning an appropriate response."

"Will do," Grady said, and hoped they planned a silent response where they cordoned off the exits and didn't race into the lot where they'd risk spooking Murphy.

Erik ended the call, and Grady devoted his attention to driving. He reached the street holding the shop and slowed at the corner. No way he was going to draw attention to their SUV by roaring into the lot. He turned into the parking lot.

"There!" Ainslie pointed out the windshield. "Parked out front. A white Escalade with the correct plates."

Grady came to a stop and assessed the situation. The SUV was sitting in the second parking spot, parallel to the building, the spaces in front and back open. "I'd like to block him in, but the way he parked makes it impossible."

"Likely Matt's plan." Ainslie leaned forward, her gaze focused ahead. "We're not dealing with just anyone here. He knows how to evade arrest."

Nick scooted closer and peered between the seats. "Looks like they're in the car. How do you want to proceed?"

Grady watched the vehicle. "I think the only thing we *can* do is keep eyes on Murphy and maybe take those pictures Erik asked for."

"Matt knows us," Ainslie said. "The minute we step out of the SUV, he'll take off."

"He doesn't know me." Nick rubbed his hands together. "You guys wait here, and I'll take the pics."

He slid out of the car. Cell phone in hand, he covertly

started snapping pictures of the SUV and the area. He walked up to the coffee shop, head down like he was minding his own business and went into the building. Grady could see him just inside, where he took a few more covert photos before going to the counter and ordering. He came out holding a paper cup, and he took a quick look at the Escalade before continuing on to their vehicle. He was a natural in his ability to fly under the radar.

"They're both inside the SUV, and it's running. Jayla looks terrified." He held up the coffee cup. "Anyone need some caffeine?"

"Are you kidding?" Ainslie said. "I have enough adrenaline rushing through my veins already."

The SUV suddenly roared to life and raced through the lot toward the exit.

"Something spooked him," Grady said.

"Dang!" Nick slammed his fist into the back of Grady's seat. "I know it wasn't me. He could be listening to a scanner app on his phone and heard something was going down here."

"We have to go after him!" Ainslie fired Grady a panicked look. "Jayla needs us."

"I'm on it." Grady shifted into gear and raced to the parking lot exit. He prayed. Prayed hard, asking God to show him the right thing to do before a young girl lost her life.

25

Ainslie held onto the dashboard, rolling with the vehicle's movements as Grady took the corners fast and hard. Her heart thundered in her chest, and she offered copious prayers for safety for Jayla and for them, too, while in pursuit of Murphy.

Ainslie glanced at Grady. She might be afraid, but he looked calm and deadly, navigating onto Skyline Boulevard and starting the climb into the West Hills. Driving higher. Higher along the heavily wooded road. Erik was on the speaker, and Grady gave him a play-by-play of the action.

Murphy suddenly whipped off the road into a small clearing with tall power lines.

"He's heading to Forest Park," she said, remembering her photos and wondering if she'd missed something in them.

The vehicle crashed into a barrier. Reverberated and stopped.

Grady slammed on his brakes, the SUV skidding on the wet pavement.

Ainslie held fast, but kept her attention down the road where Murphy bolted from his Escalade, a rifle over his shoulder. He ran around front. Dragged Jayla out. She fought him. Struggling. Kicking. Screaming. He cold-cocked her and tossed her over his free shoulder and ran full speed toward the path.

Grady surged forward and shifted into park at the turnoff. He looked at Ainslie. "Stay here. I can't worry about you and Jayla at the same time."

He jerked open his door and bolted. Nick was hot on his heels. Both men had their guns raised. She opened her door and thought to follow. But she couldn't distract them. And she had zero skills to chase an armed man.

"Be careful," she screamed after them.

They all disappeared on the wooded path in the very secluded part of the park. People wouldn't be out hiking at this time of night.

Ainslie didn't know what to do, so she got back in the vehicle and out of the rain to update Erik. "Matt has a rifle. I'm afraid for Grady and Nick. Matt could kill them."

"Backup's on the way but there's a major accident with serious injuries nearby and resources are spread pretty thin right now." Erik sounded frustrated. "I wish I could do more, but I'm clear across town. You'll have to count on them arriving in time."

"Thanks," she said. "I'll call back if we need you."

She disconnected and kept watching out the window, straining to see through the growing rain, her breath held. She got out her phone and looked up their location on a map program. She couldn't see much of anything, since they were on a trail, not a road, and the overhead satellite view showed only an impervious tree canopy. They would all be moving deeper into the woods. Away from her. From help. From that backup that still wasn't arriving.

A gunshot split the quiet.

"No. Oh, no." She craned her neck ahead. Saw nothing.

Oh, please, Father. Please keep them all safe.

She scooted even closer to the windshield. Reached over to turn on the key so she could get the wipers running. She craned her neck again. Struggled to look through the swipe of the blades, but the sun had completely disappeared now, and she was greeted with only a hazy glow from a faraway street light.

"Where are you, Grady?" she asked. "Are you okay?"

Her heart clipped at a high rate, but she sat quietly. The window started to fog, and she fiddled with the controls to get the fan running.

Her car door was suddenly jerked open. She spun. Matt stood, handgun aimed at her.

A bolt of terror shot into Ainslie's heart.

Jayla was still hanging limp over Matt's shoulder next to that long rifle. "Get behind the wheel and drive."

She couldn't move. Not a muscle as she looked down the muzzle of his gun. How had she been so careless that she'd let him sneak up on her? She never even imagined he'd find a way to circle back to her.

"Move!" He glared at her. "Now, or I kill the girl."

He jabbed the gun into her side. That got her moving. She slid over the console to the driver's seat. He kept his gun trained on her and opened the back door. He was distracted. She had to act quickly. She got out her phone. Pressed Grady's icon and turned the volume all the way down so Grady wouldn't be heard. She tucked the phone by her leg just as he tossed Jayla into the back seat like a rag doll.

"Matt, hey," Ainslie said loudly. "You should let Jayla go. You don't need her anymore, and you're hurting her by throwing her in the backseat like that." Her statement sounded stilted, but she had to get as much information out as possible so Grady knew that Matt was with her.

He snorted and slammed the door, hitting the child's beat-up sneakers and shoving her forward.

"Get going." He slid into the front and jerked his door closed, the sound feeling like he'd pulled down a coffin lid on them.

No. Don't think that way. Think positive. Find a way out.

She couldn't die here. She couldn't let Jayla die here. Ainslie had to stall. Give Grady and Nick time to come back. If she drove off this site, Matt would kill her. "You don't want to do this, Matt. Put the gun away. You can't come back from murder."

"Hah!" He waved the gun. "Like you know what you're talking about. I'm already on the hook for murder."

"Neil?" she asked. "You killed Neil, didn't you?"

"Well, duh! Yeah. He had to go." His earnest tone lacking even a crumb of remorse shocked her. "Won't take your super geeks long to figure out the unknown DNA profile found on Neil's shirt belongs to me."

He'd done it. He'd killed Neil. Meant he wouldn't likely hesitate to kill her, too. "You were involved in killing him? But how? Ethan didn't see you."

"That's because he ran off like a little chicken before Neil died. Wade choked Neil, but as usual, he couldn't finish the job, and he let Neil go when he passed out. Then he took off after your brother, and I had to take it over the finish line. A perfect quarterback sneak." He gave a sick laugh and waved the gun. "Now get going."

She reached for the key in the ignition and let her hand rest there. "But why kill him?"

"He figured out Wade and I were Stoner's suppliers and was going to report us. Wade could go down for that, but not me. Couldn't have the star quarterback's rep tarnished from drug sales. Wouldn't get me where I wanted to go in life."

"You supplied drugs to our local dealer?" she clarified for Grady.

"Him and a dozen others in the county." He lifted his shoulders with pride.

Out of the corner of her eye, she caught movement in the backseat. She slyly glanced at Jayla and saw her messing with her shoelaces. What was the girl planning?

"Surprised, right?" Matt said, catching her unaware. He jabbed the gun into her side. "Now get this SUV going before your buddies figure out I doubled back."

She turned the key. The big engine roared to life, and she slowly inched it toward the road.

"Faster. Go!" He wiggled the gun.

She stopped at the road. "Which direction?"

"North. Now move."

She turned onto the road and left Grady and Nick behind. Hopefully, Matt had left the keys in the ignition of his SUV and Grady could follow her.

"So you were a drug dealer," she said to get him talking and keep him distracted so she could find a way to escape.

"No one ever found out about the drugs except for Neil. I mighta teased him one too many times in front of the school. He snapped and wanted to get revenge, so he followed me one night to a drug hookup. Then thought he could blackmail me. Fool."

She clicked on the windshield wipers and adjusted the rearview mirror so she could see Jayla. She'd removed a shoelace and was working on the other one. Was she planning to try to strangle Matt? If so, she wasn't nearly strong enough to fight him on her own.

"Neil should've thought about how strong you were before he messed with you," she said, her statement a warning for Jayla.

"Exactly." His chin raised and lowered his gun. "I'm invincible."

The kind of attitude that went before a fall. "At least while you're waving that gun around. Maybe when you shot Wade. You did shoot him, right?"

He frowned at her. "Guess you saw the video."

"We did," she admitted and let off on the gas bit by bit, hoping he wouldn't notice she'd slowed. "But why shoot him after all these years?"

"My stupid detective reopened the investigation without telling me. Wade thought it was a good time to start black-mailing me."

She glanced at him. "But you botched the job."

He grimaced, and she had to admit to some satisfaction at seeing his reaction.

"Still, it helped," he said. "Wade knew I meant it when I said I'd end his life if he didn't take the fall for Neil and even blame your brother for the shooting. Oh, and he also got me the rifle to do you in. Stood by and watched me take the shot."

"But you missed again."

He glared at her, his gaze stony and harsh. Maybe she'd pushed him too far.

"Wouldn't have," he snapped, "if I'd had more time."

"And the swatting incident at my house and the bomb? You behind both of those, too?"

He grinned. "Thought SWAT would take you out, but guess they weren't as trigger happy as I'd hoped so had to get creative."

"But why try to kill me?" she asked. "I didn't know anything."

"You told Wade you were going to get to the bottom of the shooting. Brought in the super team, and I figured you might just do it." He snorted. "Couldn't have that happen."

"You had to know if you killed me that the team would come after you, right?"

"Actually, I didn't know that. Figured with you gone, they'd drop it. Then I saw you all in action, and I knew the bonds were tight. If I took you out they'd keep after it."

"And now?" she asked and continued slowing. "Where will you go, and what will you do with us?"

"Coast and then Mexico. You and the kid are going to be my insurance."

He clearly hadn't thought this through, which surprised her. "I don't have a passport with me. Jayla doesn't either. We'll be stopped at the border, if you even make it that far. It's a long drive."

"Don't need one. I got a boat at the coast ready to smuggle me aboard, and you two will be taking a permanent nap in the ocean."

She could easily imagine him tossing them overboard and laughing while doing so.

"You slowed down. Press on that gas." He pointed his gun at her. "Now! No more stalling."

She met his gaze. "You won't kill me if I'm your insurance policy."

"Only need one person, and I got the kid." He leaned closer, a growl in his tone. "Either speed up this vehicle, or you die now. Got it." He jabbed the barrel hard into her ribs.

She sucked in her breath and clamped her mouth closed so she wouldn't cry out and let him know he'd hurt her. She couldn't stall any longer. She pressed her foot on the gas.

Matt rested his gun on his knee but kept his focus on her. She quickly glanced in the mirror at Jayla. She had both shoelaces free and tied together. Her gaze met Ainslie's. Her eyes narrowed, and she gave a tight nod born of fear and determination.

Ainslie didn't want to have to count on a teen to save the

day, but she nodded back. Her life was in the hands of a teenager.

~

Grady didn't know if his heart was bursting from running full stop or from listening to the calm conversation Ainslie was having with Murphy. Grady didn't know how she was doing it. Keeping the guy talking when he had a gun trained on her—was threatening her with every other sentence. Snapping. Barking. Shouting.

She needed him. Now!

He tried to kick up speed, but his side hurt. A stitch. A bad one. He could hardly keep moving. But he had to. He couldn't stop for a little pain. Not when Ainslie was counting on him. He churned his legs. Knew Nick was behind him but didn't slow to check.

They crested the last hill, the cold wet night stretching out in front of him, the wind buffeting his body. He barreled down, his legs pumping and barely keeping up with the downhill momentum.

His foot caught a rock. He stumbled. Righted himself and continued. He reached the turnoff and confirmed the SUV was gone. Grady bolted for Murphy's vehicle and glanced at Nick. "Keys are in the ignition. Let's go."

Grady didn't wait for Nick to agree but hopped into the vehicle and cranked the powerful engine.

God, please. Please.

Nick jumped in, and Grady raced for the road.

God, I need help. Now. Please. Now.

A gun report sounded over the phone.

"No!" Grady shouted, his heart shredding as he floored the gas, terrified of what he might find when he reached them.

~

Ainslie had gotten the SUV to the side of the road and was grappling with Matt's gun hand while he clawed at the shoelaces around his neck with the other one. Little Jayla held firm, and a gurgling sound came from his throat. The gun poked toward the roof. Fired. Once. Twice.

Her life flashed before her eyes. She could die here. Tonight. Ethan's and Grady's faces flashed before her eyes. She had to live for them. For the life they could all have when Matt was behind bars.

Matt's strength took over. Pressing on the gun. On her arm. Inching down. Her muscles cramped. Trembled. Failed. The gun came down further. Further.

Directly facing her. The cold steel barrel eye level. Her arm muscles turned to spaghetti. She couldn't hold him off any longer.

Father, please. I don't want to die. Help me. Oh, help me.

The passenger door jerked open. Grady appeared. He grabbed Matt's shoulders and ripped his body from the SUV, a feral growl grinding from Grady's mouth. Matt's hand jerked up. The gun fired. The sound slammed into the air, deafening. The bullet went wide, whizzing by her head and shattering the window.

Grady tossed Matt to the ground and dropped down.

She touched her head. Just to be sure. Felt for an injury. A bullet graze. She was fine, but could hardly breathe. She dragged in a breath. Another and another. She recovered enough to slide over and look down at Grady. He flipped Matt over and started pummeling him with his fists. Hard. Fast. Punishing.

Nick trained his gun on Matt. "Whoa. Man. Back off. I got my gun on him."

Grady glanced up, held his fist in the air. He shook his

head then slammed his knuckles into Matt's face again. Ainslie didn't like violence, but the crunch was satisfying.

Grady flipped Matt onto his stomach, grabbed up his hands, and put a knee in his back.

"Ainslie?" Grady called out. "Are you hit?"

"I'm fine." She shifted into park, her hand shaking like a frightened puppy. She looked back at Jayla who was breathing hard, but okay. Ainslie smiled at the girl, who wrapped her trembling arms around her waist and fell onto the seat. "Jayla's okay, too. We're both fine."

"There're zip ties in the glove compartment," Grady said. "Can you bring me a few?"

Ainslie reached out to get the ties and pressed a hand on Jayla's knee. "It's okay, honey. This is all over."

"I got him for you, didn't I?" Her voice trembled.

"That you did." Ainslie smiled again, but she had to force the gesture. She wanted to curl up in a ball and cry but she opened the glove compartment instead. "You're a hero."

"Yeah. I am." She grinned, but it quickly faded at the sound of sirens in the distance. "I want my mom."

Poor thing. "We'll get you to her as soon as possible. For now just hang tight, okay?"

"Yeah. Maybe a little rest." She curled into a tight ball and closed her eyes.

Ainslie grabbed a few zip ties and climbed out. Surprised her legs held her, she hurried around the front of the big SUV. Sirens sounded in the distance as she handed a zip tie to Grady, and he tightened Matt's hands together behind his back.

"The others." He held out his hand, and she planted the remaining ties there.

He combined them and secured Matt's ankles.

"There," he said. "Tied up like the pig he is."

273

Matt grumbled and tried to jerk free. "You're going to regret this, man. I'm a sheriff, not a common criminal."

"Right. A murderous, kidnapping sheriff." Breathing deeply, Grady came to his feet and looked at Nick. "You got him?"

"Yep."

Grady dialed Erik and gave him their new location. "We've got Murphy zip tied, and Jayla is fine. Officers are nearby. Make sure they know we're armed and not the bad guys."

Grady listened for a moment then shoved his phone into his pocket and closed the distance to Ainslie in a quick burst of speed. He searched her face and raised his voice, allowing her to hear above approaching sirens. "You're sure he didn't hurt you, because if he did..."

"I'm fine. Jayla saved the day." She made sure to take a breath and smile to assure him. "She was in the backseat and took out her shoelaces. She started to choke him, allowing me to grab hold of his gun hand."

Grady shook his head. "That was risky."

She nodded. "But we had to do it. He was going to kill us."

"Yeah, I heard it all." He shuddered and took her hands. "But when I heard the gun go off, I thought I'd lost you. I..." He shook his head and took a long shuddering breath. "Thank God, you're fine."

"Yes, it's all thanks to God." She remembered her prayers, which she could finally say had been answered. "Everything. He protected us."

Emotions flashed over Grady's expression, tumbling over each other, and she couldn't get a read on what he was feeling. He groaned and swept her into his arms, tightening them as lights swirled through the sky and the local police arrived.

"If I'd lost you, I..." he whispered, his breath warm against her neck.

"Shh." She raised her arms over his shoulders and snuggled closer. "I'm fine. You're fine. It's all good."

"Is it?" He leaned back to look at her, his eyes tight and tense. "You never told me what you thought about my confession. I know you're probably disgusted with me."

"No." She was glad to see the pain evaporate from his face. "I can totally understand your reaction as a kid. I can't put myself in your place or know how you felt. Or know why you didn't tell anyone. You didn't do it to hurt anyone but to protect the people you love. I've had plenty of time to see the wonderful man you've become. A man of honor who is going to report it now. I respect that. Respect you."

He shook his head. "I don't deserve that."

"Yes, you do. We all deserve respect."

His eyebrow went up. "That includes you."

She nodded, surprising herself at her instant reaction. "I know that now. I honestly do. It's going to take some work to let go of the old feelings, but I know I'm loved by God, and I am worth so much more than I give myself credit for."

"It's not just God," he said tentatively. "I've fallen in love with you."

Her heart soared, and she blinked, trying to process his words.

"Too much too soon?" he asked, once again sounding unsure.

"No. No. I feel the same way." She touched his cheek. "That brush with death told me as much."

"Then if you'll have me, I want that relationship," he said more confidently. "After I talk to my family and the sheriff back home, that is. I hope this doesn't involve any kind of jail time for me, but I won't know until I report it. I'll be sure to run it by Malone before then."

She could imagine how hard telling his family was going to be for him. One of the hardest things of his life. She wanted to help ease his uncertainty. "Would you like someone to come to Nebraska with you?"

His eyes widened. "You?"

"I know what you're going through. Kind of, anyway, after seeing Ethan's struggle and..."

He squeezed her hard. "Please. Yes. And more. I want more with you. So much more. I want a forever."

His long-term thoughts scared her a bit, but she wanted the same thing. Still, she had to accept that she deserved it.

"Me too." She smiled at him, making sure to put all of her feelings into it.

He locked gazes with her, then released her and wove his fingers into her hair. Slowly, ever so slowly, he lowered his head. His lips pressed against hers. Warm and cool at the same time. Gentle at first. Then growing insistent. Passionate.

The moment cocooned her. Warmth. Love. That future and forever seeming very real.

"Um, guys." Nick's voice broke through. "The police want to talk to us."

Ainslie didn't move. Couldn't break contact. Just couldn't. Not yet.

Grady groaned and lifted his head. Breathing hard, he searched her gaze. Smiled. Sweetly, softly, for her only. "They'll just have to wait a few more minutes."

Ainslie paced the sidewalk outside the detention center and willed the door to open. Ethan should have been released by now. What was going on? Once Matt had been arrested, Wade had recanted his claim that Ethan shot him, but she was starting to think the DA had changed his mind and figured out some other charge to hold Ethan on.

"Hey, relax." Grady cupped her hand in his big warm fingers. "He'll be out soon."

She looked into his eyes. "What on earth is taking so long? Maybe they changed their minds."

He drew her closer and smiled. "They have no reason to do that. Ethan is innocent. We found all the proof needed, and he deserves to be released."

"But..."

He pressed a finger against her lips. "But nothing. Government never runs swiftly. Give it time."

She looked over her shoulder, and the door finally opened. Ethan stepped out and held a hand over his eyes as he searched ahead.

She raced toward him, but her heart broke at the sight. His clothes hung on his already slight frame, and he had that fragile look of a sick person. Pale. Weak. She would make it her mission to fatten him up. But first she needed to hug his skinny neck. She flung her arms around his thin body. He felt like bones held together by his clothes, and she was afraid she might hurt him. But she was overreacting. He'd only been in jail for a little more than a week. He was fine.

He started crying, his body jerking with the release. She tried to hold back her tears, but they overcame her willpower, and she let them flow. Happy tears. Joyous tears. His release was likely a mixture of relief and so many other emotions that she could only imagine. She never wanted to know exactly what he experienced behind bars. It had to have been horrible.

He stepped back and swiped a hand over his eyes to look up at the sky. "A week in jail, and I missed the fresh air. The sky. The sun. Even the rain." He chuckled.

She nodded, though she could only imagine it. "How about good food? Miss that, too?"

He nodded and glanced over his shoulder, a nervous tint to his expression. "Right now I just want to get as far away from here as possible before they change their mind and come after me."

"That's not going to happen." She tucked her arm in his. "C'mon. I need to introduce you to Grady. He was a big help in getting you released. And saving my life a few times."

She walked her brother over to the man she loved more than life itself.

He shoved out his hand. "Grady Houston. Glad to meet you."

"I owe you, man. Big time." Ethan clasped Grady's hand and pumped it hard. "And I'll pay you back somehow."

"No need." Grady shook his head. "The only payback I want is to see your sister happy, and you being released today has done wonders for that."

Ethan gave a firm nod. "Yeah, for me, too."

"Should we go get some lunch?" Ainslie tugged on Ethan's arm and started down the sidewalk.

"Honestly," he said. "I'd like to go see that Jayla kid. Tell her thanks for being so brave and making sure that video survived."

Ainslie peered at him, searching for any hint of what he was feeling. "Are you sure? We'll have to go back to your old neighborhood, and your place is toast."

"Was nothing in there worth keeping anyway." He frowned. "Mind if I stay with you for a while?"

"Mind?" She smiled at him. "Of course not. I insist on it."

Grady used his key fob to unlock his truck, and she slid into the middle, Ethan hopping in next to her. After she put her seatbelt on, she patted Ethan's knee and smiled at him.

"Thanks, sis," he said. "I know I was a royal pain,

doubting that I'd be freed. I should've known you'd come through for me. You always do."

Her efforts on his behalf were motivated by love, and love never needed thanks. "Don't even think about it. I would've probably acted the same way."

He shook his head hard, his hair whispering with the movement. "No, you would've stayed strong. You always have. Taking over when Dad walked out and Mom couldn't cope. Taking care of me. You're my rock."

He sucked in a breath and let it out slowly. "But that changes now. I'm really gonna step up. Take control of my life and make something of myself. This was my wakeup call. And I'm going to get it right this time."

"I know you will." She squeezed his hand and released it, praying that he really would follow through and finally live the life that God wanted for him, just as she was going to try to do.

EPILOGUE

Grady pulled into the long gravel driveway leading up to the modest ranch house painted a crisp white with black shutters. Sun shone down on his mom's perennial beds that were dormant and brown with tall brown grasses and seed heads dotting the beds.

In the summer, those beds came alive, surrounding the house with bright, happy flowers. No matter the season, the house was filled with love all year round. But he didn't feel that love right now. Right now, his gut was tied in a knot, and he wanted to reverse out of the drive and fly back to Portland. To run. Fast and far. But he couldn't. Not and live with himself. Or have a future with the brave strong woman sitting in the passenger seat.

He glanced at Ainslie. "This is where my parents have lived since they lost the farm."

She smiled at him. "It's cute, and someone obviously loves roses."

He looked at the large rose border by the drive. "My mom brought them from the farm. Some of the bushes have been in the family for generations."

"It's nice that she could bring something with such meaning to her."

"Yeah. It was hard when they lost the farm, but I also think they felt a sense of relief." He pulled out the keys and got out to open her door. She slid down and, instead of moving ahead, she raised her arms around his neck and kissed him hard.

He didn't object but returned her kiss, still reveling in the newness of his love. In the pure joy she brought to his life. When she ended the kiss, she leaned back, a sweet smile on her face.

He caught his breath. "What was that for?"

She tightened her hold. "For courage to do the right thing even though it's going to hurt the people you love so much."

He shook his head. "I don't deserve you."

"You deserve all the happiness in the world."

"And so do you."

She didn't argue or even frown, showing him how far she'd come in the last few weeks. "Then it's a good thing we found each other because we make each other happy."

He kissed her. Hard and solid, to tell her that he believed in her. Wanted her in his life forever. He tightened his arms. Clung to her. But then his thoughts drifted to his family waiting inside.

His heart constricted. He wanted to continue kissing her. Holding her. But now his heart wasn't in it. He was just stalling, and it wasn't fair to her or his parents. He released her and slid his hand down to take hers while pulling in a cleansing breath.

"At this time of day," he said, leading her toward the back door. "They'll be in the kitchen having a cup of coffee and something Mom baked. I hope she made her famous chocolate chip cookie bars. My favorite."

Ainslie looked up at him. "I'm not much of a baker, but I'll have to ask for the recipe."

"Hmm," he said and grinned. "I don't know if she's shared it with anyone so that might be a challenge."

"I'll just have to charm her."

He planted a kiss on her nose. "I have no doubt you can do that."

He opened the door, releasing a mouthwatering scent, and he instantly felt at home, though he'd never lived in this house. It wasn't the walls. It was the love. The aromas. He hadn't visited for a year, but the place smelled the same as if he'd stepped back in time and through a door into an outdated kitchen filled with the scents of roasting beef and onions, mixed with the sweetness of freshly baked bread. And the safety of his parents' home.

They sat at the round eat-in kitchen table. His dad nodded a stoic hello and offered a tight smile as was his customary greeting.

"Son." His mom jumped up, leaving behind her cup of coffee and a plate of those famous chocolate chip cookie bars. She raced over to him.

He'd video chatted with his parents nearly every week since his last visit, but in person he could see they'd aged in that time, and it left his heart heavy.

She twined her arms around him, smelling like vanilla and the flowery perfume she'd worn as long as he could remember. He hugged her hard, holding on because he was about to rock her foundation.

She pushed back and searched his face. "What's wrong, son?"

He took a long breath. "Can we sit down and talk?"

She shifted her gaze to Ainslie, who stood behind Grady. "After you introduce me to this lovely young woman. You must be Ainslie."

"I am." Ainslie held out her hand. "Nice to meet you, Mrs. Houston."

"It's Irma." She ignored Ainslie's outstretched hand and swept her into a hug, leaving a flash of surprise on Ainslie's face. "I know you're special because you're the very first woman Grady's brought home to meet us."

His mom stepped back and gestured to Grady's dad. "This is my husband, Lyle."

"Nice to meet you, Ainslie." His dad offered his hand, which Grady knew would be callused and rough from his woodworking hobby. "Welcome to our home."

Grady looked at his parents through fresh eyes to see what Ainslie might be seeing. They were in their early sixties, both with dark hair highlighted with liberal gray and both still fit, though they didn't have the same physical demands as on the farm. His dad had a full beard, more silver than black these days, and new wrinkles crinkled by his mom's eyes from her endless smiles.

They wore jeans and denim shirts as if they'd decided to coordinate, but he knew it was all just an accident. Neither of them would primp for any event, even Grady coming home after a long time away. Well, maybe his mom would make sure her hair looked good for meeting Ainslie.

As if she knew he was thinking about it, she smoothed her hand over her chin-length bob. "Can I get you a cup of coffee, Ainslie?"

Ainslie smiled. "That would be lovely."

Grady moved toward a barrel shaped chair on casters. "She likes it black and strong."

"Oh, a girl after my own heart." His mom waved a hand in front of her face and laughed. "Sit. Please. And help yourself to—"

"The best bar ever." Grady pulled out a chair for Ainslie and, after she'd sat, dropped into the one next to her. He plated a golden brown bar for her then chomped off a big bite of one of his own. He groaned and swallowed.

Ainslie took a small nibble of hers. "Oh, my. It's wonderful. An explosion of vanilla."

"Once you're a member of the family," his mom said. "I'll give you the recipe."

"Member of...we..." She shot Grady a panicked look.

He patted her hand but glanced at his mom. "You're getting a little ahead of us, Mom. We just started dating."

She waved a hand. "But you're in love. I can see it's just a matter of time."

He didn't doubt that they were both glowing. They'd been nearly inseparable since Ethan had been released two weeks ago, even finding time at work to sneak into secluded spots to steal a quick kiss. He'd wasted so many years when he could've had such love in his life, but he didn't regret a bit of it. If he'd handled this situation earlier, he might have met someone else and never have Ainslie in his life. He knew deep in his heart that she was the woman God had chosen for him.

His mom set a mug of steaming black coffee in front of both of them before grabbing the pot and topping off the other mugs. She took a seat across from Grady. "Now, what is it you want to talk about?"

Grady's appetite vanished, and he set down his bar. He took a sip of his coffee, the brew strong, the way his mother had always made it. "You remember when that vagrant was run over when I was a kid."

"Yeah, sure." She looked confused by the topic. "It had the whole town in an uproar for a while."

"Never did find out who hit him or who he was." His dad held his mug midair and frowned. "Bad thing that was."

"I know who did it." Grady blurted out before he lost his nerve.

"You what?" His mom gaped at him. "But how?"

He cupped his mug and thought about how to start the conversation. "You didn't know this, but Uncle Tommy was teaching me to play poker. I snuck out every Friday night and went to his place."

His dad grinned. "We knew about the poker."

"You did?"

"Sure," he said. "Nothing much went on with you kids we didn't know about."

"Why didn't you stop me? I mean, poker for a nine-year-old?"

His mom set down her mug on the print tablecloth with a little ball fringe lining the edge. "You were having fun. Bonding with Tommy. And he really needed that in his life back then. He's always been a loner so it was special for him. For the two of you, actually."

His dad met Grady's gaze. "But what does that have to do with the vagrant?"

Grady swallowed. Formed the words in his brain. Tried to get them out, but his mouth was too dry. He took a drink of the coffee. Nearly scalded his mouth, but it didn't help.

Ainslie took his hand and clutched it tight. She met his gaze and held it.

He could do this with her help. He took a breath. "The Friday night after the guy died, I went to Uncle Tommy's place. He was in the garage instead of his apartment. He was fixing his truck. It had front-end damage like they'd reported for the vehicle that hit the vagrant."

His mom leaned back and arched her eyebrow. "So?"

"So Uncle Tommy had to have hit the guy," Grady said frankly. "And he was fixing his truck at night to cover it up."

His mom shook her head. "No, son. Tommy hit a deer, and he was fixing his truck at night because he worked on his customers' vehicles during the day."

Grady's mouth dropped open, and it took him a moment to regain control of it to speak. "You knew about it? About the truck damage?"

"Sure," she said. "Tommy had nothing to hide. In fact, when he heard about the vagrant dying and that his vehicle matched the hit-and-run driver's vehicle, he went straight to the police so they'd know about the deer and could check out his truck."

Grady sat forward, Ainslie's hand dropping away as his brain worked to process this information. "And he wasn't just using that as a coverup?"

His dad shook his head. "They swabbed the blood on the front just to be sure."

"Plus, he had an alibi for the time the vagrant died," his mom added. "And the deer was on the side of the road where he hit it, and the damage matched a deer, not a person."

Grady sagged in his chair. "Then Uncle Tommy didn't kill that guy."

"No." His mother pressed her hand on his. "Have you thought all these years that he did?"

Grady nodded. "I was afraid to come forward because I thought it would tear the family apart."

"Oh, my poor boy. That's a lot to carry." She squeezed his hand.

He felt like that nine-year-old kid again, only this time he'd finally been able to tell his mom about the terrible secret he'd been carrying. The relief nearly overwhelmed him, and he had to think hard about breathing.

Breathe in. Out. Inhale. Exhale. He had this. It was over. He could move on. Finally. Move on. Live life like God intended. Free and in His will. A heavy weight floated from his shoulders.

"It's over. All over. And everything is fine." He looked at

Ainslie, who had a broad smile on her face. "More than fine."

Her eyes glistened with tears. Of joy, he hoped. "I'm so happy everything worked out like this."

Grady wished he was alone with her so he could draw her close and talk about that forever with her. "I'm just sorry I wasted so many years when I could've been free from it."

"God works everything for our good." His mom planted her hands on the table and came to her feet. "Now, if that's all you needed to talk about, I want all of you out of my kitchen so I can finish getting supper ready. Everyone should be arriving soon." She made a shooing motion with her hands. "I mean it. Skedaddle now. You too, Lyle."

Grady took Ainslie's hand and helped her to her feet. "I want to apologize in advance for what I'm about to put you through."

"Now come on, son." His mother swatted a hand at him. "I know you don't have a lot of practice bringing a girl home to meet us, but you just got her here. For heaven's sake, don't scare her away."

"Don't worry." Ainslie locked gazes with Grady. "I don't scare easily, and it'll take a lot more than his comment to get rid of me."

～

But maybe she did scare easily.

When the family room—a roaring fire blazing in the fireplace—filled with Grady's three brothers, two sisters-in-law, three nieces, two nephews, the infamous Uncle Tommy, Grady's great aunt, and his grandma, Ainslie was overwhelmed. She'd never been in a room with so many family members in her life.

Grady took her hand. "You look shell-shocked."

287

"Honestly, I am," she readily admitted. "I didn't expect a big family dinner tonight. I thought that, once you broke the news to your parents, it would be called off."

Grady shook his head. "I should have told you Mom wouldn't have canceled, no matter what happened. Sunday night dinner has never been called off. Not for the birth of a grandchild. A tornado. A flood. She's very serious about it."

"I guess so." Ainslie admired the commitment to family that she'd sorely missed and had always wished she'd been a part of. Even now, overwhelmed or not, joy, good-natured ribbing, and love filled the room to the rafters. And what a blessing that was. She didn't know how Grady had ever left it behind.

His eyes narrowed with deep concern. "Do you think you can handle it, or do you want to take a quick walk to clear your head before we sit down to eat?"

Oh, the walk. That would be perfect. She moved closer to him. "Would you think less of me if I opted for the walk?"

"Of course not."

"But I bragged to your mom that I didn't scare easily."

"You're not really scared, right? Just a bit overwhelmed."

"I don't actually know. Let's take that walk and talk about it."

"I'll grab your jacket." He squeezed her hand and eased through the crowded space, dodging an unsteady toddler wobbling toward a table for support, a stuffed bunny in his arms. Ainslie loved seeing the children most of all. She could easily imagine having Grady's children and bringing them up in the way she'd longed to be raised.

Irma came out of the kitchen and brushed the back of her hand over her forehead. Her cheeks were rosy red, her floral apron dotted with fresh stains. She zoned in on Ainslie and made her way across the room. "It's a lot to take in with such a small room."

Ainslie nodded. "If it's okay, Grady and I are going to take a little walk. Just to clear my head."

"Oh, I get it." She smiled. "I remember meeting Lyle's family for the first time. There were three more brothers in that family, and they all had four children apiece. We met in the small farmhouse that we came to live in after we got married, and I swear there were kids hanging from the dining room chandelier." She chuckled, and her eyes crinkled with joy.

"I have a much smaller family. Just me and my brother." Ainslie didn't know how much to share, but Irma was so warm and open that Ainslie opted to continue. "And I've never gone home to meet a guy's parents either."

Irma searched her gaze. "You love my son, though, right?"

"I do," Ainslie said, putting as much oomph behind her words as she could so Irma didn't doubt Ainslie's commitment to Grady.

"Then all of this?" She waved a hand. "This isn't important now. Just love him, and you'll find a way to incorporate what he loves into your life."

Ainslie instantly knew she was going to come to love this woman. "I might need some help."

"With the family?" Irma's gaze narrowed.

Ainslie shook her head. "Football. I really hate it."

For a moment Irma didn't move, but then she tossed back her head and laughed, her red cheeks rising.

Ainslie had no idea what she'd said to cause this reaction. "What's so funny?"

Irma inched closer. "I don't like football either. Not one little bit. But I've learned how to hate it in full view of everyone else and not let them know. You ask my Lyle or Grady—anyone here really—and they'll say I love the sport."

Something cemented between them at that moment. Something even more important than getting the recipe for the cookie bars. "Then you'll have to share your secret with me."

"No secret." She settled her hands on her curvy hips. "I just love Lyle and he—"

"Loves football."

"Exactly."

Grady came back with her jacket and helped her slip into it. He looked between them, a question in his eyes. "You two look like you've got some big secret."

Ainslie faced Irma. "Secret? Not really. Just some very sound advice being passed along that will make our relationship so much stronger."

"Ah, she's telling you to run for the hills while you can, right?" He chuckled.

She tucked her arm in his and winked. "Let's make a break for it."

His smile faded, and he led her outside. The moment she closed the door, he turned to face her. "You're kidding, right? You do want to come back after the walk?"

"Do you want me to?" she asked.

"Of course."

"Then, Grady Houston, I will be back today and as many times as you want. Because you are the man I love, and I want to see you happy."

He cupped the side of her face. "And I want to see you happy, too. Forever happy with me."

She smiled up at him, and he swung her into his arms. She didn't need more than his arms tightly folded around her to know that their dreams had come true and their forever together had just begun.

ABOUT SUSAN

SUSAN SLEEMAN is a bestselling and award-winning author of more than 35 inspirational/Christian and clean read romantic suspense books. In addition to writing, Susan also hosts the website, TheSuspenseZone.com.

Susan currently lives in Oregon, but has had the pleasure of living in nine states. Her husband is a retired church music director and they have two beautiful daughters, a very special son-in-law, and an adorable grandson.

For more information visit:
www.susansleeman.com

NIGHTHAWK SECURITY SERIES
Protecting others when unspeakable danger lurks.

Keep reading for more information on the additional books in the Nighthawk Security Series where the Cold Harbor and Truth Seekers teams work side-by-side with Nighthawk Security.

A woman plagued by a stalker. Children of a murderer. A woman whose mother died under suspicious circumstances.

All in danger. Lives on the line. Needing protection.

Enter the brothers of Nighthawk Security. The five Byrd brothers with years of former military and law enforcement experience coming together to offer protection and investigation services. Their goal—protecting others when unspeakable danger lurks.

Book 1 Night Fall – November, 2020
Book 2 – Night Vision – December, 2020
Book 3 - Night Hawk – January, 2021
Book 4 –Night Moves – July, 2021
Book 5 – Night Watch – August, 2021
Book 6 – Night Prey – October, 2021

For More Details Visit -
www.susansleeman.com/books/nighthawk-security/

THE TRUTH SEEKERS

People are rarely who they seem

A twin who never knew her sister existed, a mother whose child is not her own, a woman whose father is anything but her father. All searching. All seeking. All needing help and hope.

Meet the unsung heroes of the Veritas Center. The Truth Seekers – a team, that includes experts in forensic anthropology, DNA, trace evidence, ballistics, cybercrimes, and toxicology. Committed to restoring hope and families by solving one mystery at a time, none of them are prepared for when the mystery comes calling close to home and threatens to destroy the only life they've known.

For More Details Visit -
www.susansleeman.com/books/truth-seekers/

HOMELAND HEROES SERIES

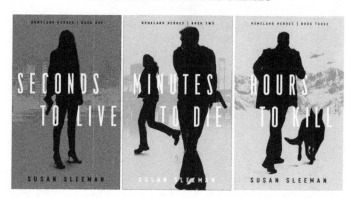

When the clock is ticking on criminal activity conducted on or facilitated by the Internet there is no better team to call other than the RED team, a division of the HSI—Homeland Security's Investigation Unit. RED team includes FBI and DHS Agents, and US Marshal's Service Deputies.

For More Details Visit -

www.susansleeman.com/books/homeland-heroes/

WHITE KNIGHTS SERIES

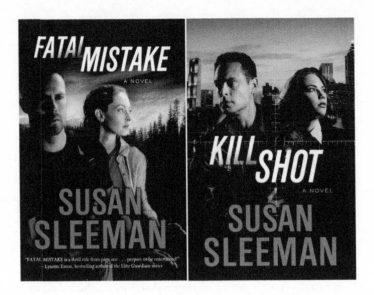

Join the White Knights as they investigate stories plucked from today's news headlines. The FBI Critical Incident Response Team includes experts in crisis management, explosives, ballistics/weapons, negotiating/criminal profiling, cyber crimes, and forensics. All team members are former military and they stand ready to deploy within four hours, anytime and anywhere to mitigate the highest-priority threats facing our nation.

BOOKS IN THE COLD HARBOR SERIES

Blackwell Tactical – this law enforcement training facility and protection services agency is made up of former military and law enforcement heroes whose injuries keep them from the line of duty. When trouble strikes, there's no better team to have on your side, and they would give everything, even their lives, to protect innocents.

For More Details Visit -
www.susansleeman.com/books/cold-harbor/

Made in the USA
Monee, IL
27 April 2021